BOBBI SCHEMERHORN

TOR

BOOK THREE IN THE *REALM WARDENS* SERIES

OTHER BOOKS BY THIS AUTHOR

THE REALM WARDENS SERIES

Blood Magic
The Gift
Tor

THE MECHANICAL DRAGONS SERIES

Fire and Water
Spirit
Earth
Air
Reunion

STANDALONE TITLES

Bounty

ACKNOWLEDGMENTS

Ah the acknowledgments, it's like my own special awards ceremony. I get to thank everyone that had a hand at getting this book here.

I'd like to thank my beta readers; if not for you I wouldn't have been able to spot those nasty little time jump mistakes. To my editor, Jennifer Dinsmore, for catching not just the big grammar issues but the little ones as well. To my amazing artistic team at Streetlight Graphics for the cover art and formatting. I would also like to thank you, the reader; you make it possible for me to continue to write every day.

And, lastly, I'd like to thank the academy. It was nice just to be nominated.... Um, yeah, sorry about that. I mean to say, thanks to everyone, enjoy your further journey into the Realm Wardens universe, and I will catch you on the other side!

The owls do not know you,
So they cannot speak your name.

~From the musing of Gronk in The Chronicles of Gronk~

CHAPTER ONE

H UES OF REDS GLOWED OVER the hill on which Tor sat, the orc village of Kalfskeen decimated from the attack moments ago. It was not even a kilometer away, yet it felt like millions as her home burned. Tor gripped her father's limp body tight as her childhood home became cinders, the heat singeing her skin. Her arm throbbed, bleeding from the gash one of the bandits had administered while she'd tried in vain to defend the youngest of her brothers. But it wasn't the orc's way to wallow, and she knew she needed to get up and go after those who'd killed her family and burned her village.

In other races of the region, hatred for the orcs ran deep—going back centuries. Even though the orcs rarely, if ever, crossed the swampland dividing theirs from that of men, man continued to cross into their land. The time for another war was coming. Even though Tor was a woman of healing now, her orc side wanted revenge.

Tor wasn't even supposed to be home, she'd only returned for her brother's joining ceremony. When Tor had received word her brother had been chosen as a mate her heart had filled with joy for him. It was supposed to be a happy time, the meeting of the two families from different villages and their coming together as one. It was a great honor to be chosen, and proved his prowess as a hunter and a warrior had spread far and wide. She had been gone for nearly ten years, learning how to be a healer at the Rejuvenation Monastery. So, her elation on just being invited—included—had her floating on air.

Tor held her father until there were only embers left of their home, the sun peeking over the horizon. Gently laying her father on his back she got to her feet, legs stiff and back sore. She took in a deep breath before moving toward the home, searching for the remainder of her family. Her two eldest brothers were laid out feet from each other, weapons in their hands.

Their eyes, now turning a milky white, stared toward a sky of radiant reds and pinks. Kertugrat, the eldest, was missing an arm, and a large gash opened his chest. Grammook, the second eldest, the one who was to be joined, had a blade protruding from his heart, and from the dark stains she knew he had a belly wound as well. Tor searched for another hour but couldn't find Thrasoot, the youngest of the four. The last she time she'd seen him he'd been running toward the house before it was set ablaze.

He had not been formally weapon-trained, but he was twelve and at the age to start learning. She'd thought he was perhaps running for his weapons, but now she feared he'd never got out.

Tor spent the rest of the day building three pyres for two of her brothers and her father, and a vigil for the brother who had presumably burned. She prepared their bodies: washing them, stitching their injuries, dressing them in their war colors, and then placing them on their pyres with the weapons they would use to fight in the afterlife.

Tor wasn't the only family member readying for the death ceremony; not one of the homes was left standing. There were at least two thousand in Kalfskeen Village, but it looked as though many were now ash like her own.

The men who'd come through numbered at least ten thousand, a small army. Tor didn't know if they'd come from the north or the south, and she hadn't recognized their colors. They wore cloaks, covering their faces, and held weapons she had not seen before. She'd felt the static emanate from those on horseback, a sign they were using magic. What kind she didn't know, but it had left a metallic taste in her mouth. This was not normal for the magic in their realm, or any other she knew of. But it had been powerful enough to create a drop in the air pressure.

As the sun began to set once again a distant drumming could be heard, a low chant building behind it. Tor closed her eyes, tapping her chest along with the beat of the drum as she began to chant the death song. The words would carry her brothers and father to the afterlife. A battle cry warning the dead of their arrival.

She set the pyres alight and stepped back, still singing the words in her native tongue. Tears streaked her face. If only she had arrived sooner, she may have been able to save them. Tor shook the thought from her mind; it would poison the death ceremony and taint her family's entry to the afterlife. They were capable warriors and did not need saving.

The ceremony lasted until the next sunrise. Tor was exhausted, but she had to remain on guard all night to ensure the fires did not go out until her father and brothers were nothing but ash. There was to be nothing left of their bodies in order for their souls to fully release.

As the embers died down she prayed to Goddess Thanroota, asking she take her family so they could once again dance and fight in the afterlife and be reunited with her mother, Abellah.

She turned her attention to the area around her home. Bodies of the enemy were strewn about; her family had put up a valiant fight. Before she'd arrived, her brothers and father had killed at least twenty of the enemy. It had been the last one standing who cut her arm before her father, Torerook, ran him through. Torerook had suffered his fatal blow just before, and the final look in his eyes, as he gazed at his daughter before he took his dying breath, would stay with her forever. He'd been disappointed in her as a warrior when she was young, and it was why she'd been sent to the monastery—at least part of the reason. And he had clearly been disappointed in her now as an adult, having not defended herself.

She had spent ten years at the Rejuvenation Monastery, becoming a cleric and learning the religion of healing, and was no longer considered a warrior amongst her people. Being sent to the monastery was more of an exile, since the clerics taught against everything with which she'd been raised.

Tor sighed as she bent down to pull the hood off one of the dead. He belonged to a race she had never seen before, with a deep set eyes and a square jawline. There were ridges above his eyes, his hair blacker than she had ever seen. The sight gave her a small chill. They were not men of Totriga, but the tattoo covering half his face intrigued her. Kneeling down next to the body, she grabbed his chin and turned his face to see the entire marking. Did it indicate a rank of some kind? Perhaps his tribal markings? The long, thick black lines ran from his ear to under his eye, and from his forehead to his strong jaw. Wiping her hands on her pants, she stood.

She checked a few more of the dead, hoping to find some sort of clue as to who these people were, and found both male and females amongst the dead. All with the same facial tattoo. She couldn't leave the bodies where they were; she needed to pile them up and burn them. She grabbed the wrist of one of the females and the dead's sleeve slide down, revealing more tattoos. Tor stopped to study them and saw hers was a simple straight line up the arm, with lettering she had never seen before. She had studied many languages, but this was not one of them. Perhaps a language from the four dead races? Was it possible they were not dead after all?

What realm did they come from? She could recognize all twelve races; were they from a distant land on Totriga? Tor furrowed her brow as she again took note of the lettering. When she returned to the monastery she would look it up in their extensive library.

Committing it to memory, Tor continued to drag the woman away from the village. She rolled the female onto her stomach, then returned for the rest. She piled them on top of each other, each facedown. They would enter the afterlife with their backs turned so everyone would know they were cowards.

It took her to just past midday to complete her task. She was washing up when she spotted a young woman standing at the top of the hill overlooking the village. Tor climbed up to stand next to her, and the two shared a quick glance. Ormhilya was a cousin of hers. They were close in age, but Ormhilya had joined two years prior and had since bore a child. Her face was covered in blood and soot, but both her tusks gleamed white as ever.

Tor unconsciously touched her own face, highlighting the absence of her tusks. She had lost one in a grappling match with her eldest brother when she was twelve. In defiance of her father's comments that she was no longer a proper warrior, she ripped the other out on her own to prove her worth. She'd thought this would make her more fierce, because what orc would be brave enough to do that to themselves? Only the strongest would dare such a feat. But she'd been wrong and won no favors from her father. An orc with no tusks had no honor, power, or strength. It was why he'd sent her away to the monastery. In his eyes, she was no longer an orc.

Ormhilya turned to watch Tor. "What will you do now, cousin?" Her voice was thick with the emotions she was keeping in check.

Tor shook her head. "I can't stay here. Father barely tolerated me, and those left certainly won't want me."

Ormhilya nodded. "Perhaps you shouldn't have returned at all." She glanced over her shoulder to where Tor's family now lay. "At least you sent them to the afterlife as they deserved. Perhaps Goddess Thanroota won't pay mind to your lack of tusks. As long as you chanted the words fiercely." She didn't wait for a response,

5

but headed back into the village. A small child was handed to her by an elderly orc.

The woman—her mother's sister—looked up at Tor. She touched her tribe tattoo on her upper arm, and Tor mirrored the old lady. Her tattoo was covered by a bandage, but the familial gesture was still the same. The woman did nothing more to acknowledge Tor, and walked away.

Tor heaved a heavy sigh, grabbed what was left of her things, and headed east to the monastery. Although the clerics welcomed her, she knew she didn't really belong there either. An orc among humans was thought to be unnatural by many.

CHAPTER TWO

IN THE EMPTY LIBRARY OF the Rejuvenation Monastery, Tor pored over the old healing tomes. It was where she spent most her time when she was not taking formal lessons. The cleric's library was vast, from healing to prophecies, from languages of the many races to the different magics used by each realm and race. She now split her focus between healing spells and defensive spells. Once she left the monastery for good she knew these spells would be required. She was a healer now, not a warrior. She'd renounced her orc side and everything that it entailed. Mostly.

Her religion, her life's meaning, was now healing. Even though she wore the cleric's robes she would still be seen as an orc. Anywhere that wasn't orc lands was dangerous for her to be. Her kind was despised by humans, thought of only as warmongers. It was true once, many centuries ago, when the orcs crossed into the land of men and burned villages near the Fairy Fields. It was after this short war the swamps had been created by elves' and sprites' magic.

The creak of the door echoed through the rows of books and down to the far end of the tables where Tor sat. It was a long walk for the High Cleric to make. She knew he was coming to her, and not to the prophecies section of the library where she sat. He believed much of this section to be the ramblings of a crazy old man, regardless if many of them had come to light. It seemed to take an eternity for him to make his way to her, and she tried to pretend as though she didn't know his destination.

High Cleric Whillem Haglund stopped in front of her but Tor kept her eyes down, avoiding contact. He cleared his throat. She hated when he did that; it was rude, just say hello. Tor brought her gaze up to meet the cleric's. She sat back in her chair and did her best to look obedient.

"It is time for you to make your pilgrimage," he said, his nose slightly elevated so he could look down on her more than he already did.

Tor's mouth dropped open. She had hoped it wouldn't be so soon. She didn't feel ready. Eight years was all that had passed since she'd returned from burying her family. Other apprentices had to wait at least twenty years before being sent on a pilgrimage. "But I'm not—"

"You are as ready as you will ever be. You will leave tomorrow." He turned on his heel and strode back down the aisle he'd come.

"But where am I to go, High Cleric Whillem?" she called after him.

"The High Kingdom," he said, without slowing or turning.

Tor slumped in her chair, her mind racing. She needed to speak to the only cleric that would give her council. He was much older than the rest, and more tolerant. He'd never judged Tor for being an orc, and had taken her into the monastery with open arms. When she'd returned eight years prior he consoled her as she worked through the loss of her family.

Tor shot out of her chair, grabbed her notebook, and rushed from the library, giving no other thought to the mess of books she was leaving behind. She rushed through the halls to the living quarters, where she knew her friend would be. It was midday, and he would be waking from his nap.

Her knock on his door was loud and impatient.

"Come in, Tor, come in." His voice was weary, but more from age than from grogginess.

"Abacuss," she said as she opened the door. He was sitting on the edge of his bed, brushing down his mess of hair. Tor closed the door behind her and pulled the only chair from the corner of the tiny room. She placed it in front of the old man and sat.

"You are to go on your pilgrimage. I know," he said, meeting her eyes.

"I'm not ready." Tor rung her hands and slumped her shoulders.

"No, you are not. You still have much to learn, but you will be needed in the High Kingdom so it is important you leave tomorrow."

Tor never fully understood how Abacuss knew the things that he did, and his prophecies were amongst the most detailed. She had studied some of his older texts, but found she preferred not to know the future.

"Who will be needing me?"

He shook his head. "Travelers from the Dwarf Kingdom, Theakredel."

"Dwarf Kingdom?" she wrinkled her nose. "High King soldiers?"

"No. They are delivering precious cargo to the High King. One will need your healing gifts."

"What cargo? Dwarf gems?"

"No. She is the unbalance in our magic."

"What unbalance? I haven't noticed any shifting in the static."

"You will." He smiled and patted her hand. "You will. Your sensitivity to the static is what will save you from what is to come."

"Who? The travelers?" Tor searched her mentors face for answers she knew he wouldn't give. He had deep-set wrinkles, and his hair line had receded nearly to the very back of his head. She'd often told him he should just shave but he refused.

His eyes were set back, and the wrinkles on his forehead were so deep they looked like ridges. But he still had a strong jawline.

"It is imperative she survive," he said, pulling Tor from her studies.

"She who?"

"But she is not the only reason you will be going to the High Kingdom."

"Abacuss, you are giving me incomplete information. Is this girl the one who is injured?"

"That is not the question you should be asking." He patted her hand as he got to his feet.

"Then what should I be asking?" Tor pivoted in her chair to watch as the old man put his clerics' robes on over his clothes.

"It has been a question on your mind since you returned eight years ago."

Tor leaned back in her chair and stared at the floor. "What does this have to do with the men who burned down my village and killed my family? These people I'm to meet in the High Kingdom, are they the ones who killed my family?"

"No, of course not. What have you found in the library about the language you found?"

Tor leaned on the back of the chair. She had been searching all the books for years, looking for the strange letters and markings of that race. They haunted her dreams and she continued to come up empty-handed. "Nothing."

He faced her as he tied his robes. "Are you certain?"

"Yes, of course. Don't you think I would have said something if I had?"

Abacuss smiled. It was kind and understanding. "The High Kingdom will have the answers you seek."

"Do they have a library?"

He laughed. "Oh my, no. At least not as extensive as our own."

Tor sighed. "Then how will I find my answers?"

He cupped Tor's face in his wrinkled, bony hand. "Trust that I know the answers you seek wait for you there."

"Is this another one of your crazy prophecies?" Tor gave the man who'd practically raised her a crooked smile.

"My prophecies are only crazy when they do not come to light. Otherwise, I am wise and insightful."

Tor laughed lightly. "People can be fickle."

Abacuss laughed gently. "Fickle indeed."

"Will you give me more information, old man, or will you force me to enter the city with no knowledge?"

Abacuss returned to his bed and sat on the edge, resting his hands on his knees. "Knowledge is also fickle. It can only suit you if you know what needs to be known. My dear Tor, I have given you all that you need to know."

Tor shook her head and stared at her mentor. He was of one of the twelve races, she just could never figure out which one. She knew he wasn't human, nor elf, but that was all. At one point she had thought he could be fae, because of his prophecies and tendency to speak in riddles and games. But he was old and frail, and fae were timeless.

"So, I'm to leave tomorrow for the High Kingdom. Am I traveling with others?"

"No. You are the only one going on this pilgrimage."

Tor sighed. The thought of being alone on the road, in the land of men, scared her more than anything she had ever had to face in her life. As an orc, this fear brought on a deep-seated shame; warriors do not have fear. For a brief moment, she'd thought her Goddess Thanroota would no longer hear her prayers.

Her internal struggles must have shown on her face because Abacuss spoke. "You have been studying things that a healer should really have no knowledge of. It will keep you safe. It was smart you studied these things."

"Are you talking of the defensive magic?"

Abacuss smiled and cupped her chin once again. "As I have said, you have all the knowledge you need."

"What if I'm forced to defend myself and someone is hurt?" As a healer cleric this was a fear, as an orc warrior this was a fact of life.

Abacuss put his hands out for Tor to help him off the bed. She rose and assisted him, even though he was quite spry for his age. They stepped into the hall and he put his arm through Tor's as they headed down the hallway. "I can only tell you to trust your own judgment. You will know, when the time comes, how you must react. You have good instincts." He patted her arm. "And perhaps you can speak with that goddess of yours for spiritual guidance."

Tor stiffened. She'd been warned very early on in her life with the clerics that her beliefs in deities would not be tolerated. It was superstitious nonsense meant to cause man to stray from the path of truth. For those at Rejuvenation Monastery, the path must only be healing; that was her religion now.

"How did you—"

Abacuss laughed lightly. "You were a headstrong child when you came to us. I knew that when you were done with your cleric training for the day you would seek council from your goddess. She brought you comfort."

"You didn't say anything?"

"Who you choose to speak with is not my business. Some of the men of this land are very closed-minded. Some of the men in this monastery are closed-minded."

Now able to speak openly, Tor had questions. "How is it that no one else prays to a deity?"

"What makes you think that orc's are the only ones who pray to a higher power?"

"I've never known anyone who does."

"Ah." Abacuss lifted his hand and pointed his finger at her. "So you have met everyone there is to meet."

Tor snorted. "No, of course not."

With a chuckle and smile he said, "Then how do you know such things to be true?"

"You're right. I apologize for making such a broad assumption."

They stopped at the end of the long hall of the living quarters. He faced Tor. "Get yourself ready for your journey. I will see you when you return. Remember, my dear Tor, you are not to judge. You are only to heal; it is not your place to judge who comes to you for help. You are but a humble servant to the Rejuvenation Monastery and are no better than any man. We live to serve, to share our religion openly."

"Yes, of course."

Abacuss turned and continued back down the hall, leaving Tor alone. She sighed heavily, watching until her mentor disappeared around the corner before heading for her own room on the far side of the monastery. She was not just an orc but she was also the only female, so they'd separated her from the men. Not that there was any fear of her fraternizing with anyone.

As she shoved her things into her bag she grabbed her notes of herbs, plants, and other healing items along with the different incantations needed for certain aliments. She flipped to the back of her book and looked over the defensive magic. Her studies were incomplete. She only knew a handful of defensive spells. Good enough against one man, but many? She would have to wait and find out in person.

She grabbed her talisman; an inverted triangle with a teardrop opal in the center, the symbol of the Rejuvenation Monastery. It would help to identify her as a cleric. Tor put her head through the hoop of the leather band. It hung gently around her neck. She tucked the emblem into her shirt, grabbed her robes and pulled them over her clothes, then headed for the library. Running wasn't allowed in the monastery, so she walked as quickly as she could.

The books she had used earlier were still on the table where she'd left them.

She pushed several of the larger tomes aside, finding a small book the size of her palm. *The Language of Defense* was burned into the leather cover. She shoved it into her pack, then hastily packed up the rest of the books and returned them to their proper homes. It was rude to leave a mess for someone else to clean up.

She headed for the main hall, where Abacuss and the High Cleric would likely be. When she entered all eyes fell on her. She wasn't a high enough ranking to be in this hall, but Tor didn't care. She wasn't going to wait until morning to leave; she was leaving now and needed to say goodbye.

Before the High Cleric could speak Abacuss rose to his feet. "I figured you would not wait until morning."

She took his outstretched hands. "I will miss you."

"Remember what I told you," he whispered.

"I will."

He squeezed her hands and bowed his head.

Tor dropped to her knees, a sign of obedience and respect. She placed her forehead against one of his hands, and he placed the other on the top of her head. "Go forth and share our beliefs freely. We are no better than any man. It is our honor to serve and heal those in need."

Tor repeated the words, and when he lifted his hand from her head she stood, nodded to the High Cleric, and left the hall, the monastery. She turned her eyes to the High Kingdom and started down the road.

CHAPTER THREE

THE RAIN PELTED TOR RELENTLESSLY as she trudged down the road toward the High Kingdom. It was the second day. She had left the monastery so late the previous day she'd had to stop early on. As the rain soaked her she thought of Abacuss and his words. She truly loved that man, and he was more a father to her than Torerook had been.

She knew there were several small villages along this route, and hoped they would give her shelter for the nights she was on the road. There was already shelter waiting for her in the High Kingdom, one that all the clerics used when on their pilgrimages. She would serve as a healer to the lower and middle class in the city, though she doubted either would accept her help.

Tor needed to remind herself of the true purpose of her going: the travelers Abacuss had spoken of. She wasn't certain, but Abacuss was likely the reason the High Cleric had sent her now and not in a few years. If it were any other cleric, she was certain High Cleric Whillem would have fought to keep them longer to train more. But he'd never wanted her there even when she knew him as Whillem, just a cleric like herself. Once he was promoted, Tor knew her days were numbered.

Almost as though the weather sensed her foul mood it began to pour harder. She let out a low growl of disdain and discomfort, and pulled her hood down over her face to prevent the water from going into her eyes and down her back. She tried to distract herself by naming off what ingredients to use for the more common aliments among the poor in large cities.

When that didn't work she went through her own personal inventory of herbs and plants, counting off the quantities and the varying species of flowers in her head. She had been stockpiling them for a few years, something all the clerics did as part of their healing education to know what ingredients came from where and how to obtain them.

It wasn't enough to occupy her mind, however, so she switched to the simpler of the defensive spells. They required specific incantations and movements of the wrists, hands, and fingers in varying degrees. Some were more subtle than others; just a small flick of the wrist and a few words could cause someone to lose their balance. A large circular motion would allow her to erect a shield, but this was a bit trickier as the wording was hard to get her tongue around. She ran through them in her head, careful not to speak out loud and complete the spell with her hand gestures. The last thing she wanted was to actually cast one. This was enough of a distraction that, when she came upon the first of the tiny villages, she didn't realize it until she heard another voice.

"What in Gronk's beard are you doing here, orc?" The voice was deep and angry. "I could see ya coming from kilometers away."

Tor lifted her head and pushed back her hood, revealing herself completely. "I'm a healer from the Rejuvenation Monastery. I'm on a pilgrimage to the High Kingdom."

"An orc healer?" The man barked out a laugh. "Since when do the orc care about healing?"

"I'm merely passing through, my good man. I wish no harm." She took several steps back when the man blocked her path. He was about a foot shorter than her six. "Please, sir, let me pass." She kept her chin low and her hands folded in front. *I am better than no one.* Abacuss's words echoed in her mind, a lesson in humility.

"What if I don't, orc? What if I just run you through right here?" He produced a poker metalworkers' used to stoke their fires.

"I am but a servant, good sir. I wish you no harm." Tor readied to take a knee when another voice came from behind.

"Let her pass, Covan. The quicker she gets out of town the better."

Tor didn't dare lift her eyes to meet the man's. She didn't want to give him any reason to think she was becoming aggressive.

"Fine." Covan growled. "Get out of our town, and don't come back!"

Tor nodded and stepped around the man. He shoved her hard as she passed, and was knocked off balance, slipping on the muddy road and falling into a puddle. He laughed a full belly laugh, and Tor lifted her face enough to scan the area. Many of the villagers were watching, most laughing along with Covan.

She sighed inwardly and got to her feet. Knowing it would seem prideful and be frowned upon, Tor lifted her face and raised her chin, holding herself high and confident. She didn't care. She strode out of the village, meeting the eyes of everyone she passed and sending them cowering into their homes. When she was out of the village, and far enough away she couldn't be seen, she covered her head once again to protect herself from the weather. It did little good, since she was already soaked through. A shiver ran through her. "What I wouldn't do for a fire right now."

After another couple hours of walking, it was now just past midday. The rain had stopped a half hour before, and Tor was glad for the reprieve. The sun wasn't doing much to warm her up, but at least her coat was drying some. In the distance she could see the next village. It was bigger, more of a traveler's haven, and there would likely be a tavern and an inn. If she were lucky, they would serve her a hot meal.

As she approached she heard a cry of pain; it was a young-sounding voice, a child. Without hesitation Tor ran toward the screaming child and found him in the stables, cradling his arm. She noticed the ladder leading to the loft and the broken rung. It had likely gave way under his weight, causing him to fall at least seven feet.

She was only able to take one step toward the child when a man rushed in behind her and pushed past. "What happened, boy?" he asked.

The boy gestured to the ladder, as Tor suspected.

"I'm a healer. I can help," Tor said, reaching for the talisman. The young boy's mouth dropped open at the sight of her and the man did a double take, as if seeing her for the first time.

"Gronk's hairy balls you will! Step back, orc!" the man screamed.

"Please—"

A woman now rushed to the boy's side. "What happened? Tagger, are you all right?"

"Why are you still here?" The man said to Tor, standing tall with fists tight.

The woman did the same double take as the man, taking in Tor's presence. A small crowd had begun to form and Tor was beginning to feel threatened. She was trapped now in the stables with a great deal of pitchforks.

She bowed her head, dropping her gaze to the ground. "Please sir, ma'am. I am a healer from the Rejuvenation Monastery." She showed her pendant without looking up. "Allow me to help."

The man scoffed, which did not surprise Tor as that seemed to be everyone's opinion. "Like I would trust an orc to touch my boy."

Tor gave the boy a quick glance. "It looks as though he has dislocated his shoulder. It would not take much to put it back in place. But the longer we wait, the more likely the damage will be permanent and he will lose full use of the arm."

The man and woman exchanged a glance.

"Please, Mamma, it hurts."

"Let the orc help," the woman said after much too long a silence as the crowd inched ever closer.

"Edenth, are you insane?" the man said.

Edenth pointed at the boy. "Busharde, he cannot work the horses with one arm." Her look was one that made even Tor want to step back. "Let the orc help."

Tor watched the reluctance cross his face, but he then clenched his jaw and nodded toward the boy. Tor rushed forward, taking off her pack then removing a second one that looped over one shoulder and across her chest. She unzipped the pouch and unfolded it, revealing a number of vials, smaller leather pouches, several tools, and a small stone bowl.

Tor grabbed a pouch and pulled out an odd, five-pronged leaf. It was a greenish-purple and she offered it to the boy. "Chew this; it will dull the pain."

The boy's eyes wide with both fear and pain, he looked to his mother for guidance.

"It's all right, Tagger, go ahead." Tor could tell Edenth was trying to sound reassuring, but her own uncertainty was apparent. The boy took the leaf and shoved it in his mouth. His face contorted.

"It's sour."

"Yes, I'm sorry, but make sure you chew it completely then swallow." As the boy did as he was told Tor readied a bandage. She made a triangle with the cloth and laid it out.

"Okay," Tagger said. "I swallowed it."

Tor smiled gently at the boy. "Good." She turned her attention to the mother, who was now watching intently. "What I am going to do is rotate his elbow inward, then pull. This will allow the shoulder to pop back into place. Although I have given him something to dull the pain, it will still be quite painful for him."

Tor looked at the father. "He will yell out, and may even pass out. Please do not kill me. I can only numb some of his pain."

Busharde seemed surprised by Tor's comments, until Tor's eyes dropped to the pitchfork he was holding. He nodded and put the weapon down, which made Tor breathe a little easier.

"Ready?" she asked the boy.

"No," he said with a weak smile.

"Deep breath in," Tor said as she gripped his wrist with one hand and his elbow with the other. "And breathe out." As Tagger let the air out Tor twisted and pulled. He did as she said he would and screamed so loud it made her ears ring. But the shoulder slid back into place. Tor quickly put his arm to his chest. "Keep your arm there." She turned to Edenth again. "Watch how I put this on him, so you can duplicate this on your own."

The woman nodded and watched intently. Tor put the sling on the boy and tied it behind his neck. "He must sleep with this on for at least seven days. Then he can take it off to sleep. When he is working, or about during the day, he needs to wear it for at least three weeks. Allow the shoulder to heal properly, or this injury will consistently reoccur."

"I understand."

Tor turned to Tagger. "You may remove the sling to bathe, but it is important you not use this arm for three weeks and keep it bandaged."

Tagger nodded.

"I will give you some herbs to put in his tea, which will help with the swelling and the pain. I'll give you enough for a week."

"I don't drink tea."

Tor smiled. "You will this week."

"Come on, boy." Busharde grabbed him from under his good arm and helped him off the ground, then escorted him out of the stables along with everyone else.

Tor packed up her medical supplies. As she zipped up her

pouch, Edenth spoke. "You look as though you got caught in that storm this morning."

"Yes, ma'am. Unfortunately I had nowhere to seek shelter." Tor stood, putting her packs back on, and Edenth followed. "I will continue on. Thank you for allowing me to help."

"You must be hungry." Edenth's words were, kind but her wringing hands told Tor she was extremely nervous. "Most healers require payment of some kind. I can offer you a place to stay and a warm meal. The sun will be setting soon, and you won't be able to see in the dark. Plus, it will allow you to dry your clothes. Don't want you catching ill." She managed a smile that looked genuine and Tor decided to believe it was.

"That would be lovely."

"Follow me, then." Edenth led them out of the stables and next door to a tavern that was also an inn. Edenth stepped behind the bar and grabbed a large book. Penning in a number she then looked up. "What was your name?"

"Tor, ma'am. Just Tor."

Edenth nodded and wrote the name down, then put the book back behind the bar and grabbed a key. "Up the stairs and down the hall. If you would like a hot bath, I can ready it for you after you have a meal. I hope you understand that I must ask you to eat in your room."

Tor nodded. "I'm grateful for your hospitality."

"I'll have it brought to you."

"Thank you." Tor followed the directions, climbing the narrow stairs and walking to the end of the hall—far away from every other room. No matter. It was a warm, dry place to sleep that night, and better than the ground and a risk of another storm.

She took no time in taking her wet jacket off and hanging it on a hook. As she was pulling clean, dry clothes from her pack there was a knock on the door; or, rather, a pounding.

Tor opened it to find Tagger holding a tray. He must have

kicked the door because he had no free hand with which to knock. He seemed to be struggling with the weight of the tray, so Tor took it from him and said, "Thank you, Tagger."

He smiled, nodded, then left without a word.

Tor took the tray to the bed. There was nowhere else for her to sit, no table but the nightstand. So she pulled it closer and used it as a table as she sat on the edge of the bed. Her meal was a stew, likely rabbit, with large chunks of potatoes and carrots. There were several hunks of bread in a bowl next to it, and a mug of steaming tea that smelled of berries.

Relatively certain they weren't going to poison her, Tor dug into the meal and was grateful for every bite. When she was done she continued with her unpacking. It wasn't long after that another knock came and a voice shouted through the door.

"Your bath is ready across the hall." Tor then heard footsteps scurry away.

Tor sighed. She hoped the people of the High Kingdom would be a little more tolerable, but she doubted it.

She took her hot bath, soaking long enough to make her fingers wrinkle. Many believed orcs to have tough skin, perhaps because their color tone was green. But Tor was always very good at ensuring her skin was soft and supple. When she returned to her room, her dirty dishes were cleared and there was a pile of firewood next to the hearth. Tor quickly checked her supplies, having the fleeting thought that they may have robbed her as well as cleaned up. Everything was as she'd left it.

She made a fire, unfolded the extra blanket over the bed, and crawled in. The crackling of the fire was the lullaby that put her to sleep.

CHAPTER FOUR

TOR ROSE JUST BEFORE THE sun, happy to find her coat and bag were dry. She dressed, folded the blankets and placed them at the end of the bed, then packed the remainder of her bag and left. She wanted to be out of the village before everyone else was up and about.

She left a pouch of extra tea leaves for Tagger on the book behind the bar, along with a note of instructions and a couple pieces of copper. She didn't feel right about not paying for at least a portion of their hospitality.

When she stepped outside there was a mist in the air, a light fog. It must have rained for most the night as the road was muddier than the day before, if such a thing was even possible. Tor did her best to avoid the larger mud puddles, and made quick time getting out of town.

She kept a steady pace, and when the sun rose she stopped to have a small bite to eat to cease her stomach's growling. She had saved several of the hunks of bread from last night's dinner, and she had dried fruit and nuts from the monastery. For an orc this was a meager meal, one that would cause most to rip the arms off the person closest. But Tor was used to eating much smaller portions.

Although she spent most her time quite hungry, she was taught early on that clerics were not better than others and therefore shouldn't get more food. She didn't always agree with that assessment, whether or not she was better than someone else she felt she shouldn't be expected to starve if there was enough food to go around. In the monastery there had always been enough, but it had become her new normal, and when she was younger she had just been happy to have a bed to sleep in.

When done with her meal she started back onto the road. The castle's turrets could be seen in the distance, but it was still at least one more day away. She would likely have to sleep on the ground that night.

Her day of travel was met with no further resistance, no people at all for that matter, and she was relieved for it. As the sun was about an hour from setting, Tor found a flat spot off the road where she could build a lean-to and set up a little camp. She'd start a fire, and perhaps catch a bird for dinner.

All skills and practices she'd learned while she lived with her family she'd continued through the years in the monastery. Sometimes, a bowl of porridge for dinner just wasn't enough. So she would sneak out and supplement her meal. Her hunting skills were quite remarkable given she was so young when sent away and none of the clerics had trained her.

As she worked on her camp she kept checking over her shoulder, the feeling of being watched nagging at her. But whenever she stepped out of the firelight and waited for her eyes to adjust there was no one there. She was on her own but for the bugs and the wildlife, and Tor was confident the fire would keep predators away.

Once she finished plucking the small bird she'd caught, she put it on a stone she had heated on the edge of the fire. It wasn't the best, but it was all she had. The idea of bringing cooking implements had never crossed her mind, and she wished she had brought a small pan.

Tor stared into the fire, listening to the wood pop and crack against the quiet undertones of the sizzling bird, when she felt a static in the air. The hair on her arms and back of her neck stood on end. The only reason she'd feel static was if someone nearby was using magic. It was weak, but growing stronger. The taste of flowers and spices formed in her mouth. The mixture was odd, and she wrinkled her nose and tried to swallow. She had been around magic all her life, but never had she tasted such a mixture. She had no idea what type of magic was being used.

Tor rose and stepped in front of the fire to block its glare. She squinted into the darkness. The longer she stood the stronger the static grew, until she saw the shimmer. Tor tilted her head to the side and stared at the spot now shimmering in front of her. There were no veils to the other realms around here, and the closest was at least several months' travel in any direction. Lavender and pepper had become the forefront tastes.

As she stared a female stepped forward, accompanied by two others who stood at either side. They were dressed all in white, their skin pale. Their hair was short and also white, and they glistened like they had just stepped out of a bath. She knew this race, but only by pictures and descriptions. She had never encountered them in person, and not many had from what she knew. This wasn't good.

Tor narrowed her eyes at the first of the three. "How are you doing that?" Tor pointed with the stick she was using to rotate her bird. "Your veil is nowhere near here, and it's sealed. How are you here, fae? What magic did you use?"

"We have a message."

"What kind of message?" Tor folded her arms. "I have no intention of making a deal with you." Making deals with fae was a dangerous idea. They twisted their words, played games, and always found loopholes to get out of their end of the bargain but still held you to yours. Fae were powerful beings, but tricksters and incapable of entering this realm. Their own had been sealed four thousand years ago. *How are they able to be here now? Are they really, or is it an illusion?* Tor's mind raced.

"We ask for no deal, only a request," the first fae said.

"Deal, request, same thing."

"The child must survive," the fae on the right said.

"What child?" Tor dropped her hands.

"The one who brings the unbalance to all magic," the fae on the left said.

The first spoke again. "Totriga and her realms will not survive if the child dies."

Tor shook her head; it made no sense. "How would our world die? What child are you talking about? And what unbalance of magic?" The shimmer around the fae flickered a deep purple, and Tor knew whatever magic they were using to punch through their veil and appear in front of her did not come naturally. "You're Destiny Custodians." She was not asking.

The fae stepped back into the shimmer. "If the child dies, all will die with her."

Before Tor could speak the three disappeared, and she was once again alone with her crackling fire. The static dissipated, along with the nasty mixture of lavender and pepper and the nagging feeling of being watched. When she smelled something burning, she spun to find her tiny bird blackened on one half but cooked well on the other. She dropped to the ground and sighed as she ate around the charred parts of the bird.

Thoughts of this mystery child ran through her head. Tor wondered if this child was amongst the travelers Abacuss told her she was to help. The wording, the warnings, they were much the same as Abacuss's. Aside from the world dying. That was new information. As for this unbalance, she didn't feel it, but she hadn't used any magic since leaving the monastery.

"At least now I have something to think about on my final stretch to the High Kingdom," Tor mused aloud as she threw the bones of the bird into the fire, added another log, then crawled into her bed.

The next day seemed to go on forever. Heavy winds coming from the Tilinrich Mountains in the east made the cold rain slanted. She was freezing and miserable by the time she reached the final hill looking down on the high stone walls surrounding the High Kingdom.

But even through her misery she'd been able to go over the previous night's events. Destiny Custodians were a rare breed of fae, more so when it came to females. That was what unnerved her the most, what caused her to get little rest the night before. Whoever this child was, their death would bring on a catastrophic event. Female fae only show themselves in such circumstances. Male fae enjoy the chaos, and will show themselves to those they know can cause the most destruction. Encounters with the fae were hardly heard of anymore and all knowledge of them now in books, kept in the monastery library along with the rest of Totriga's history.

Clerics had taken on the task of keeping the world's history long before any of the major wars. The race that had started the monasteries were scholars, mostly. Knowledge was their religion, and over the millennia they began to branch off and create other religions based on magic, such as healing. It was around that time the beliefs in gods and deities fell away.

With these thoughts of the world dying, and not knowing who this child was or where she might find them, Tor stood on the hill looking down the road leading to the walls of the High Kingdom. Her map pointed out each gate and she hoped the guards would allow her to pass, uncertain how many orc—if any—had ever come to the Kingdom. It worried her greatly.

Tor pulled on the leather strap around her neck, exposing the pendant bearing the symbol of the monastery. This would be her identification to get her through the gates. It was the only proof she had of her intentions in the city. She hugged herself tight and trudged down the remaining hill.

Tor approached the back gates. She was entering through entrance for the beggars and the lower class, knowing better than to try and enter through those for the higher class. The sun was starting to set. A guard stood on a stone platform, looking out over the crowd trying to enter the castle walls. Two other guards stood on each side of the gate, stopping and checking the people the guard on the platform told them to.

Tor hoped she would be allowed to pass without question, but she was an orc and there was no hiding that. As she expected, a guard stepped in front of her.

"Where do you think you're going, orc?" He sneered as he looked her up and down.

"I'm here on a pilgrimage from the Rejuvenation Monastery." She presented her pendant. "I'm a healer." Tor once again adopted a submissive stance and waited.

"What's she doing here?" the man on the platform shouted.

"Says she's a healer from that bloody monastery." The guard was practically screaming in Tor's ear. She fought to keep her face neutral, her jaw relaxed, and her breathing steady.

"You sure?" Platform Guard asked.

The one standing in front of her got up close. "Do you have proof? Don't you healers carry some sort of identification?"

Tor slowly and carefully held out the pendant once again, as the guard obviously hadn't paid attention the first time.

He snatched it from her hand, yanking on the leather strap. If she was a smaller person it would have knocked her off balance, but given her size she barely moved. "How do I know you didn't kill the poor sucker who owned this, and are now posing just to get into our great city?"

Tor looked the man in the eyes as she took the pendant back. "You don't. You will just have to trust me. Whether I'm an orc or not. I mean you and the people of this great city no harm. I only wish to heal and to help."

He eyed her for a long minute.

Platform Guard called out. "It's getting late, just let her go."

The guard before her sucked his teeth and said, "We'll be keeping a close eye on you. You stay to the lower city. If we find you straying outside those parts we'll have your head on a spike."

"I understand. Thank you for allowing me to enter. Do you happen to know where the healer's home is?"

"Gronk's beard! Get out of my sight!" he shouted as a bit of spittle flew from his mouth and landed on her cheek.

She fought the urge to wipe it clear. Doing so would give him reason to take it a sign of disrespect and strike her down.

I am a humble servant of the Rejuvenation Monastery, and am no better than any man. I live to serve, to share my religion openly, she said to herself. Tor stepped away, and when she knew he was no longer watching she wiped the spit from her cheek. A hand grabbed her arm and pulled her to a stop, and she took a deep breath to ready for the strike.

"Follow this road to a t-shaped intersection, take the left, then a right, and another left. You can't miss the shack when you see it." The man giving directions was her height and looked quite young, his armor a little too small as his large belly poked out.

"Thank you." Tor smiled. He released her and she followed his directions. When she reached the shack she saw the guard wasn't wrong about not missing it.

It had the monastery's symbol on the front, but it looked in complete disarray. It should have only been empty for a month or two. The last cleric had been asked to move into the castle to care for the king himself.

Tor entered the shack, seeing it was in worse condition on the inside than it was out. The front room had a rickety table, on its side, and four chairs that looked like they would turn to kindling if she sat on them. To the right was a bed, likely for patients. A large hearth sat in the center of the room, separating the front from the back. The air was stale and the distinct smell of waste hung. Tor wrinkled her nose. A chamber pot must have been left full when the previous resident left.

Tor moved through the shack. The kitchen was small, but it would do for just herself. As she'd suspected, there was another room at the back where another bed sat, and she was relieved to see it would be big enough.

It was late, and Tor was in no mood to clean anything. She attempted to secure the door, not wanting any uninvited guests in the middle of the night. If they really wanted in, they could just crawl through any of the three broken windows.

She fixed the bed the best she could and crawled in. When her full weight settled on the frame it creaked and moaned. With a loud crack she found herself on the floor and the frame in pieces. Tor sighed and laid back down. Tomorrow was going to be a busy day of cleaning, fixing, and letting the locals know they had a new healer in town.

CHAPTER FIVE

TOR SPENT THE NEXT SEVERAL weeks cleaning and fixing what she could with the hovel she was expected to live in. She missed her tiny six-by-six stone room at the monastery. At least the roof didn't leak, and the furniture to sit on and not better used as wood for the fire. Every morning, she put out the sign indicating a healer was present.

She would get many visitors at first, but the moment they spotted her they would turn and leave. Tor needed to find a way to convince the people of the lower city she could be trusted. That's when she'd decided to seek out the orphanage. Every lower city has an orphanage. Perhaps, if she endeared herself to the Mothers, they would spread the word.

The next morning, Tor packed her pouch of medical supplies, took down the sign she was available, and headed for the orphanage. At least, in the direction she was relatively certain it would be: the center of the lower city.

It took a little time to find, but she smiled when she heard the children, on the other side of the tall wall, shouting and laughing. Tor followed the wall to the front gate, which was open, so she stepped in. One child screamed, drawing the attention of the others and causing them to scatter and run for the building.

"It's okay," Tor said, raising her hands. "I won't hurt you." She'd taken another step into the compound when a woman, likely in her seventies, stepped out of the building and stood on the front step. Her presence was both intimidating and comforting. She stood tall and looked down at Tor.

"Is there something I can help you with?"

"My name is Tor and I'm a healer from—"

"I am aware of who you are. Everyone is aware of the orc healer." The woman crossed her arms.

Tor risked stepping further in, but she didn't know if the Mothers would harm her. Their only job was to protect the children, and Tor doubted they had an oath about not harming others. "I thought I would see if you needed any medical assistance. I would love to serve you and yours." Tor bowed her head low when she heard a second voice.

"Head Mother, his fever is much higher. He is becoming delirious."

Head Mother said, "Has there been any word from the High King? Will he send his healer?"

"No, Head Mother, he has denied our request."

Tor lifted her head enough to peer out under her lashes. "Please, allow me to help."

There was a long silence, so long it made Tor uncomfortable. If the Mothers were going to kill her, she wanted to be standing tall. She met Head Mothers' eyes.

"Very well, follow me. But if you try anything—"

Tor raised a hand. "I understand."

The second Mother opened her mouth in protest, but said nothing as Tor stepped past. She quickened her pace to catch up with the Head Mother, the gazes of the children and the five other Mothers in the room following her.

Tor was led to a secluded room at the back of the orphanage. It was smart they had separated the child from the others to prevent the spread of a possible infection. A single bed, chair, and night table occupied the room. A small child lay on the bed, soaked in sweat. He was moaning and speaking, but not making any sense.

Tor took off her medical bag and placed it on the table, handing the bowl of water to the Head Mother. She unzipped her bag, then leaned in close to the boy. His breathing was fast and erratic.

"How long has he been in this condition?"

"He fell ill five days ago. He complained of a sore throat, then his temperature began to rise," Head Mother said.

Tor pulled back the soaked blanket and dropped it to the floor. "Could you fill this bowl with fresh water, as cold as you can get it, as well as bring a kettle of the hottest water?" She directed her request to no one in particular now she was drawing a small crowd, and didn't take her eyes off the boy as she pulled a rare root out of her bag. It had taken her months to get it, to convince the fairies she was worthy.

When she took out her blade there was a collective gasp. Without looking up, Tor said, "It's all right, I just need to use it to shave some of this root." She ran the knife down the strange root, letting a long, thin peel drop onto the cloth she'd draped across her legs. She placed the remainder and the knife back into her pack, then took the shaved part and lay it across the boy's forehead. The root went from a stark white to a deep purple in an instant.

"Hmm." Tor grabbed the small stone bowl she carried with her supplies and put inside a leafy plant stem and a drop of oil, then began to crush the ingredients together. She chanted an incantation of healing as she worked the mixture. The static in the room grew, and when it reached its peak Tor stopped mixing. A puff of pink smoke rose from the bowl. Tor smiled.

She was about to speak when two Mothers returned with her requested items. "Thank you," she said as she took the kettle and added the mixture, then stirred it and replaced the lid before placing it on the ground. She then took the bowl of water and added several flower petals of an orange and green color to the bowl.

Swirling it, careful not to spill anything, she chanted again—a different incantation this time. The smell of wood and dirt filled her nose and she smiled again, placing the bowl on the floor.

"Cloth?" she asked Head Mother, who was watching intently. She stuttered slightly before handing Tor a clean cloth. She dipped it into the bowl, letting it soak up the mixture before rinsing it out. She took the root shaving from the boy's forehead and started wiping him down with the cloth. She was meticulous, starting from the top of his head and working her way down his tiny body.

The entire time she chanted a healing spell, the static holding at a steady level. Head Mother helped roll the boy over so Tor could wash his back, from head to toe. When she was done she handed the bowl to a Mother, whose eyes widened at the sight of the near-black water.

"It's the illness being pulled from his body," Tor said, answering the unasked question. "Please dispose of it immediately. Somewhere people will not come into contact with it, and try not to touch it."

The Mother nodded and rushed from the room. Tor dressed the boy in clean, dry cloths and propped him up. His eyes opened and he looked from Tor to the Head Mother, then back to Tor. "Am I dead?" he asked quietly.

"You are not," Tor said, gently and with a smile. She lifted the kettle and swished the contents, then poured it into a mug. "Drink this, little one. It will help your throat and further bring down your fever."

He reluctantly took the mug and sipped. His eyes then brightened and he gulped down the rest. "May I have some more?" He held out the mug.

"In a few hours. Now rest." Tor helped him to readjust and again lie down, then covered him up. She handed Head Mother the kettle. "There is enough in there for three more treatments. Every three hours, no matter the time of day, he is to have one mug until all of the mixture is gone. No matter how much he says he is feeling better, do not allow him around the other children until he has finished this mixture."

"What did you put in it?" Head Mother asked. "He seemed to enjoy it."

Tor smiled. "I added a bit of sugar to it. Normally, it is quiet sour and potent. But we need him to drink it, so I added the sugar. It does not alter the medicine."

Head Mother laughed. "I'll need to remember that trick. Thank you, Healer. I'm sorry I judged you. It's just— You understand."

"I understand." Tor packed up her medical supplies and stood. "If any of the other children start to feel ill, you will come and get me?"

"Yes, of course. Thank you again."

"And, if it's not too much to ask, let others know I am only here to help."

Head Mother took Tor's hands into her own. "I will spread the word. But, before you leave, perhaps you can look at one more child?"

"Of course, lead the way."

Head Mother led Tor back the way they'd come, and took a turn from the main room to where she could hear children speaking in unison. When they reached the door Tor spotted a Mother at the head of a room half full of children sitting at tables, facing her. They were reading from the board on the wall.

"You have a school here as well?" Tor asked.

Head Mother smiled. "Yes. We teach reading and mathematics to the children in the area, not just those in the orphanage. There is nowhere else in the lower city for children to get any type of education." She turned back to the classroom. "Excuse the intrusion Mother, Faiddian please come."

All the children's eyes fell onto the young boy. Perhaps ten, although his size would indicate younger. He stood, and Tor saw he was thin and gangly. His hand was wrapped poorly in a dirty bandage. He came to stand in front of Tor, his head back as far as it would go as he looked up at her.

"May I take a look at that?" Tor asked, pointing at the hand he'd put behind his back. "Why don't the three of us go to the front room, where I can see it better."

His eyes darted back and forth, from Tor to Head Mother. Head Mother smiled and put an arm around his shoulders, guiding him to where the children ate their meals and slept. They sat at a table, and Tor knelt in front of the boy so he could look down at her.

She held her hand out and smiled. "May I?"

Reluctantly, he put his bandaged hand into hers.

"Playing in the dirt, were you?" Tor smiled again.

Faiddian said nothing.

Tor unwrapped his hand, the bandage getting cleaner as it unraveled. Then it turned a brownish-red. When she finished she could see two of his fingers were angled oddly, crushed. Tor's shoulders slumped as she inspected the injury. The only good news was there was no infection, but the damage had been done well over a week ago and the injury could not be fixed. No amount of magic or incantations she knew could restore his fingers.

"What happened?"

Head Mother nudged Faiddian. "I-I fell from a tree."

Tor narrowed her eyes at him and puckered out her lips. "This is not an injury of a fall from a tree. What really happened?"

"It's true. I fell from a tree," he insisted.

"All right. Then what happened?"

He fidgeted in his seat, gaze darting to the Head Mother.

"Head Mother, could you get me some clean bandages?" Tor asked. Head Mother nodded, smiled, and left the two of them. "All right, what really happened?"

He hung his head, and Tor could now see the shame he felt. "I was pushing one of the other boys. He fell and I kicked him."

"Okay, so what happened to your hand?"

"He kicked me in the balls, and when I fell he smashed my hand with a rock." He rushed the words out, as if quickly pulling a blade from a wound to get it over with.

"I see. You were being a bully and your victim got tired of it."

"Yes."

"Have you learned your lesson?" Tor lifted the boys chin to look into his eyes. "Will you pick on others?"

He shook his head, but Tor could see he hadn't fully learned his lesson. If it weren't for his hand, he would likely have sought revenge by now.

"I'm afraid there is nothing I can do to heal your hand. But you are a smart boy, and I suspect you already knew that. I will have to remove these two fingers before they become infected and you lose the entire hand."

The boy began to sob.

"As cruel as this sounds, Faiddian, you have been cruel to another and this is the punishment. I also suspect that this wasn't the first time you'd picked on this other boy. Was it?"

"He made fun of me. Said I had no parents, but he did." He wiped at his face with his good hand.

Tor glanced toward Head Mother, who had been listening in the entire time. "He should not have said those things, but we don't solve disputes with violence. He goes home with two good hands, and now you will only have two fingers on this hand. How will you ever count to ten?" Tor gave him a gentle nudge and a smile.

He snorted and wiped his face again.

"Have you really learned your lesson?"

He nodded. Tor really didn't believe it, but she wasn't his spiritual adviser or guardian. She wasn't there to judge this boy, she was only there to heal him.

"Bring him to my place in a couple days," Tor said to Head Mother as she rewrapped his hand. "I will have a sterile place to remove the damaged fingers. I'm sorry I am unable to repair the damage. Perhaps if he were brought to me sooner."

Head Mother dipped her head. "Yes. My own prejudice prevented that from happening. It will not happen again. I will have him brought to you in two days." Head Mother opened her mouth, then shut it again.

Tor could see a question cross the woman's face. "You want to ask me something else? Is another not well?"

"No, Healer, it's not that."

"Then what is it?"

"It's just that I've heard of healers fixing broken and crushed bones before. So I'm a little—"

Tor stood to her full height. "Yes, the healing magic of the tree sprites. It is, unfortunately, a magic I was never taught. Tree sprites are very secretive about their magic, since it is natural. It comes from their blood, so you can imagine that if others knew what was needed to use their magic—"

"Sprites would be hunted."

"Exactly." She turned to grab her medical bag. "Perhaps I can find a sprite who would be willing to share their knowledge with me. I hear there are several forested areas in this region that are cared for by sprites."

"Jannar Forest," Faiddian blurted out.

Both Tor and Head Mother had thought the boy had left he had kept so quiet.

"Yes, it's the closest I'm aware of." Head Mother nodded, then pointed to the boy to indicate he return to class. He skittered away. "The only other woods with sprites I'm aware of is the Whispering Oaks Forest. But that is a several weeks' walk south toward the Knolnt River."

Tor nodded. Perhaps she would try the Jannar Forest in a few months, but for now she needed to remain in the city so people knew where to find her for help. She swung her pack over her shoulder. "I'll see you in two days then?"

Head Mother nodded. "Yes, two days. Thank you again, Healer Tor." Her smile was warm and welcoming, and not so intimidating anymore.

Tor bowed her head and left the orphanage with a warm feeling. She had been there for most of the day. When she returned home, she put her sign back out for a few hours before calling it a night and turning in.

It didn't take long for Tor to forget about the fae and the child. She had her hands full with fixing up her shack and tending to those who were willing to trust her. Word spread quickly about her healing the boy at the orphanage, and most days there was a lineup of people seeking medical treatment of some kind outside her door.

Tor had adapted a bartering system for her services: food, clothes, work to be done on the shack. Before long she had everything she needed to live and a shack she could now call home, with no drafts, the windows fixed, and a roof that no longer leaked. There was still some mistrust, and her home had been vandalized several times, but nothing she couldn't handle herself.

She was going over her notes and some basic defensive spells, practicing the finger placements and wrist movements, when she heard a small child cry out. It wasn't an injured cry, but a distress call. Without a second thought, Tor bolted out of her shack into the street. A boy no more than three stood over a woman lying in the middle of the road.

A small crowd had begun to gather around her, but parted when Tor approached. She swallowed hard as she knelt next to the unmoving woman. Tor rolled her over onto her back, seeing the dark circles under her eyes were a deep contrast to the paleness of her skin. She was ashen, her lips gray. The young boy clutched at the woman.

"Momma, Momma."

Tor glanced up at the sea of faces around her, all familiar and thankfully all friendly. "Does anyone know this woman?"

There was a murmur from the crowd, then a voice from the back said, "I think she's one of the field workers. I've seen her leave the gates some mornings, when she passes my stall."

Tor nodded. It didn't give her much to go on, but at least she knew this woman was a laborer. Tor lifted her out of the mud and dirt with ease and carried her back to the shack, the small boy in tow.

"Do you need any help, Healer Tor?" a voice called out.

Without turning, Tor said over her shoulder, "Could you check to see if she has any other family, and if any of them are ill?"

Another murmur came from the crowd, with several agreeing to the task.

Tor pushed open the door to her shack and placed the woman on the bed for patients. Then she began to mix several ingredients into a bowl. What ailed this woman, Tor didn't know, so she made an elixir that would treat several different illnesses. While she waited for the water to boil she knelt in front of the small boy.

"What's your name, dear one?" Her voice was soft, soothing.

He looked her straight in the eye, perhaps the first child Tor had ever encountered who didn't seem afraid of her. "Parin." His tiny voice could be barely heard.

"How are you feeling, Parin?"

"Fine."

"Do you mind if I touch your head?"

He shook his head, and with it his whole body seemed to follow as he swayed back and forth. Tor smiled and placed a palm to his forehead, then spoke a simple incantation under her breath to draw out any heat that may be gathering from an early fever. But there was nothing.

She smiled at him again. "Would you like some stew? It's deer."

His eyes brightened and he nodded.

"Okay. Take a seat at the table." Tor quickly moved to the kitchen, pulling the boiling water from the fire and adding it to a kettle, then dropping her mixture into it. She then ladled out a bowl of stew, which was simmering on the other side of the fire. She grabbed a large knife and cut chunks of bread from a loaf, put them on a plate, and returned with the meal to Parin, who was sitting at the table.

He didn't hesitate, and dug right into the meal. Tor then turned her attention to his mother. Her fever was high, and her heart raced. Tor worked quickly to clean the woman and cleanse her body. She recited her incantations and concocted different mixtures of herbs throughout the night.

Parin slept in her bed while Tor stayed vigil over his mother, worried she may not recover at all. Tor sat in a chair next to the bed, her arms and legs crossed and her chin dipped low to her chest. She snored lightly. A moan from Parin's mother woke her. It was the wee hours of the early morning, the sun only starting to show the colors of its arrival.

The woman blinked and squinted at Tor. "Healer? I don't remember making it here."

Tor smiled. "You didn't quite. I found you on the street, just a few buildings up the road."

"How long?"

"Just the night."

She shot up. "Parin, my boy—"

Tor placed a hand on her shoulder. "Sleeping in the other room." She went to the kitchen and grabbed a pot. "I'll be right back. Please don't get up."

The woman nodded and Tor left to fetch water from the well down the street. The streets of lower-town were quiet, no one yet out, but as she passed by some dwellings she could hear chatter as people got ready to leave for work for the day. It took Tor less than five minutes to fill her pots and return.

Parin's mother had fallen back to sleep by the time she came back. Tor prepared another rinse to clean her patient, as well as a tea she would drink to help with any remnants. By the time everything was done, the sun was up and the streets outside her little shack were bustling.

Parin's mom and Parin were both up. The boy enjoyed another hot meal for breakfast, and his mother drank the tea Tor had made.

"Thank you, Healer, for everything you have done," Parin's mom said as she handed Tor the empty mug and swung her legs over the edge of the bed.

"Please, call me Tor," she said, taking the mug. "You will still be quite weak, and a little light-headed. I would prefer that you stay for at least another day."

She smiled at Tor and patted her hand. "Call me Darla. I appreciate everything you have done for me and my son, but we have imposed enough." She reached into her pocket and pulled out one copper piece. "This is all I have, I'm sorry—"

Tor closed Darla's hand around the piece. "No need. You keep that for you and Parin. If you need anything else." Tor helped Darla to her feet, who took a moment to steady herself. Tor rushed to the kitchen grabbed the remainder of the bread and a bowl, which she filled with stew and covered with a cloth then secured with twine. Then took a small satchel and placed inside the dry ingredients for the tea mixture.

She placed all the items in a cloth bag and brought them to Darla. "For later. Make sure you have two mugs of the tea mixture a day, for the next week. There is more than enough. One spoonful in a mug of hot water. It wouldn't hurt young Parin to have a bit as well."

"Thank you again...Tor." Darla cradled the package in her arm like a small baby and ushered Parin from Tor's home.

Tor waited at the door, watching as the two eased their way down the street and out of sight. Parin turned just before they were completely gone and waved. Tor waved back, then let out a heavy sigh. She was concerned Darla may fall ill again, being up and about so soon, so decided that over the next week she would visit the two every night.

CHAPTER SIX

I T HAD TAKEN ALMOST TWO years for word to reach the city's middle class of the new healer, and before her services were requested. Yet she was still not allowed to leave the lower parts of the city. All mid-town clients were forced to come to her, although most sent messengers, not wanting to dirty themselves.

Those of middle class who did come were not shy about show-ing their disdain. To them, the idea of having to cross into lower-town was distasteful. But they paid their fees with actual currency: gold bars and gems. Tor did not refuse because she knew she would eventually have to barter with real money.

Tor was at the back of her shack, tending her garden of herbs for natural remedies, when she heard her front door open. It had a distinct creak as the wood protested the movement. One of her patients had offered to fix it but one night while she slept, after being vandalized and attacked, that creak had warned her someone was coming.

She stood and wiped her dirt-covered hands on the leather apron she wore over her handkerchief-type top and baggy pants, which were held up with a leather belt—all items given for services rendered. When she stepped into the front room she found a King's Guard. His armor was much too small, his large belly forcing its way out. His hair was short, but not cropped, and his baby face was closely shaved. Tor knew this man; he'd helped her the day she arrived.

"How can I help you today?" Tor asked, grabbing a cloth to properly clean her hands. "Are you injured?"

"No," he said as he looked around the cozy room.

"You're ill then?"

"No, I'm not here for me." He fidgeted on the spot, playing with the hilt of his sword and shifting from one foot to the other.

Tor slouched and dropped her chin slightly, adopting a submissive stance. She normally held her head high, back straight, but to many that was terrifying. "Who requires my services?"

His gaze fell onto her, and he glanced her up and down. He then cleared his throat and lifted his own chin. She knew he was trying to appear authoritative, but his baby face and nervous gaze gave him away. "There's a small hut, three streets over and down a short side street of tightly packed homes with red thatched roofs."

"I know it well." Many of the elderly lived in the area. They kept an eye on one another, but it was the poorest part of lower-town. If that was even possible.

"It's the fourth from the left when facing the street. An old man requires immediate medical attention."

Tor lifted her head, and without thinking straightened her back. "What ails him?"

The guard took a half step back, then composed himself once again. "He's bedridden, non-responsive. Won't eat or drink."

"How long?"

"A week, maybe two. Will you help him?"

"Of course." Tor moved to her kitchen and readied her medical bag, grabbing her stone mixing bowl and several kinds of herbs, oils, and plants. She turned to speak to the guard, but the creak of the door told her he'd left. She finished packing, took off her apron, and put on her coat. As she buttoned up there was a light knock and the door creaked open again.

A small boy popped his head in. "Tor?"

"Parin?" He was five now. "What are you doing here? Is your momma all right?" She had run a fever for several days, and had been near death when Tor had met her two years prior. By the time Tor was done treating her, she was healthier than she had ever been her entire life. She worked the fields and had paid Tor with refined oats.

"I can't find her. She not back from fields. I'm hungry, Tor."

Tor knitted her eyebrows. It was near dark and all the field workers would have re-entered the city walls by now, so the gates would be closed. "Come in and sit." Parin did as he was told and climbed onto one of the kitchen chairs. Tor always had a soup or a stew of some kind simmering. When some patients didn't want to take their medicine she would add it to the soup or the stew and offer a warm meal.

Many only had one meal a day, so they never refused. Tor spooned out a helping of chicken, carrots, and some sort of noodle into a bowl. She placed it in front of Parin, then handed him a spoon. Without question, he dug into the meal.

Tor took off her coat and sat across from the boy. His momma usually cared for him well, and kept him in as clean and as fresh of clothes she could manage given their living situation. But he looked as though he hadn't washed in days; his clothes were filthy, and the way he dug into the soup meant he hadn't eaten in some time. Her heart ached for him.

The slurping of the young boy as he sucked up the noodles filled the air, making Tor smile. A vague thought ran through her mind, wondering if this was the child the fae had spoken of two years ago. But Tor felt no static. He had no magic, nothing natural anyways, and the likelihood a five year old could master incantations was next to nothing.

"What are these?" Parin asked as he pulled a long, string-like item from his bowl.

"It's called pasta, and it's a delicacy in mid-town. Do you like it?"

He opened his mouth and tilted his head back, dropping the noodle into it. "Very much," he said with a full mouth.

When he'd had his fill, he pushed the bowl away and rubbed his belly. Tor took the bowl and came back with a wet cloth. She proceeded to clean his face and hands, and as she did she checked him for marks, bruises, cuts, scrapes. He had a great deal of dirt under his nails, which had not been properly trimmed for a while, and it looked as though he chewed on a few.

His appearance was really that of a young boy who liked to play in the dirt. "Parin, how long has your momma been gone?"

He looked down and counted on his fingers. He held up one hand with four fingers. "That many."

"Four days?"

He nodded.

"Did somebody come and pick her up? Did she fall ill again?"

Parin shook his head. "She went to the fields like she always done."

"Where have you been staying?"

"I go with other kids every day, like always. But alone at home at night, waiting for momma to come home..." Large fat tears ran down his cheeks, and Tor wiped them with the back of her hand. The kids he spoke of were mostly street kids and ones who lived in the orphanage. Head Mother had brought many children in for deep cuts or running noses over the years, but Tor never questioned why so many children were in the orphanage.

It was like every major city with a poor end of town that was rampant with ill-treated diseases that took the lives of parents and children.

"I don't want to go to orphanage." Parin blinked his large eyes at her.

"You can stay here tonight. You look quite tired."

"I scared without momma at night. Too scary to sleep."

Tor nodded. "Okay, come lie down in my bed." She stood and held out her hand. He slid off the chair and took it, and Tor led him into her room and pulled back the large quilt and sheets—payment from a mid-town woman. Tor then went to a chest and pulled out a clean top. The boy would be swimming it, but she didn't want him in her clean sheets wearing such dirty clothes.

She was about to hand him the shirt when she paused. "I think you should have a bath first, don't you?"

Parin looked down at himself and shrugged. Typical of a boy his age, but she prepared a hot bath and helped him to clean himself. He was fascinated by the bubbles the fancy soap made when water was added, and it smelled of lavender and roses. Once clean she dressed him in the fresh shirt and put him to bed. He was asleep before Tor left the room.

She closed the curtain that separated her sleeping area from the rest of her home. Grabbing her notebook, she sat at the table with a hot tea and went through her notes on different magics. It had been two years; when was this child supposed to come? Had Abacuss been wrong about his vision? Was Parin the child she'd been waiting for? If he was, she needed to figure out how he was causing an unbalance.

Tor furrowed her brow. There hadn't been any unbalance. She used magic more now than she ever had for her healing, and never encountered any issues. Tor tapped her pencil on the piece of paper as she fell further into thought. For all the time she had known Parin and his mother, she had never felt any static from either. Perhaps he had a type of magic she couldn't detect by the static, a magic that doesn't expel static when used. But, through all the studying of different magics, one that fits that description doesn't exist. Not to her knowledge.

It's no wonder the boy couldn't care for himself. She would take him to the orphanage tomorrow, and ask Head Mother to watch him until Tor could find his momma. She would try to speak with the guards at the back gate, where all the field workers exit and enter the city. These workers are tracked by the guards, because they are the king's workers.

She put another couple logs into the hearth and banked the fire, moving the simmering pot of soup to the edge so as not to burn it or have it cool off too much and spoil. Her shoulders slumped when she spotted her medical bag and remembered the old man she was to visit. Leaving Parin on his own was out of the question, and it was getting a little late.

"First thing after I go to the orphanage," she said, then went to the back room to sleep. She found Parin lying diagonally across the bed, all his limbs spread out.

Tor smirked, grabbed an extra blanket from the chest, and slept on the small cot in the front of her home. She had to lie on her side, her knees hanging over the edge of the bed. She was much too large for it, and Tor made a mental note to have it made slightly larger. Parin wasn't going to be spending another night, so at least she would be in her own bed tomorrow.

CHAPTER SEVEN

T HE NEXT MORNING, AFTER THEY'D had a meal, Tor reluctantly helped Parin back into his dirty clothes. She had nothing else for him.

"This bed is very soft." He smiled wide as he passed by the mattress. "Mine is hard and lumpy. Straw pokes me in the back. Your straw is nice."

"That's because it isn't straw, it's made of feathers and soft materials." Tor could feel her face heat up with embarrassment at admitting she slept on such a luxurious mattress. Her bed at the monastery was quite hard, she'd been taught it was part of learning humility.

"Where did you get it?"

"A very nice man in mid-town was thankful for my help in healing his foot."

"You think, if I help nice people in mid-town, I can get a bed like that?"

Tor smiled at his bright face. He did look as though he had a solid night's sleep, probably the best in his short life. "Perhaps."

He gave one curt nod, satisfied with an answer of possibility.

"Come, let's go see Head Mother at the orphanage. You can spend the day there while I look for your momma." Tor led him out of her home and put up a notice that she wasn't in, but would return shortly. When they stepped into the middle of the street, Tor caught a glimpse of a man in a cloak. He was poorly hiding himself, and she could see the shine of his chest plate. Even after two years, the King's Guard still watched and followed her.

Parin stayed close as Tor strode down the streets. People stepped out of her way and nodded. Many smiled and wished them a good day. In the time Tor had spent in the city, she had helped save many lives. A great deal of the clerics sent to the High Kingdom on their pilgrimage took little time to forget their oath that they are better than no man. They would stay only long enough to check on a few of the poor, then move to mid-town or the upper regions of the city.

When word reached the monastery, these clerics would be recalled or sent on pilgrimage to a different place. She thought it hypocritical that many of the clerics before her would ingratiate themselves with the rich and ignore the poor. It was against everything their religion taught. She'd been punished when, younger, she'd tried to maintain some of her orc ceremonies, yet others were allowed to forget their oaths altogether.

Even though Tor was unable to leave the lower levels, she still tended to the poor as she would the better off. Her oath of servitude was all she had, money and high status meant nothing to her.

As they approached the orphanage, a group of boys around Parin's age filed out the front doors. They laughed and screamed out in joy as they chased each other around. The orphanage Mothers took exceptional care of the children, doing the best they could with their resources. Tor donated her time and skills, and bartered services to send goods to the Mothers.

Parin was bouncing on the balls of his feet, excitedly watching the other children play.

"Go," Tor said. "I will see you later."

Parin hugged her and took off, screaming with joy.

Tor watched him with great affection, and when she turned to the orphanage she found Head Mother standing on the front steps, her arms crossed and smiling at Tor.

"I do not need your services today, my friend," she said as Tor approached.

"I'm very pleased to hear that. I have brought some supplies." Tor stood at the bottom of the stairs and looked up at the Head Mother, raising the bags she held in one hand.

Head Mother smiled warmly and took the bags full of fruit, meats, and blankets.

"However, my main reason for coming is of another matter."

"Oh? How can the House of Mothers' Foundlings help you?"

"Parin's momma has not come home for four days. Do you have a bed he may sleep in until I find her?"

Head Mother dropped her hands, her smile dropping with them. "Come inside."

A pit formed in Tor's stomach. That was an ominous response to her request, and she knew she wasn't going to like what was coming. Tor followed Head Mother into the building. She stopped only briefly to hand over Tor's offerings to another Mother, then lead Tor through the main living area, the dining hall, and then to the back offices.

Head Mother sat behind a heavy wood desk, papers laid out everywhere. She pointed to a rickety-looking chair and told Tor to sit. Tor eyed the chair, unsure if it would hold her weight. She made a mental note to have a woodworker fix it for the Head Mother.

"I'm sorry, Tor, I can't take Parin in."

Tor was taken back by the response. She had never known them to turn any child away. "Why?"

"We are past capacity as it is, and the children are already sleeping two to a bed."

"I don't understand; how could you possibly be full? How are there so many orphaned children? I haven't been getting any terminal or extremely ill patients."

Head Mother took in a deep breath and leaned on the desk. "There have been reports of missing people, for months now. Many of the children are here because their parents have gone missing. They leave in the morning for work in the fields, and don't return. We have tried to place many of the children with family, but times are hard here in the lower city."

Tor rubbed her face.

"Does Parin have other family here?" Head Mother asked.

"I don't believe so. But I can't say for certain. He is a bright boy, a fast learner. There must be something you can do."

Head Mother gave a sympathetic smile and shook her head. "Perhaps you can take him in, teach him in the ways of healing, and when the time is right he can go to the Rejuvenation Monastery."

Tor gave a tight smile, her shoulders dropping, but not enough for the Head Mother to notice. Her mind drifted. Is this what Abacuss meant? The fae had told her the child must survive. Perhaps Parin was the child. He must be, for everything to come together in such a way: the chance meeting two years before, Tor coming across Parin and his momma just as she'd collapsed from fever. She was now being forced to have Parin stay with her, the orphanage full and having to turn him away.

If Parin was to live on the streets, he would surely die. Tor still didn't feel any type of static from him, and he had shown no sensitivity when she used magic around him. Perhaps he will grow into it.

"If you were to take him in, we would still gladly teach him reading, writing, and mathematics." Head Mother smiled as she kept leaning toward Tor.

Tor sighed inwardly. "Of course, I will take him. He will make a wonderful apprentice, as he is always eager to learn. But I would still like to find out what happened to his momma. Do you know anything more about the disappearances?"

"No, I'm afraid not." Head Mother sat back in her chair. "We are not in the business of solving mysteries."

"How many children have come to you because their parents have gone missing?"

Head Mother swallowed. Her eyes widened, not in horror but in a sadness Tor had only seen once before. "At least twenty-five."

"In how long?"

"The last two to three months."

Tor's mouth dropped open, and she didn't know what to say. "Have you gone to the King's Guard? Told them of the disappearances?"

"It is not our job. We have many to care for, and we don't have time. We check to see if the children have other family they could go to, but that is all we can do."

Tor stood, and her abruptness obviously startled Head Mother as she flinched. Ignoring the reaction, Tor said, "I will do some looking into it myself, then. Perhaps King Thomas doesn't know his people are disappearing. If I can get one of the guards—"

Head Mother shook her head and scoffed. "There isn't anything that goes on in the High Kingdom that King Thomas doesn't know about. After two years of being in the city walls, I thought you would have learned that. Trust me, Tor, King Thomas knows."

Tor tightened her lips and sighed heavily. "Thank you for your time, Head Mother. I will be back for Parin at the end of his teachings for the day."

Head Mother stood and bowed her head. Tor made her way out of the building as the children were being called back in for their midday teachings.

She spotted Parin with two other boys. "Parin," she called, and he ran to her. "You will stay for your days' teachings, and I will return for you this afternoon. You will be staying with me for now. All right?"

His face lit up and he nodded his head vigorously.

"All right, off you go before I get scolded for holding you up."

Without a word, he ran to catch up with his classmates and they all filed into the building. Tor gave a small wave and smile to the waiting Mother, who nodded and closed the door.

Tor needed answers. If over twenty children had lost their parents, but not to illness, someone must know what was happening. There was only one place she could think of going. As she stepped out of the orphanage compound, she glanced down the street and set a grim stare on the man hiding beside a building.

Or at least he was supposed to be hiding, he just wasn't any good at it. Tor strode toward him, and when he realized his cover had been blown he tried to scurry away. But the streets were packed with midday travelers and merchants. Tor grabbed the hood of his shabby cloak and dragged him down a side path between buildings.

She stood at least two feet taller than him and he was forced to look up at her. Tor was certain this height advantage would suit her well in the interrogation.

"The Head Mother at the orphanage has informed me of an alarming amount of people have gone missing."

He stood a little taller, perhaps feeling braver, and said, "What does that have anything to do with me?"

"At least twenty children have lost both their parents, and many have just up and disappeared." Tor still had a grip on the man's cloak and she lifted her arm, forcing him to his toes. Not so brave now.

"I'm but a lonely beggar, and I have no idea what you speak of. These are hard times, perhaps they ran off."

Tor narrowed her eyes at the man. She dropped him and ripped open his cloak, revealing his chest plate with the crest of the High King. She rapped her knuckle on it, like she was knocking on someone's door. "You are no more a lonely beggar than I am a damsel in a tower. Tell me what I want to know, or tell me where I can find out." She stepped back from the man. "You knights have been following me from the first moment I set foot through the gates two years ago. You know every move I make, and I can only assume you inform the king. Which also leaves me to believe you guards know things that you don't inform King Thomas about."

"I still have no idea what you are talking about," he said, lifting his chin high.

Tor sighed, loud and impatient. "There are children involved."

The man scrunched his face and attempted a shrug through his armor.

She studied the guard. She knew him, not by name or personally, but she knew of him. Many of the guards at the back gate had roots in the lower parts of the city. The lower-town was where many lived. The two stared at each other for a short time, then Tor realized exactly where she'd seen him for the first time.

She smiled, and the guard seemed to lose all confidence. "How is the wife? And your...son, correct? You had a son about a year ago. You were on duty, and couldn't be at his birth. But I was there."

He swallowed hard, his eyes narrowing and his bravery returning. "What do you want, orc?"

"Information, that's it. I just want to know where these people are disappearing to." She put her hands on her hips just as she felt the static in the air rise. Dropping her hands, Tor glanced about. It was a strong static, powerful magic was being used. Clouds grew, dark above their heads, and with a slight drop in air pressure lightning streaked across the sky as the static dissipated. When she brought her eyes back to the guard he was watching her.

"Strange storms we keep having, don't you think?" he asked.

Tor thought she hid her surprise at the question well. "Strange indeed. Unfortunate there is no rain for the fields." She felt as though they were now talking in code, and she hoped she would be able to figure it out.

"Yes, it is unfortunate, but many of our field workers are leaving their jobs, making them difficult to maintain."

"Are they finding work elsewhere?"

"Nowhere you would want to go on your own."

"Forced labor?"

"Tell me, orc, do you believe in religion? A higher being?" He leaned against the wall, attempting to be casual, but Tor could see the conversation was making him uncomfortable. Perhaps it was a topic they were not to discuss.

"My religion is that of healing."

"I once heard that orcs believed in gods. That you worship deities."

"In the land of men that would be considered blasphemy. It would be suicide if I were to do such a thing." Tor looked both ways down the path. Was he biding time for others to come? Was he really giving her information she needed? It was starting to feel like a trap.

"Do you think if a man was worshiped he could become a god?" the guard asked.

Now she couldn't hide her surprise. "Man cannot be a god, they do not exist."

"What if they did? What if a man figured out how to become a god? How would he gain his power? How would he rise to such heights?"

"Are you saying that there is someone who has discovered such a thing? That they need worshippers to become a god? Are you saying the king is recruiting worshippers?"

"Recruiting?" The guard's laugh was hollow and his eyes darted up and down the ally. "No, I wouldn't say that at all. In the beginning, one can't just recruit. Perhaps one day, yes."

Tor had a feeling she knew what he meant. Whoever was causing the storms, with no rain, was taking the workers from the fields, trying to find the perfect magic. Once they figured it out, they would then gather a following. "We need to stop them."

"*We?* There is no 'we,' and you will be hard-pressed to find anyone who will help. If they know what's good for them and their families." He pushed himself off the wall and stepped in close. "If you know what's good for you, orc, you'll keep your nose out of it. Or you may wake up one morning and find your new pet missing." He nodded toward the orphanage, and Tor didn't need a translation to know he was threatening Parin. He shoved past her and strode out of the path and into the street, disappearing around the corner.

Tor stood between the buildings as she tried to make sense of everything. She had studied many of the tomes in the monastery's library, and when she wasn't studying her medicines, healing, and defensive magic she would study history and other topics. One topic that interested her was that of strong dark magic. She would never use it herself, but she was fascinated as to the effects dark magic had on the user. There were theories, that if the proper dark magic was used at the right time, a man could become god-like. Extremely powerful, but great sacrifices needed to be made.

There was one more factor that would be needed: worshippers. People who gave their undying devotion, their souls, to this man. With their very life force, the proper dark magic, and the perfect time of year, along with a specific chant, could result in very powerful, god-like powers.

Perhaps that was why she was here, why Parin had come to her. Was he to be protected because he housed the very magic that would be needed for the ceremony? If so, the best course of action was for her to take the boy away from the city.

There were two problems: she had yet to meet travelers with an injured man, the group Abacuss told her she needed to meet; and the biggest problem was that the guards at the gates would never allow her to leave with a human child, no matter the situation. If she tried to sneak him out, and was caught, they would kill her, and nobody knows what they would do to the boy.

Her hands were tied. As much as she wanted to do right by all those children, without help she could do nothing. She would need to protect Parin, to teach him, and when he turned seventeen, the age of consent, she would take him to the monastery.

Tor set her shoulders and headed back to her shack. She was certain there would be people waiting for treatment. As she made her way through the streets she made a note to herself to practice her defensive magic.

CHAPTER EIGHT

THE NEXT MORNING TOR READIED her medical supplies and walked Parin to the orphanage. She headed to the small home she was supposed to visit two days before, but felt distracted.

Tor made her way down the muddy streets of the poorest part of the High Kingdom. She had been there for two years, but there was no sign of the people her mentor, or even the fae, had spoken about. Three travelers, with one injured, had not yet visited her. She began to doubt her mentor's prophecies, perhaps another one that would go by without coming to light.

But the child the fae had spoken about, the precious cargo Abacuss mentioned.... Were they the same thing? What was it about this child that they were all so worried about? Tor had heard of children who had mastered magical powers at a young age, but they were mostly from other realms—like the elf realm, Aweens. Perhaps even the fairy's young learned early on. But neither of these races would allow their young to be transported by humans and a dwarf. A war would be waged before that would happen.

The more Tor thought about it, the more she felt she was right about Parin. The fae had to have been talking about the boy, and they mentioned nothing about travelers. She shook the thought from her head as she approached the hovel.

She knocked on the side of a door frame, the door made from

a shredded sheet. A hunched woman answered, craning her neck to see Tor's face. "You the healer?" she croaked.

"I am," Tor said with a slight bow. Humility was the first lesson she'd learned at the monastery—no one was beneath her.

The woman squinted at her. "You're an orc, ain't ya?"

"I am that as well, yes." Tor smiled, used to the odd stares and snarls thrown in her direction.

"You came from the monastery?"

"Madam, I understand your caution. If I were in your position, I would do the same. But I promise you I am from the monastery. I am a healer, and I am only here to help."

The woman snarled, but Tor wasn't sure if it was actually just due to the fact she had to crane her neck to look up at her. Yet she stepped aside, and Tor ducked to enter the dwelling. It was dark, the fire in the hearth burning and the air was stale. It smelled of human waste and vomit.

Tor did her best to keep her face neutral, even though the stench was burning her nose and throat. The woman led her into the back, where there was a bed. If the woman hadn't grabbed the old man's hand, Tor would never had seen him.

He was so fragile looking, and he lay in the center of the bed—but could have fit in a drawer, given his size. Tor took off the leather pack. Stepping around the opposite side of the bed, she knelt next to it. She didn't want to sit on the bed, as it didn't look as though it could hold her weight.

She listened to the old man's raspy, uneven breathing. There was a rattling at the end of each breath. Tor checked his eyes, which in the dim light it wasn't an easy task, but she could see they were yellow around the edges. Pulling the covers back to get a better look at his body, she saw his skin was pale and seemed to just hang off his bones.

He had barely any muscle left, and he had soiled himself several times—which was where the smell came from. Obviously, the old woman could only do so much given her own condition. When Tor met her eyes she cast them down, shameful, and covered her husband. Tor stood and placed a hand on the old man's head. He was so small her hand nearly covered it entirely.

Tor knew there was nothing she could do for him, no amount of herbs, medicines, and not even magic could help. His body was shutting down, and the last of his days were upon him. Knowing full well that humans didn't believe in any deities, and that her own religion was that of healing, she still gave a silent prayer to one of the orc gods. She asked her Goddess Kadianea, the goddess of a simple death, if she would take this man who did not die on a battlefield, and to take this night, peacefully in his sleep, so that he may once again run and dance free in the afterlife.

Her own people would be disgusted she had given such a blessing to a non-orc, but Tor couldn't let this old man journey to the afterlife alone.

"What are you doing?" the old woman asked. "Are you healing him?"

Tor lifted her hand and stood to her full height. She gestured for the woman to go to the other room. Once in the front room, the old woman sat in a chair. She was still horribly hunched over, and had to crane to see Tor.

Tor dropped to her knees in front of the woman, sitting back on her heels and bringing her face down as low as she could so the old woman didn't have to crane her neck any more. "Do you have other family?"

The old woman narrowed her eyes. "Grandchildren."

"You should have them come and say their goodbyes now."

The old woman bit her lower lip as her chin began to quiver. "There is nothing you can do?"

"I'm afraid not. His illness, and his age, make healing impossible. I am truly sorry."

"How long?"

Tor sighed. "Another night, maybe two."

"What were you doing to him in there?" The woman's eyes hardened.

Tor cleared her throat, knowing it wasn't a good idea to tell her anything. But maybe it would bring the old woman some comfort. "I asked for my goddess to guide him into the next life. To take him gently, so that he may run and dance once again."

"No such things as gods," the old woman said, snarling.

Tor smiled. "You don't need to believe." Tor came to her feet, and as she did she glanced at the hump on the old woman's back. "How long have you had that lump?"

"Eh? You looking to make more money from me? You didn't even do anything for my husband, but I sure bet you want to be paid."

"I don't believe there was an answer in there."

The old woman snarled at Tor; grief and pain was all she could see on the woman's face. "Several years," she finally said.

"Did you fall? Did it appear after an injury?" Tor leaned over the woman and gently felt around the hump.

"No, it just started growing."

"Did you see any other healers about it?"

The old woman laughed a bitter laugh. "None that would barter. We couldn't afford any treatments. I thought you healers were better than no man?" She shrugged away from Tor's hands. "I don't have more than a few copper pieces. It's all we have, and that's your fee. So take it and go."

"You don't wish for me to treat this?" Tor took a step back and looked around the little house. "You bake?"

"Eh? Do I bake?"

"Yes, do you make breads? Pies?"

The old woman grunted. "Since I was a young girl. I make the best sour bread."

"I love sour bread," Tor said, smiling. She had actually never even heard of sour bread, and wasn't sure it was something she wanted to try. "If you bake me a loaf of your sour bread, that will be your payment for this visit. Including my taking a look at that hump of yours."

The woman's eyes lit up. "You'd take sour bread as payment?"

"Yes ma'am."

"I would have to bake it."

"Even better; nothing better than warm, fresh bread." Tor smiled again, as it was true: warm, fresh bread was the best in soothing a soul. So her mentor would say when she was young and missing home.

The woman nodded and Tor, who took off her jacket and medicine bag. She opened the curtain, just a dirty piece of cloth, but it let in enough light for Tor to get a look at the hump. She poked at it a few more times, noticing it wasn't a solid mass. It was filled with fluid.

"Do you lie on your back when you sleep?"

"Terrible pain when I do, and there's the wetness that happens too."

"Wetness?"

The woman shook her head. "I wake up with my back wet, my bed soaked. Always thought I was sweating, but never understood why as it never gets that hot at night."

"The next morning...how do you feel?"

She shrugged. "Better, I suppose. I can stand a little taller, but after a day or two I'm back to being all hunched again."

Tor nodded. This wasn't a growth; it was a cyst, a pocket of fluid. It was likely she'd sustained an injury of some sort and the pocket had begun to form. It had been left untreated, and had just continued to grow over the years. Tor was relatively positive she could drain it and straighten the old woman's back, relieving her pain.

She moved to her medicine bag and took out a hard case. She

placed it on the table, then pulled out a small vial of liquid, some herbs, and a stone bowl.

"You always carry a stone bowl around with you," the old woman said, nodding toward the item.

Tor smiled. "Strangely enough, yes." She put several leaves, pines, seeds, and then the oil into the bowl and grounded it down while chanting an incantation under her breath. The static built and a green smoke rose from the bowl. Tor stopped mixing and took a bandage, rubbing the mixture into the cloth. She placed it on the table next to the bowl, then opened the case. Inside was a metal plunger, with a tube connected to it, and in a neat row were several different-sized needles.

Tor chose the largest of the needles and screwed it to the end of the plunger. The old woman's eyes widened. "What do you plan on doing with that?"

"I'm going to drain the hump on your back. Then, I will put this mixture on it and, finally, put the bandage on. In two days, I will return and do this all over again. I think it will take at least four, maybe five, drainages. Then, we can work on straightening your back." Tor stood and moved behind the old woman. "You will feel a pinch and a bit of discomfort, but then you will find relief. Ready?"

The old woman grabbed the edge of the table and braced herself, then nodded. She grasped tighter as the needle broke the surface of the skin, but her body began to relax as Tor drained the fluid. When the plunger was full, Tor used their chamber pot to dump it. She needed to drain it three times before all was left was the saggy skin where the hump once was.

Tor rubbed the mixture into the skin, then put the bandage on, making sure to cover the spot where the needles were injected. She washed her hands, then cleaned up all her supplies and the needle. For the first time the old woman smiled, sitting a little taller and starting to reach toward the spot on her back.

"Don't play with that," Tor said as she put the remainder of her things in her bag. "Leave it be. I will clean and change everything in two days, when I return. Don't overdo it, though. I know you will be feeling much better, but try not to sleep on your back."

The woman stood and took one of Tor's hands, patting it. "Thank you."

"Take care of your husband." Tor patted the old woman's hand in return, then put on her coat and medicine bag. She had headed for the door when the old woman spoke.

"In two days, I will have your bread ready."

"I look forward to it, ma'am."

"Granadha. My name is Granadha, but you will call me Gran."

Tor nodded and took two steps out of the dwelling, then turned back. "Try to let some fresh air in. I know your means are small, but try to clean as much as you can. It will help to keep out further sickness."

"I will have my grandson help me. He's a good boy. Thank you, Healer."

"Tor. My name is Tor."

"Of course." The old woman nodded.

Tor stepped out into the street and took a deep breath, not sure how long she'd been in that stifling little hut. She hoped Gran would do the best she could to clean and air out the home, but she had other things to worry about with her husband.

As Tor made her way back to her own tiny home, only one thought ran through her mind: What is sour bread?

CHAPTER NINE

TWO DAYS LATER, TOR RETURNED to Gran's house. She brought Parin with her, since every five days the orphanage gave the children a day off from learning. Tor thought this would be a good time to start Parin's training.

"Why are we going to this house?" Parin asked. "Why do they not come to you?"

"They are elderly and cannot travel. Sometimes, we must go to patients' homes in order to ensure they get proper treatments."

"Like you did for momma when she was sick?"

"Exactly." They stopped at the hut, and Tor knocked on the doorframe. A moment later, Gran answered. She was hunched over, as Tor had expected.

"Come in." Her voice seemed small.

Tor ushered Parin in first, then she ducked through the door. The house was in much better condition. It had been aired out, and the smell of waste had been mostly cleared. Tor stepped in to look into the back room, and found the bed was empty. Gran's husband had passed within the last two days.

Tor knelt in front of Gran and sat back on her heels. "When did he pass?" she asked.

"The night you were here." Her voice cracked. "My grandsons had time to say their goodbyes."

"I'm truly sorry for your loss."

Gran nodded and dabbed at her eyes. "You said he didn't have long." She strained to look Tor in the eyes. "Do you think your goddess came for him?"

"I thought there was no such thing as gods?"

The old woman set her jaw and Tor took her hands. "Kadianea is a loving goddess. She is the guide for gentle souls. I know she led him into his afterlife, and showed him happiness and freedom once again."

Gran sobbed into a cloth and Tor continued to hold her hand.

"Who's Kadianea? What's the afterlife?" Parin's voice seemed to echo through the shack, and Tor turned her head toward him.

"Hush now, Parin. You are never to speak of Kadianea again. You understand? Never again." She sent him a glare and used a tone she hoped he would fully understand; there were consequences if he spoke of it again.

Parin pushed out his bottom lip and shrugged.

"Promise me, Parin."

"Promise." He sniffed and wiped away the tears running down his face. Tor's heart dropped, and Gran gave her a look of disapproval and nodded at the boy.

Tor sighed. "Perhaps, one day, when you are older, I will teach you. But, for now, you must not speak her name."

Parin raised his face and smiled.

Tor turned her head to hide her own smile. Teaching Parin her orc ways made her happier than she thought she could be. Gran squeezed Tor's hand, obviously reading her expression. Tor straightened and attempted to become all serious, then took in a deep breath. "Okay, let's start some water for a tea and I will get the mixture started for your back."

Gran sniffed and nodded. She made to stand, but Tor put a hand on her shoulder.

"I can see the kettle, and young Parin can get some water from the well." Tor held the kettle out to the boy, and he jumped off his chair and took it. He ran from the home, and Tor opened her medicine bag and got to putting the mixture together.

"Where did you get the boy from?" Gran asked.

Tor looked from the door to Gran. "I knew his momma well."

"There wasn't an answer in there."

Tor chuckled at the use of her own words. "You're right, that was not an answer."

"His momma is dead or missing?" Gran asked.

Tor sat back, pausing in her task. "Missing, maybe dead. Parin came to me two days ago to tell me she hadn't come home for four days."

Gran's eyes narrowed. "Why is he not with the Mothers, then?"

Tor understood why Gran didn't quite trust her. They had only just met, and seeing an orc with a human child would turn many heads and cause concern. "The Mothers have no room. They are over capacity as it is. Head Mother asked me to take Parin in, since the boy already knows and trusts me."

Gran nodded, grunting, seemingly satisfied with the answer. Parin returned with a much-too-full kettle, spilling water on the floor. His tongue was sticking out, and he was desperately trying to keep the water in the container.

Gran got to her feet. "I'll take that." She dumped the excess into a large pot sitting by the hearth, then put the kettle in the fire. When she took her seat, Tor was twisting the needle onto the plunger.

"Come over here, Parin," Tor said. "Now, see how this is soft and you can move it with your finger?" Tor gently probed the cyst.

Parin's eyes were wide, and his mouth open. He reached up to touch it but Tor stopped him.

"One day you can touch such things, but today you will just watch and learn. Okay?"

Parin nodded, staring intently as Tor positioned the needle.

"You'll feel a pinch," she said to Gran.

There wasn't nearly as much fluid in the cyst as the day before, but Tor was pleased with the progress. She added the mixture and the bandage, then cleaned her tools. By the time she was done, Gran had poured the hot water for tea.

"You will sit and visit," Gran said as she placed the mugs on the table.

"I have other pat—"

"You will sit and visit."

Tor smiled and took a seat. "I will sit and visit for a bit."

"Tell me more of the boy's momma. How did you come to know her?" Gran handed Parin a small cake, and he sat at the opposite side of the table and ate it quietly.

"I healed his momma several years ago. Through the years, she would come to me for other injuries or illnesses."

Gran nodded. "And you decided to keep him instead of taking him to family once the Mothers turned him away?"

Tor took a sip of the tea, which was mostly just water. Tea leaves were expensive. Tor reached for her bag and searched inside as she spoke. "He has no other family in the High City." Tor pulled out a small leather pouch. She opened it, and the smell of berries filled the air. She took Gran's mug and her own, and dumped the liquid out.

"Hey, that was the last of my leaves," Gran shouted.

Tor poured new, hot water into the mugs, then added leaves from the pouch. She brought the mugs back and set them down in front of the old woman.

She smiled when the smell of berries hit her senses. "This is lovely, extravagant."

"I had a patient from mid-town, whose baby was quite ill when born. She gave me a plant that produces leaves for tea, and berries to eat. It is quite soothing."

Gran took a long sip, and hummed as the liquid made its way down her throat. "And the baby?"

"She is about five months now, and very healthy." Tor's gaze dropped to her own mug. Parin patted her arm, and Tor realized she must have had a sad expression. She put her hand on Parin's and smiled warmly at the boy. So young, and so much empathy; he would be a wonderful healer.

"If the child survived, then what saddens you?"

Tor heaved a sullen breath and looked Gran in the eye. The old woman was now sitting up straight, the cyst having been drained. "Because I was not able to cross into mid-town, the baby nearly died."

"But she didn't."

"This time."

Gran grunted, nodding. She'd taken another sip from her mug when there was a voice at the door.

"Knock knock, Gran." The man stepped into the house, but stopped at the sight of Tor.

Tor came to her feet, meeting the man's gaze. He was in a leather-and-suede coat, one that was usually worn under armor. He was unshaven, and likely had not been on duty for a couple days. Tor smiled; for a human he was quite handsome.

"Ah, I'm sorry, Gran. I didn't realize you would have company."

"Nonsense. Tor, this is my grandson, Eydis. Eydis, this is the healer I told you about."

"Yes, Gran. I'd figured, since she is the only orc in our city walls."

Tor smiled, giving a light laugh. It was nice that Gran didn't introduce her as the orc healer, as so many did, but the introduction obviously wasn't needed.

"We should be on our way," Tor said, holding her hand out to Parin as she grabbed her bag from the table. Tor turned to say goodbye to Gran. "I will return in another two days for your next treatment." She handed over her leather pouch. "I have an entire plant, so you take this and enjoy it."

Gran's eyes brightened as she took the leather pouch, then she handed Tor a warm cloth. "Your sour bread, warm from the oven."

"Sour bread!" Parin bounced on the balls of his feet. "I love sour bread! Can we have some with stew tonight, Tor?" Tor, Gran, and Eydis all laughed at his delight.

"Yes, of course," Tor said as she put the loaf into a different bag.

Eydis leaned toward Parin. "Gran's sour bread is the best you will ever have."

Parin's eyes widened in delight, and he bounced even more and clapped his hands. Tor put a hand on his head, and with a smile said, "Two days, Gran. Eydis, it was nice seeing you."

Eydis bowed his head.

"Wait," Gran nearly shouted. "Why not ask Eydis?"

"Ask me what?"

Tor took a step and shook her head. "It won't do any good, Gran. Trust me."

"Ask me what?" Eydis repeated.

Gran put a hand on her grandson's forearm. "Tor needs permission to cross into mid-town. She has people there who need her help and they can't, or won't, come to lower-town to see her."

Eydis shook his head. "Tor's right; there is nothing I can do. The order comes down from the High King himself; she is not to leave lower-town."

Tor smiled. "Thank you for trying, Gran. Perhaps one day I can get a house closer to the border." She laughed at the notion, then bid her goodbyes again and followed Parin out of the house. As she returned home, her thoughts drifted to the idea of getting a slightly larger home on the border of mid-town and lower-town. A shelter, with at least a room big enough for two beds, would be better. Twelve years was a long time to share a room with a growing boy.

She shook the idea from her mind. She was a healer from the Rejuvenation Monastery. She was better than no man, and she was never to live in luxury. Even though she slept on a bed of feathers and soft materials. She smiled again at the irony.

When they rounded the corner to their home they found a lineup of ten, waiting for her to open her door.

CHAPTER TEN

LIKE ANY OTHER MORNING, TOR and Parin woke early and prepared several different remedies for ongoing clients. Tor beamed at Parin. At seventeen years old, his skills were nearly that of a master. She had hoped that his magic would begin to show itself, but after so many years she still couldn't feel any static about him.

He crushed some herbs and oil in a stone bowl as Tor cut up carrots and potatoes for the day's meals. She smiled and hummed as she worked at her own task, thinking about how happy she was in that moment. Life still wasn't easy, and no matter how many people she had helped there were still twice as many who only saw her as an orc.

She and Parin had secured a slightly larger home eight years prior, where Parin had his own room, on the very border between mid-town and lower-town. Her higher-end clients were willing to come to this location for treatment, rather than sending messengers with poorly explained symptoms. Being able to help the richer citizens allowed her to keep the home and help even more of the poor.

The poor were mostly uncomfortable getting so close to the border, so Tor would also still see patients in the old shack, commuting between them and spending half her time at each place.

She'd even been able to get Parin into a school that suited his age; the orphanage could only get him to a certain point in his education. Many children in lower-town Parin's age would be forced into labor, and she was grateful the mid-town schools took Parin in and would teach him until he was eighteen. It saddened her that she may have to remove him from the school before then. The travelers her mentor had spoken of still had not arrived, and she wasn't willing to give up on his prophecy just yet, but she would be ready when they did. Parin, however, was ready to leave as he wanted to become a trained healer like her.

As she dumped the vegetables into the pot of water she wiped her hands on her apron. "Let me finish that up, or you will be late for school."

Parin surrendered the pestle and removed his apron, hanging it on a hook. He rushed to his room and came back with a handful of books, then kissed Tor on the cheek. "Say hello to Gran for me. Tell her I look forward to her sour bread."

"I will. Have a good day."

"You as well, Das'mut." He waved and closed the door behind him.

Tor smiled again when he called her 'mother.' He had insisted, at a very young age, to learn her language. She was reluctant, as he would never be welcome in orc lands let alone be welcome to speak with her people. But she'd taught him certain words here and there to appease his relentless badgering. Das'mut was the first word he'd wanted to learn.

When she was done with the stew, she turned to finishing the remedies. Some were natural mixtures, but others required her to work magic. The last few months she'd been having a difficult time with the incantations and using her healing magic. The static was unpredictable in its strength, sometimes making the mixture too potent and other times souring it completely, making it unusable. An unbalance had begun nine years before but the effects had been small at first, and in many cases unnoticeable.

In the beginning she was certain it had to be Parin, as she felt the timing was too coincidental. But, as he'd got older, the unbalance never changed—until the last five months, when it had drastically done so, and at times even became dangerous. And, still, she was unable to sense any magical static from Parin, now making her certain he was not the cause.

How could he be? Although he could now feel the static when magic was being used, he himself didn't seem to create the static on his own. Those with natural magic, magic they were born with, would always give off a hint. But Parin never had.

It was no matter anymore; he was her son, and she loved him more than she thought she could love anyone. Her oath to protect him, to take him from the city, had not and would not change.

The mixture she was working on was for Gran, who had developed issues with her joints. They were sore and difficult to use at times, but this would help alleviate the pain enough for her to go about her daily business. There was no cure, and even though Tor tried different magics on her they never seemed to help.

Once the herbs and seeds had been crushed she added an oil that smelled of grass. As she poured and mixed, she began chanting the proper incantation. The static in the room built, and the hair on her arms and back of her neck began to stand on end as she continued to mix the compound. She repeated it two more times as the static in the air grew stronger, then changed. There was a drop in air pressure and the sky outside the windows darkened. Her skin began to tingle painfully.

"Oh great," she said as she stopped mixing. An orange puff of smoke rose from the bowl, giving off a foul smell, followed immediately by a flash of light outside and a thunderous boom. Tor ground her teeth. For twelve years she'd tried to find out what the king was up to. People were still disappearing, and the King's Guard refused to talk about it or help.

The little bits of information she had were more rumors and conjecture, about him trying to gather worshippers and magic to become god-like. She'd scoffed at the idea, since it would be impossible to get enough of either. But then the stories about magical beings being brought into the city walls and taken to the castle began circulating. She had witnessed elves, sprites, and even a goblin being marched to the castle several times—all beings with natural magic.

The only good news about any of this was that Tor no longer had to practice her magic in secret. When the King's War had ended five years ago King Thomas instituted a law against all magic being used, so she'd had to find new ways to use it in her healing without getting caught. But she was no longer scared that she would be turned in at any time. But it did worry her that she may become a target for the gathering of magical beings.

She busied herself by making a new batch so she could see Gran before noon, which was when all her other clients began to show for their treatments. With the unbalance in the magic, it took her several tries to get the mixture and magic just right.

Her skin still tingled painfully from the spells going awry, but experience told her it would dissipate in fifteen minutes; it's the risk she took every time she used magic at the same time as a lightning strike. Tor carefully packed all her supplies into her medical bag, then slung it over her shoulder and across her body.

She left a sign indicating she was not in and headed for the tiny hut in the poorest part of lower-town. She smiled and tilted her head at those who greeted her and ignored those who spit at her. Fourteen years, and still she received very little respect from many people.

She knocked on the wooden doorframe Tor had one of her clients make. A snarling, winkled face peeked through the crack of the partially open door, but softened at the sight of Tor and she pulled it open wide. "Tor, come in, come in."

Tor ducked into the tiny home. It wasn't in such a shambles as it had once been, when Tor first met the old woman. Through the years she had become like a mother to her and a grandmother to Parin. Tor would barter and trade her services to help Gran out since she and Parin had everything they could ever need.

"You're late," Gran said as she eased herself into a chair by the fire. "The game is all set."

Tor sighed. "I'm afraid, due to my tardiness, I won't have time for stones today. Next time, I promise."

"What held you up? The boy all right?"

"Yes, yes, but it took me several tries to make your mixture. The static is very unbalanced as of late. With the blood moon being tonight, the king is causing more chaos than normal."

Gran grunted. "These are becoming dangerous times."

"Becoming? It's always been dangerous." Tor took a seat across from Gran and opened her medical bag.

"Yes, but it seems the disappearances have increased. Not just the poor are being taken."

Tor stopped digging through her bag. "What do you mean?"

"I've heard rumors."

"Oh, Gran, you know better than to listen to rumors." Tor gave a half smile and shook her head as she pulled out the bottle of the mixture she made, then an extra leather pouch.

"Eydis told me. Wants me to leave the High City."

Was this the moment Abacuss had spoken of so many years ago? What the fae had been talking about on the road to the High Kingdom? Was Parin in danger if they stayed? "Did he say why he wanted you to leave the city?"

Gran snorted. "He fears I will be taken as well. What would the king want with an old crone like me anyway?"

"It may not be a bad idea to—"

"Oh, now you stop." Gran pointed a crooked, bony finger at Tor. "If anything, you should be getting that boy and yourself out of this city. With the blood moon these next few days..."

"I don't think I can leave just yet."

"It's that nonsense your mentor told you, isn't it?"

"It's not nonsense. Abacuss is a very wise—"

"Did he not send you to a city of men?"

Tor knitted her brows and slumped. "Yes."

"Told you travelers were going to need your help? That you must save the child."

"Yes."

"But didn't tell you who or when they would show up?"

"No, but—"

"Well, have you met any travelers with a child needing saving?"

Tor tightened her lips. "I don't think it's that simple."

"Ha!" The old woman threw her head back in mock humor. "Fourteen years you have been here, and I must say I'm surprised you've survived this long. But don't you think these travelers would have come by now? No, my dear Tor, it's time you take that Parin to your monastery and get out of the city of men. I worry for you every day." Tears filled Gran's eyes. "When you are late to meet I fear the mobs have finally achieved what they have been threatening to do for so long."

Tor reached across the table and touched her hand. "I don't want to leave you." The idea of losing another mother, even a surrogate, broke Tor's heart. She hadn't known her own mother for long, as she'd died in childbirth while delivering her youngest brother. Tor had only been three at the time. "There is also the issue with Parin's age. He is not yet able to consent. No guard will let me leave the city with him."

Gran nodded. "You know one guard that will help you. Besides, the boy is nearly seventeen. Only a few short months away. If it weren't for you getting him into that school, he would be working the fields."

"Eydis can only do so much, and that is very little if he is surrounded by others."

"You will figure it out." Gran heaved herself out of her seat and went to the hearth. She came back with a bundle and handed it to Tor. It was still warm from sitting by the fire.

Tor smiled. "Parin has been looking forward to your sour bread all week."

Gran eased back down. "The boy knows how to make it. Why doesn't he make it himself?" Her gruff but loving tone made Tor smile.

"You know how it is. He can never seem to get the one ingredient you use right."

She scrunched her face. "What ingredient is that?"

"Love."

She rolled her eyes and Tor laughed. "Out you go now, my dear Tor. Go help others, and watch that shift in the static. And be mindful of your words. You speak too openly about the static and the king. One day the wrong person will hear you."

Tor smiled warmly. "I will watch my words." She rose and moved to lean over and kiss Gran on the cheek. "I will stop by in a couple days."

"Yes, yes." She waved her hand, shooing Tor away. "Thank you for the berry tea as well."

Tor smiled as she left the little dwelling, tucking the loaf of bread into her bag and heading home. As she walked through the street the static began to grow once again, the air pressure dropping, and she braced for the flash of lightning and the crack of thunder. The lightning struck near the well in the center of the square, sending rocks in every direction. The crack of thunder was so loud Tor thought her bones were going to break under the pressure.

People had scattered about, but were now coming from their hiding places. She'd taken a step back toward Gran's house when the old woman stepped out.

"You all right?" Tor shouted as she strode toward her.

"Ears are ringing a little, but I'm all right."

Tor quickly checked her over before she shooed her away again. Tor checked several others with minor cuts and scrapes, but nothing serious. It was another hour before she was heading home again. To her surprise, no one was waiting by the time she arrived. She checked the timepiece on her wrist, the result of a barter she had done with a timepiece maker when he'd got his finger caught up in several large gears.

The tiny arms pointed to the twelve and the one. "Hmm, strange," she said as she entered her home. She was about to put the open sign out when a voice spoke behind her.

"Please don't open just yet."

Tor turned to find a slight woman standing in front of her. Her hair was short and white, and her clothes were dark, slim-cut, and fit tight. Although there was a little dirt smudge on her face, she still looked as though she had just stepped out of a bath.

Tor narrowed her eyes at the woman. "What do you want, fae? Where's your trio?"

The secrets are not lost, but waiting.
You must ask the nymphs, for they can tell you.

~From the musing of Gronk in The Chronicles of Gronk~

CHAPTER ELEVEN

T OR STARED DOWN AT THE tiny woman, who had her hands on her hips, and Tor could only find the image amusing. Taking a seat at her small table, Tor crossed her arms and legs and lifted one eyebrow at the woman. It looked as though someone had shoved her to the ground at one point, or perhaps she had tripped.

"I've come a long way to speak with you."

"I have no use for fae. Where is your trio?" Tor again narrowed her eyes at the woman.

"It's a long story."

Tor lifted both eyebrows. "I have nothing but time."

"Time is something you don't have. Like I said, I have come a long way and I need you to come with me."

"Go with you where?"

"Passed the Fairy Fields." The fae took a seat.

"Why in the world would I travel so far west? And in the winter, of all times?" Tor snorted a laugh as she rose from the table to get a drink. This whole situation was strange and very unsettling. First the trio of female fae had come to her on the road and now this one, who somehow seemed to be on her side of the barrier. How did she get out of her realm? Why was she alone? Tor took her time pouring herself a mug of tea.

"Please, I need your help."

Reluctantly, Tor poured the fae a drink as well. Her training in the monastery, of taking care of those around her, kicking in. She placed the mug on the table in front of the fae and returned to her own seat. "I'll consider your request, but I have conditions." She knew she needed to tread carefully, agreeing to anything a fae wanted would come with consequences and favors asked down the road.

The fae put the mug to her lips, but before taking a drink she paused and stared at the liquid.

"I have not poisoned you."

"It's not the poison I fear, it's the ingredient you have added." She placed the mug back on the table. "I thought clerics were honest people, and yet you try to trick me with your serum. I have no reason to lie to you, so why attempt to drug me?"

Tor smiled; it was polite, but not kind. "I may be a cleric, but I am also not stupid."

The fae's eyebrows came together. "I never believed you to be stupid. I just can't risk you asking me the wrong question, your serum forcing me to speak the words."

"I know fae to be tricksters and you want me to go off and make my way across the country, to go against my vow and leave my oath and pilgrimage behind. Leaving the sick and vulnerable, and many depend on my services here. You want me to do this on nothing more than you saying I must go. No, you'll answer my questions and, if I'm satisfied, I will consider your request."

The fae sat back in her chair. "Ask your questions, but I can't guarantee I can answer any of them."

"Where is your trio?"

There was a slight pause as she opened her mouth to speak then closed it again.

"As you've already pointed out I'm a cleric, a healer. I intend you no harm unless you try to do something first."

"I am alone. I have no trio."

"How's that possible? Fae can't function without each other, so how are you still alive?"

The fae wrinkled her brow. "Where did you hear that?"

"Everywhere."

"It's utter nonsense. Our living essences aren't connected, so if one dies the others don't follow."

Tor put her hand up. "Okay. The fae are a mystery to most, so we're bound to get some things wrong. Are your trio dead? Is that why you're alone?"

"They are on the other side of the veil. I was trapped and separated from them."

Tor studied the tiny woman, who somehow looked smaller seated. The fae reached for the mug and brought it to her lips, stopped, let out a low growl and put the mug back on the table. Tor returned to her kitchen and poured a clean cup of tea for her *guest*. When she handed it to her, the fae immediately took a drink.

"Ask your other question, or are you done?"

The thought of being separated from something that was a part of her was a feeling Tor could not imagine. She was certain she wasn't going to get the fae to elaborate on the separation but, if she remembered her history, the only time this would have been possible was during the invasion of the Shadow Realm. That was over four thousand years ago. The rumors of fae being immortal must be true if she has been on this side of the veil for that long.

"What's happening at the Fairy Fields that you want me to see?"

"Not see, do."

"Okay then, do."

"My friends are in trouble, and they need help. My vision told me to come to you. That only you can complete this task."

Tor scrutinized the fae. "Where did you say you traveled from?"

"I didn't."

"Then I think you should now."

The fae sighed heavily. "I reside in the Great Walled City of Andria."

"Really?" Tor crossed her arms again. "What kind of work do you do in the Walled City? Brothel?"

The fae's expression changed for only a brief second.

"Not a brothel, then. What kind of work?"

"I work for the Agency."

"Really? Cleaning rooms?"

Again her face contorted and Tor knew she was insulting her. "Assassin or spy?"

"Not your concern. Will you help my friends?"

"I have no use for assassins or spies. You're not as trustworthy as you allow people to believe." Tor shook her head as she took a long drink. "Why not go after them yourself? Why travel in the opposite direction for five months?"

"Because they are trapped, and if I go I can be trapped too."

"Trapped how?"

"By the time dilation."

Tor furrowed her brow, not attempting to cover her confusion. "And what exactly is a *time dilation*?"

The fae rubbed her hands together. "It is a place where time no longer runs at the same speed as the surrounding area. It will either speed things up, or slow them down. They can be very dangerous to maneuver."

Tor crossed her arms and nodded. "So, are orc's immune to this time dilation?"

"Of course not." The fae's tone was annoyed and impatient.

"Then why me?"

"You were in my vision, so you are the one who needs to be there. Only you can do what needs to be done." The fae's tone changed to one of panic.

Tor leaned on the table. "What needs to be done?"

The fae shook her head. "I don't know. Without my trio my visions are muddled, fractured. Sometimes I receive mixed messages, or they are out of order."

She lifted an eyebrow. "With this being the case, you still believe I need to go?"

She nodded.

"Who are these friends?" Tor leaned back again and took a sip from her drink.

"I can't tell you that."

"Why not?"

The fae bit her lip. Again she appeared to be unsure of herself, her confidence sliding. Perhaps being out of the Walled City was too much for her. It was possible she wasn't a spy or assassin at all.

"I have a task to complete here first," Tor finally said.

"Then you will go?"

"I haven't decided yet."

"But you must," she said, coming to her feet.

Tor sighed and stood as well, towering over the fae like a mother would a child. "I *must* do nothing. Especially for a fae. I'll think on the situation."

"Perhaps if you pray to your Goddess Thanroota she will give you guidance."

Tor stared at the fae, contemplating her words. Fae know things, and there was no good trying to hide it. "Perhaps." Tor raised her arm, pointing to the door. "I'll find you, fae, if I choose to take on this quest of yours."

The fae quirked an eyebrow. "Quest? Interesting term, but I suppose it could be considered a quest."

Tor cleared her throat, moved to the door, and opened it.

"You'll know where to find me?"

"I'll find you. If I want to."

The fae straightened her leather coat and lifted her chin, giving her a regal look and commanding a great deal of attention.

Tor blinked several times at this tiny woman's transformation, from meek and pleading for help to fierce and someone who could handle herself.

The fae stepped out into the street and within seconds could no longer be seen, as if she had vanished into thin air.

Tor nodded. "Huh, very impressive indeed." She didn't think it was magic at work, as she didn't feel the static that comes with the use of natural magic. Perhaps this fae was using a different kind, or none at all. She was from the Walled City, home of one of the assassin academies. Disappearing into a crowd was a skill they not only learned, but mastered.

CHAPTER TWELVE

T OR FINISHED CLEANING THE MUGS used during the odd visit from the fae, then grabbed her medical satchel and two other bags. She would spend the day in the old shack, but she didn't keep much there since it had been broken into many times after she and Parin moved. So she always brought everything she would possibly need.

Entering the shack, she opened the windows and started setting up for the day. The stew she'd brought from home was put by the hearth, and she lit a fire to heat it. On the counter were several containers of fresh water for teas and elixirs. Tor had decided to make herself a tea when she heard the distinct creak of the door. She turned to see who had entered the clinic as a slight girl stepped in.

Tor knelt in front of the skinny, travel-worn child. "Don't you have pretty eyes?" Tor noted the color of the child's skin, her hair, and the deep brown eyes. She could feel the magic coming from the girl. Her static was strong, but strange. There was something natural, yet also unnatural, about it. It was uncommon for Tor's skin to tingle when spells were not being cast, as it was now, but she was certain this child was not casting any spells.

Tor's studies told her this child held a powerful magic, but not that of nature. A slight hint of bitterness lingered in Tor's mouth, another strange thing to happen when magic wasn't being used.

There was something about the child that didn't seem right, and she knew the travelers Abacuss had spoken about had finally arrived. In that instant, she knew beyond any doubt that Parin was not the child she was to help survive.

Tor studied the girl for a moment longer, again taking in her eyes, her skin tone, and the taste of her magic. She had never experienced these things firsthand but Tor had studied it thoroughly at the monastery. This girl's origins were becoming apparent.

The girl smiled and broke into Tor's thoughts. "Enya bring Jardeth. Jardeth need help."

"Who?" Tor asked as the door behind them opened for a second time and a woman with fire-red hair stepped in. A mark ran down her face, coming to a point on her cheek.

She was laden down by a man, who appeared to have extreme difficulty keeping his feet under him. Not paying any mind to the couple, Tor kept her attention solely on the child. She understood now why it was important she come to the High Kingdom. Everything was starting to piece together.

The girl reached up and touched the chunky red stripe in Tor's otherwise all-green hair. "I want."

Tor smiled and touched the girl's dingy gray hair. "You could use a little color."

The woman, who Tor assumed must be Enya, cleared her throat to announce her presence.

"I'm aware you're here; no need to be rude. A simple hello would have sufficed." She stood to her full height of six feet.

"I apologize, but it is a matter of urgency. I was told a healer named Tor lived here."

"Yes, that's true, but I'm really more of a cleric than a healer."

"What's the difference?"

Nothing really, since healing was her religion, but she had never been asked the question before and didn't see any reason to explain. "Place your friend on the bed over there and I'll have a look."

"So, you're Tor then?"

"Surprised I'm an orc?" Her smile was polite but not friendly.

"I was, but I've had a couple days to get over the shock of it." Enya did her best to relieve herself of the man she was carrying. With a grunt, she practically dropped him onto the bed. Tor used the back of her hand to feel his forehead, then placed her ear to his chest. "What happened? Disease?"

"No. He was struck in the arm with a knife and shot in the side with an arrow, which went all the way through."

Tor removed the man's cloak and shirt. There were black lines, sprawling like spider webs across his torso from the injury in his side. She leaned in then recoiled, wrinkling her nose. "It has festered. How long did you say it's been?"

"I didn't, but it's been about seven days, maybe more. The days seem to have blurred together."

Tor got up and went to the back of the tiny shack. She grabbed her stone bowl and started dropping different dry ingredients into it. She chanted the incantation silently to herself as she pounded and stirred the contents. The poison used on the weapons was a strong one, rare. She could smell the hint of gykkeem root—a plant that could only be found in Cinalaneekk, the Goblin Realm.

Tor poured in thistle oil, made from the fruit of the same name grown in the Fairy Fields. She continued to chant in a low tone, so only she could hear the words. The static began to build, and she hoped it would work the first time. Many of the ingredients she was using were extremely rare and near impossible to come by. When the static reached its peak, there was a subtle drop in air pressure and a greenish-gray smoke rose from the mixture.

She smiled, sighing in relief that the mixture had not soured. Tor returned to the injured man's side and began to rub the salve into and around his wounds, all the while speaking the incantation.

When she was done, she covered the wounds with bandages. "I need to make him some tea; it will take an hour or so to steep." She grabbed her stone bowl and returned to her kitchen. "You can tell your dwarf outside that he can take your horses to the stables down the road. Tell them I sent you. They'll be sure to care for your beasts and your belongings as if their lives depended on it."

Enya hesitated, then let go of the child's hand to relay the information.

When she returned, Tor said, "You must be quite hungry. I have a rabbit stew, which is quite good, keeping warm by the fire. Would you and your friends like some?" Tor could see, from the look of both, that they had not eaten in several days, possibly longer.

"Yes, that would be nice."

"Excellent. Have a seat." Before Tor poured the bowls of stew she added an additional ingredient, chanting several words before a puff of brown steam rose from the bowls. Certain her guests didn't see she placed the two bowls in front of the woman and the child, then came back with some bread and cheese.

Enya glanced about the room.

Tor answered the unasked question. "I take food and other supplies in trade for my services."

"I wasn't—"

"I know what you were wondering. Just as I know you're trying to figure out how an orc became a cleric. Let's just say that I've showed special talents and gifts since I was young." There was nothing in her religion that said she couldn't lie. "My father thought I would do better with the clerics, if they would take me. They did, and I learned many things, and now I'm here. That's all you need to know." Her tone was final, silencing the woman. Tor watched as the two ate in silence, until the door swung open and a dwarf appeared in the doorway.

His military ranking showed clearly from the size of his beard, mustache, and muttonchops. "Ah, Master Warrior," Tor said. "Welcome. Would you like something to eat?" She couldn't fully see if he had all-gold rings on his beard or silver, but his rank of Master Warrior could not be mistaken.

The dwarf narrowed his eyes at her then scanned the other two, who had their cheeks full. "How ye feeling, lass?"

Before she could say anything, Tor answered for her. "I haven't poisoned them, if that's what you're worried about. I won't hurt you here, Master Warrior. I'm no warrior myself. I have no quarrel with your kind."

The dwarf grunted and pulled out the last chair set around the small table. He grabbed a piece of bread and a hunk of cheese while Tor poured him a bowl of stew. When Tor returned, the child lifted her bowl up to her. "Please more."

Tor cupped her chin in her hand. This child was no longer the same being she'd been when she entered their world. Tor could feel it in her bones, but the magic she felt was from the child. She wanted to be wrong, but she feared she was right about the child's origins. "Sure, sweet thing." She took the bowl and filled it a second time. Tor sat as she placed the bowl back in front of the child. "Why don't you explain to me how you got your hands on a Shadow child, and what exactly have you done to her?"

The other two stopped eating; Enya in mid-chew, and the dwarf with his spoon frozen halfway to his mouth.

"She is a gift for the High King from the Dwarf King," Enya said around the food in her mouth. Her eyes then went wide with the fact she had revealed this information.

"King Firth wants King Thomas dead. She's going tae murder him with her blood magic, sae King Firth can have these lands," the dwarf added, showing an equal amount of surprise.

"Ha, truth soup." The child giggled.

"Yes, I'm afraid she's right. I put a little garrulousni weed, along with a small incantation, into your meals. Oh, don't worry, it won't hurt you, and the effects should wear off in a few hours."

"Why?"

"When a dwarf, two Dragon Clan members, and a Shadow child walk into my shop I have a right to be a bit concerned."

"Two Dragon— Jardeth is the only Dragon Clan member here," Enya said forcefully, which Tor didn't like.

Tor studied her, narrowing her eyes. "Who attacked your friend?"

"There's a hit on our heads," said the dwarf, still eating. Enya put a hand on his arm, but he pulled away. "We're already drugged, lass. No reason tae let the food go tae waste."

She shrugged and resumed eating her stew.

"A hit? Who would have put a hit on all of you?"

"Your guess is as good as ours," she said.

Tor turned her attention back to the woman, her eyes lingering on the marking that ran down the length of her face. "How long have you had that tattoo?"

Enya touched it. "For as long as I can remember. I always thought it was a birthmark."

"Why would the people who gave you the tattoo not tell you what it was?"

The two strangers shared a look, then looked back to Tor. "I was raised by dwarves. My real family left me in the woods to die."

Tor raised one eyebrow. "I see. That does explain your dwarf rank." She nodded at the braids and the poorly shaved side of her head. She then stood and returned to her hearth, poured hot liquid into a mug, and sat next to Jardeth on the bed. She pulled him into a partially seated position and had him drink the liquid. Tor breathed through her mouth the best she could to avoid the putrid smell. Jardeth coughed and wrinkled his face, but she continued to force him to drink the tea.

When it was done she laid him back down and returned to the table. She watched the child sit back in her chair and play with her hair. "How long have you had the child?"

"Three months," the dwarf said, shoving his bowl away.

"Okay. How long has the child been in our realm?"

"I born here," Shadow Child answered.

"Really?" Tor moved in close. "The queen must be searching for you then." She turned to the others. "Where did you find her?"

"Queen, not mother."

Tor leaned back in her chair. How is it possible the queen didn't create the child? As far as anyone knew, only the queen of the Shadow Realm could create a child, and only one queen ruled at a time. This child must be the magic the trio had said caused the imbalance.

If used in the wrong way, her magic could end them all.

Tor contemplated the girl. The story didn't make sense. If she was created in this realm and not in the Shadow Realm, then she wouldn't have that magic. She wouldn't have their traits, regardless who created her. There was something they were hiding, or something even they didn't know.

"Dae ye mind sharin' what yer thinkin'?" the dwarf asked.

Tor realized she had been staring at the child for some time. "Where did you find her?" she asked again.

"My king had her, and asked that we deliver her tae the High King."

Tor's mouth suddenly went dry, then it hit her: the memory of a story Abacuss had told her when she was still quite young. He'd never said it was a prophecy, he'd just said it was a story. As Tor got older, she'd realized that his stories were prophecies; some came to light and some did not.

Tor must have had a strange look on her face because Enya said, "What is it?"

"There are prophecies of a child born of Shadow, but they're centuries old. The clerics never believed them to be real, just the ramblings of a crazy man. Nothing else he predicted around that time ever came to light." *No reason to tell them everything. It could still be wrong.*

"What kind of prophecies and predictions?" Enya asked.

"I don't really remember, other than something about a child born of Shadow traveling the realm. I would need to return to the clerics and check the archives to be sure. However, there *is* something different about the child."

"Pac," she said.

"What?" said Tor.

"Name is Pac. I am Pac."

Enya spoke. "She didn't have a name, so we named her."

"You named her Pac?"

"Yes, it's short for something."

"Short for what?"

"Package." The woman's eyes dropped and her cheeks pinked up. Tor glanced at the dwarf, and even he avoided eye contact with everyone. "When the king summoned Rusty, he said he had a package to deliver. And...well, she didn't talk when we first picked her up so she couldn't tell us her name. I was a little drunk at the time, and I'm going to stop talking now."

"Probably best." Tor folded her hands in her lap and crossed her legs. "I suspect Pac is not fully Shadow, or she's possibly spent entirely too much time in our realm and around humans such as yourself." She addressed Rusty. "Your king, what's his name? Firth? He's sending her to the High King as a gift?"

"Aye."

"You know why?"

"Wasn't my place tae ask."

Tor wrinkled her nose at him. "Dwarves and their blind allegiances. I'm assuming he wants her blood magic?" Now she looked to Enya. With all the pieces of the story, Tor was finally putting it all together.

"That's what Pac told us a little over a month ago."

"The king has been up to some shady business as of late. I'd say the last eight to nine months or so." If they knew the full truth, would it make a difference? Sure, she was supposed to help Jardeth, but were they so ignorant to the true plan? "Don't know what he's got going on, but there have been some odd things happening."

"Like what?"

"Large thunder and lightning storms that bring no rain. People going missing. But the most disturbing thing I've encountered so far is the fae."

"Gronk's beard," Rusty said.

Tor smiled. "Yes, indeed. I forgot how much you dwarves love that dirty, horny, green bastard. Greatest warrior, my ass. He chased people off with his giant boner. Who wants to fight a guy with a boner? Half the time it wasn't known if he wanted to fight or fornicate. And, as the legend goes, he didn't care if it was with a man, a beast, or a tree stump."

"Boner?" Pac asked, looking up from examining her hair.

"Uh," Enya stammered, "never mind. Why don't you go keep Jardeth company?"

Pac jumped down from her chair and sat next to Jardeth, and the others watched as the child picked up his hand and cupped it against her face.

"She doesn't have much Shadow left in her. Which means her blood magic isn't the same either."

"Does that mean she doesn't have any magic at all?" Enya asked.

"No, she has magic. I can feel it radiating off her, but it's different now. Look, I would normally just heal your friend and tell you to be on your way. But, I'm telling you right now, if you let the king take her blood magic, nothing good will come of it."

"We have no intention of handing her over."

"Gronk's beard, we dinnae. King Firth wants the High King tae have her and he will," Rusty shouted from across the table.

Enya got to her feet. "Over my dead body, Rusty! I am not handing her over. You will have to run me through before I stand aside!"

Tor raised her hands. "Settle yourselves. I'll have none of that in my home. Now sit."

Enya eased herself back into her chair, silent for only a moment. "Does it have anything to do with the fae?"

"Have you seen them too?" Tor asked.

"Twice. They want me to kill an elf and save the king."

Tor bit her lip as her mind went to the tiny fae who'd come to her earlier that day.

"Tor, if you know something."

"I don't know anything. Look, it's going to be a couple days before your friend is healthy enough to move. I suggest you take that time and decide—"

"We dinnae have a couple days," Rusty said, cutting her short. "We have tae deliver the bairn by tomorrow."

"Tomorrow? Why tomorrow?"

"King Firth told us to have her in the king's hands before the third full moon. Tomorrow is the third full moon."

"It is also the blood moon. Master Warrior, I don't think it's a good idea for you to even consider handing the child—"

"Ah dinnae ask fer yer bloody opinion, orc."

"Rusty, come on now," Enya said.

"What happens if you don't drop her off?" Tor asked. In unison, the visitors shook their heads. "I think you can safely bet he will send his guards to come get her."

"He has to find us first." The woman crossed her arms in defiance.

"You think he doesn't already know you're here? Do not underestimate the man. There isn't anything that goes on in his city that he doesn't know about." Tor rose and cleared the dishes from the table. "You can stay the night in the inn down the road, across from the stables. Tell them I sent you and you should get a good deal. Come check on your friend in the morning."

The three stood from the table and Enya gestured for Pac to take her hand. She led them out into the street and turned to thank Tor as the dwarf stomped past without turning back.

CHAPTER THIRTEEN

TOR WATCHED JARDETH AS HE sipped the rancid tea. She and
Parin took shifts throughout the night, checking his wounds
and changing his bandages several times as the salve drew out the
poison.

"You look much better now," Tor said as she set water on the
stove to boil for tea. "Your color is back"-she placed a hand on his
forehead-"and you've stopped sweating. That's a good sign." She
checked under his bandage and the dark spider veins were slowly
retreating toward the wound, which was nearly healed.

"I feel much better thanks to you, my dear." He smiled and
touched her hand.

Tor smiled back and returned to the kitchen to ready his tea.
She handed it to him and pulled a chair close to his bed. "Tell me
about the child."

"What about her?" He made to take a sip then pulled the mug
away. "What is this?"

"Just drink it; it's what's healing your wounds. I already know
the child is a Shadow, but you must have noticed she isn't really
one anymore."

"What do you mean? Have you encountered many Shadows in
the city?"

There was a look in his eyes that told Tor he was keeping
something from her. She debated using the garrulousni weed on

him, but it may counteract the healing medicine for the poison. "No, the library at the monastery is quite thorough. I've read much about their realm, the war, the queen, and how they work. It also speaks of their magic."

"I see, that is a very well-kept library." He smiled and winked, then lifting the mug to his mouth his face soured.

"Drink it," Tor said, nudging the bottom of the cup. "The girl, she is more a human child now—at least in appearance. Her magic has changed as well, and the static that surrounds her is...different."

"Different how?"

Tor had to find the right words to explain. She had never experienced this type of blood magic before, and certainly never Shadow magic. But even the static of the blood magic was different. "You're aware of how the different magics work?"

"You mean, from learning how to use it to being born with it?"

"Yes."

"Of course."

"You are aware of the static that builds up around those who use magic, but for those who are born with it the static never leaves. It always surrounds them. As a cleric I was trained in different magics, mostly healing. But I have become sensitive to the shift in it. I can feel even the slightest of static around those who were born with it. Such as Pac." Tor leaned toward Jardeth, hoping her size would intimidate him into telling her what she wanted to know. "Do you not feel the static around her?"

Jardeth took a hesitant sip from the mug. "Gah, this is terrible."

"Jardeth, I need to know what has happened to the child."

Jardeth pulled his attention from his drink. "No, I don't sense the static around her. I usually don't pick up on the little subtleties, which is why I don't use it. But Pac looks like Pac; she hasn't changed. Not that I've noticed."

"Then you haven't been paying attention." Tor sat back in her chair. "You'll see when they return for you." She rose from her seat and went back to the kitchen. Jardeth wasn't going to give her anything and she was a healer, not an interrogator.

It was at least five minutes before anyone spoke again. "You must journey to Tilinrich Mountains," Jardeth said in between pulling sour faces.

"And why must I do that?" Tor was amused by this human. She liked him; he was charming and, for a human, good-looking. But she liked her men to be a little greener. He had been flirting with her all morning, and it made her feel more like a woman than she had ever felt. Jardeth had an ability to see past the fact that she was an orc, and she didn't feel, nor ever see in his gestures, that he cared.

"This time of year, the mountains glisten. It's like the stars themselves have settled on their peaks." He took the last swig from the mug and hissed before handing it back to her. When she grabbed it his fingers grazed hers, and she was certain it wasn't an accident. "I'm not sure I'll ever get that taste out of my mouth."

Tor laughed as she took the mug back into the kitchen. "I'm making soup; that should help."

"Oh, and you really want to experience Ursena Lake this time of year too."

Tor stood in the archway that separated the front area from the kitchen and back room where she'd once slept. She crossed her arms and leaned against the wall. "I hear the people of Ursena don't like outsiders around during their mating rituals."

"You know about that then?"

"I'm assuming you were speaking of the singing that is part of their rituals." Tor lifted an eyebrow, giving a half smile. She moved to his side to help him out of bed and to the table, pulling out a chair and depositing him into it. "Your friends should be arriving soon. What did you say their names were again?"

"Enya Garretsmith and Dufin Rustbeard."

"Ah, yes, of course. So you have been travel companions for

some time then. It's always nice to have lifelong friends." Tor smiled, keeping her tone relaxed so he would freely give her more information. She knew he was hiding something, something about the child.

"I've only known Enya and Dufin for a few months. Met them just before we picked up Pac." He smiled as his eyes drifted. "Seems like decades since I've been home, been with my real friends."

Tor touched his arm gently to bring him back to the room and he smiled again as his eyes met hers. "Where are you from?" she asked.

"Many places, my dear, I'm from many places. Currently, though, I reside in Grashneet City. Lovely place."

"How did you end up in Theakredel? The dwarf kingdom is nearly a three month's travel southwest, and then to turn around and come all the way back? Did you meet the other two on the road?"

Jardeth chuckled gently. "I did some traveling of my own with a couple of friends. One of them had information to pass along to the dwarf kingdom, and asked if I would tag along. When I left Theakredel with Enya and Dufin, my friends decided to carry on north to the Ruins Labyrinth."

Tor returned the mug to the kitchen and was ladling more soup into a bowl, but froze partway through. Didn't that fae mention something about the Fairy Fields, and her friends traveling there? The fairies built the labyrinth as a way to keep humans from entering the fairy realm. Going to the Ruins Labyrinth meant they were going to Fairy Fields. The fae did mention it, Tor was sure of it. She brought over the bowl of soup and sat down. "Why are your friends going there? What's their purpose?"

Jardeth smiled. "Why are you so curious about all this?"

"I'm currently deciding on my next destination and was debating visiting the village outside of the Ruins Labyrinth. I do need to do some resupplying as well. The Fairies will have plants that I can't get anywhere else." It was a probable story; she was a cleric and that was what clerics did on their pilgrimages. "If something is happening there, then maybe I should leave sooner rather than later."

Jardeth sipped at the liquid and nodded. "Niviel, my friend, was meeting up with someone who'd been sent there on a contract."

"So Niviel's friend is a merchant?" Tor couldn't think of anyone else who would have a contract to go to the Fairy Fields. The only reason to ever risk the Ruins and get to the fairy veil was to purchase rare goods. There are few merchants east of the veil who the fairies would deal with.

"No. His friend is with the Agency."

"He's an assassin?"

"She's a spy, actually. Niviel is an assassin."

Tor tilted her head. "Your other friend he is traveling with is an assassin as well, then?"

Jardeth laughed. "No, Zaden is a tree sprite."

"Tree sprite? That's an odd pairing. How—"

The door swung open and Enya entered first. She smiled at seeing Jardeth sitting at the table and eating a bowl of soup.

"Jardeth," Pac called as she bounded toward him. He picked her up and put her on his lap, then stopped and stared at her for a long time, as if he didn't quite know who she was. Tor brought in two mugs and gestured for them to all sit. Jardeth couldn't seem to pull his gaze away from Pac.

"What is it?" Enya finally asked, her voice slightly apprehensive.

Jardeth looked from Enya to Tor. "You're right," he said to Tor. "I can see it now."

"See what? What's going on?" Enya said.

"Like I said the last time you were here, Pac is not really

Shadow anymore. She's been in our Realm far too long. Shadow creatures are called that for a reason."

"What aire ye bloody goin' oan about? How can she no' be a Shadow no mair? Who cares how lang she's been in our realm."

"Have you ever been in the Shadow Realm, Master Warrior?" Jardeth asked.

"Why in Gronk's beard would Ah ever go there?"

"There is no sun, no light there," said Tor. "It is a bleak, desolate place and the Shadow creatures thrive there because of it. They die in the light. This is why you never see them during the day, and if you did it would be in dark recesses of places never out in the open. She"—Tor pointed at Pac—"has been in the light for at least three months. She's changing."

"No, that can't be right," Enya said. "Pac is at least eight, maybe nine years old. Why would she only start changing now?"

"Pac"—Tor turned to her and Pac stared back—"where did you live before going with these people?"

"I live king's house." She wrinkled her face, like she tasted something sour. "It was cold, dark. I did not like it."

"Like in the Shadow Realm, she lived in the dark. I bet she had limited contact with people, too. It's likely why her gift of speech is so poor." Tor took a sip from her mug, then looked at Dufin. "Makes your plans a little more complicated, doesn't it? Now that she's more human than monster?"

Pac and Dufin made eye contact, and she gave him a knowing smile.

"She told me last night that if she dies, everyone in the Realm will die. Is this true?" Enya asked Tor.

"What makes you think I know?" Tor asked.

"You said you saw fae," Enya said. "What did they want you to do?"

"I didn't see just any fae, I saw Destiny Custodians. What made it even more interesting is that they were female."

"You never said that," Jardeth said, the color suddenly draining from his face.

"Sae what? Male? Female? What daes it matter?" Dufin crossed his arms and sat back in his chair.

Tor looked to Enya.

Enya merely shrugged. "I know as much as Jardeth does about fae, but I only met my first a few days ago and they didn't seem like anything special."

"Remember when I told you that fae are tricksters, even the Destiny Custodians, and that they love chaos and will influence events to ensure it?" Jardeth asked.

"Yes," Enya nodded.

"Those are the males. Females are rarely, if ever, seen. They care little for the chaos our world could create. They will make bargains if it works in their favor, but they are extremely difficult to find and even harder to summon. If a female Destiny Custodian comes to you, then something big is about to happen. Something bad."

"How bad?" Enya and Dufin asked in unison.

"Extinction–level bad," Tor said.

"What did these fae tell you?" Enya asked Tor.

"The child must live."

"Nothing about the High King?"

"No. Why, did the fae tell you the king must die?"

"No, the opposite. They told us the king must live but an elf assassin must die."

"What elf assassin?" Tor noticed Jardeth shift in his seat with the mention of the elf. It was subtle, and she was certain no one else noticed.

Enya shrugged.

Tor stood and gathered the mugs from the table. "I think I would trust the females on this one."

"Why? How aire yer fae any better?"

"Like I said, Warrior Dwarf, females only intervene if there is an extinction–level event happening. They step in to prevent it. Males care nothing for who lives or who dies, they just want the most destruction possible. That being said, these two groups are working against each other. I would go with the team that is rooting for our survival."

"How come they care?" Dufin asked. "Fae care abou' no one but themselves, right? Isn't that what ye said?" He pointed at Jardeth.

"Males want as much chaos as possible; they don't really care about the consequences. Females have a tendency to see past the event and look at the aftermath. They evaluate the impact of such things in relation to their own kind. Most times, an extinction–level event for one Realm has no effect on another. You don't see the females often, but if more than one Realm is going to feel the blow they tend to step in."

"Then why the damn riddles?" Dufin said. "Why no' tell us what in Gronk's beard we aire supposed tae dae!"

"Because what would be the fun in that?" Tor said. "Female fae are still fae, after all."

"Come with us tae speak tae the High King," Dufin said to Tor. "Explain tae him what ye just told us."

"What? Are you crazy?" Jardeth said. "Were you not listening to any of this? Pac has to live. If we take her to the High King—"

"It's extremely naive of you to think the king would listen." Tor smiled and started packing a bag. "Especially to me, an orc. I won't go with you because your intentions are not as pure as you want us to think." Tor had no experience with dwarves but she knew most of them wanted their mines back, to keep all their gems and gold. She also knew the High King was taking a large portion of that due to the peace treaty agreement from the Kings War. She also knew they would blindly follow the orders of their leaders, no matter the cost. She hoped this dwarf would be different. "I suggest you keep that child as far from the High King as possible." Tor spoke straight to Enya. "Because, if his taking her magic is what causes this event, then you'll have killed us all."

Pac stood up from Jardeth's lap. "I go king. I get king listen."

"No, darling Pac, that won't work. The king won't listen to a child."

"I go king. King listen like Dufin listen."

"What?" Dufin asked as all eyes fell on him.

"King listen like you. You move 'cause you listen." She smiled at Enya and showed her an apple core. "Apple man listen like Dufin listen. Like guards at gate listen." When no one seemed to understand what she was saying, she gave a deep sigh and looked determined to school the imbeciles. Tor did her best to stifle a laugh. "I tell Dufin move. Dufin move and arrow miss. I tell apple man I hungry. Apple man gave apple. Guard won't let us pass, I tell let us pass. He let us pass. I tell king no magic, king will no take magic." She moved to the other side of the table and looked Dufin in the eyes. "I tell king to give mines, king give mines. Dufin happy and Pac can live."

"What arrow?" Jardeth asked.

"That's what you took away from that?" Enya said.

"Last night," Dufin said, looking at Enya, "Ah heard a voice in my head an' it told me tae step back. When Ah did, the arrow missed me by a millimeter."

Enya dropped into a chair. "I need a drink. This is too much. Now she can mind control on people?"

"She dinnae control me, she told me tae step back. The first time Ah dinnae listen but then she said it again, only a little louder. Ah made the choice tae step back."

"Did you?" Jardeth asked, raising an eyebrow.

Dufin looked at Pac. "Dinnae Ah?"

Pac bit her lip and cast her gaze down before slowly shaking her head.

"Gronk's hairy balls," he spat.

"She saved your life," Enya said.

"She controlled me!" he shouted back.

Enya touched Pac's arm, and Pac pulled her gaze up to meet hers. "No more mind controlling friends, okay?"

"No mair fuckin' mind controllin' period!" Dufin added.

"Except for the king. We're doing that mind-control thing on the king, right?" Jardeth asked.

Tor put on her coat. She still didn't have exactly what she wanted, but she knew Jardeth knew something about how Pac had changed as much as she did. She suspected he had given her something to change her in the hopes it would destroy her magic. But she had no proof.

"I hate to break up this little party," Tor said, "but I need to go. I have to get to the monastery and search the archives for some information on the prophecy I told you about. Jardeth is on the mend, but keep drinking that tea I gave you. There's enough there for the next week. Make sure you drink it all, or the poison will work itself back into your blood." She opened the door and held it open while everyone gathered their things and left her little hovel. As Enya passed, Tor took her hands. "Whether the king lives or dies my fae didn't care, what matters is that Pac lives. Don't take any unnecessary chances. And, when the time comes, seek out your people."

"My people?"

"You know who you truly are. So, when the time comes seek them out—"

"When will that be?"

Tor let go of her hands. "You'll know." The two stepped out into the midday sun to join the others. Tor bid them farewell, and turned in the opposite direction.

CHAPTER FOURTEEN

T HE INSTANT TOR WAS OUT of the old shack she headed for
her home on the edge of mid-town. She glanced over her
shoulder in time to see the King's Guard escort the others away.
She should have taken Pac. It was her duty to protect the child. But
Jardeth and Enya had seemed capable.

She turned toward the guards and picked up her pace. Most of
the guards knew her, as she treated many of their families. They
would believe her if she told them what the fae had said. She followed them through lower-town, sidestepping and pushing through
the crowds. When the guards crossed over the threshold between
lower-town and mid-town, Tor stopped.

The multiple warnings over the years about her leaving lower-
town ran through her mind as one of the guards turned his head. It
was as if he'd sensed her. He wasn't one of the guards from this
area, but a personal guard of the king himself. She had never met
him before, and the likelihood she knew any of them was slim.

Tor swore under her breath; she had to keep the child safe.
It was why she'd been sent here. Two feet from the border, Tor
stood. If she stepped over the line, they would kill her. She could
do no good if dead. She heard children playing behind her, and her
thoughts were brought back to Parin. He would be waiting for her
at home by now, school over for the day.

She watched as the small escort disappeared around a corner.

Hoping she'd made the right choice, Tor prayed this was not the end the fae had spoken about. She spun on her heal and headed for home.

When she came through the door, Parin was right where she thought he would be: sitting at the table poring over his studies.

He looked up as the door opened. "Das'mut, I was getting a little worried. How is our patient? Would you like me to go stay with him?" Parin began to stand when Tor put a hand on his shoulder.

"He is mended, and they have gone on their way. Now we must be on ours."

Parin's eyebrows knitted. "What do you mean?"

"We must leave the city, now. Pack your things. We're going to return to the monastery. I must speak with Abacuss, and there is information I must find."

"I don't understand. I thought we were waiting until I was done the year. Completed my studies."

Tor was in the kitchen, packing all the supplies she could fit into her medical satchel. "I don't have time to argue or explain. We need to get out of the city before the gates are closed."

"Does this have to do with all the magical beings being brought to the king? About the blood moon being tonight?"

That thought hadn't actually crossed Tor's mind. But now it all made sense. She stopped packing, realizing she had made a terrible mistake. With the guards escorting the others to the castle, Pac would surely be sacrificed. But what of this mind control? Was Pac strong enough to actually do what she said she was going to do? Could she turn the tide?

"Das'mut?"

Parin's words cut through Tor's thoughts. "Yes. Yes it does. We must get out of the city. Please, Parin, put your things together."

Parin set his shoulders and nodded once. He rushed past her and disappeared into his room. She could hear him moving about as he pulled items from cabinets and chests. Tor finished packing her medical bag, then moved to food supplies. Once done, she went to her own room and grabbed clothes and a sturdy blanket for sleeping on the ground.

When she came back to the front of the house, Parin was putting on his coat and swinging his pack over his shoulder. Tor handed him the food satchel as she took the medical bag.

"What about Gran?" Parin asked. "I don't think we should leave without saying goodbye."

He was right; she was family. But the sun was getting low, and they would never make the gate if they stopped to say their goodbyes. A lump formed in her throat at the thought of leaving her surrogate mother behind, but Gran had also made it clear that she would never leave the city.

"If Eydis is at the gate we will have him pass on the message. She will understand why we had to leave so quickly." *No, she wouldn't.* Tor thought. *But we have no choice.* She tried desperately to convince herself as she ushered Parin out of their home of eight years.

Tor kept her pace steady as they headed for the gate at the back of the High Kingdom, the one used by the poor and destitute—the people the king wanted little to do with, and certainly didn't want to see enter his city. She still debated whether she was going to go to the Fairy Fields. What exactly were her friends there for? What contract were they fulfilling? Gathering more magical beings?

Tor shook the thought from her head. She needed to get Parin to the monastery. The High Cleric shouldn't have any problem accepting Parin. Parin was human, and that would play in his favor. She hoped Abacuss was still there. He'd been ancient when she left, and it was possible that over the past fourteen years he had passed away.

Parin had to jog to keep up with her pace. She could hear him panting, but she couldn't slow. Time was running out. When they reached the gate she took one last look back at the castle, and made a silent plea to her Goddess Thanroota that Jardeth and the others had fled the city with the child. It was not the warrior thing to do, to run, but they may have to battle their way out. And that was when Thanroota would show herself and battle beside them. As the thought crossed her mind, a static built in the air. Dark clouds formed above head, and a flash of lightning streaked across the sky.

Tor took a deep breath and ground her teeth. The King was practicing his magic again, but what kind of magic was he using to create such affects? "Nothing good," she said out loud.

"What was that?" one of the guards at the gate asked. He was a beast of a man, and her height. His armor was much too small for him, and his belly hung outside of the metal.

"Oh nothing, just speaking to the boy." Tor touched Parin's shoulder while keeping her eye on the sky, waiting for another lightning streak and hoping it wouldn't touch the ground. That type of discharge would mean dark magic was being used—strong dark magic. Right now, the king was merely dabbling with likely weak blood magic.

"Are you leaving us?" the guard asked. "Gran will be disappointed. She will miss you both dearly. She's come to enjoy the time you spend with her through the years."

"Eydis," she said with a warm smile. "I've decided this was the best time to take Parin to the monastery. Please tell Gran we are so deeply sorry we didn't say goodbye. Go to my home and take the berry plant from the back; it is in a separate pot from the rest. Tell her to water it every other day, and it will produce the berries and leaves for the tea she loves."

Eydis nodded, his face sullen. She had known for years that Eydis was interested in her, but just didn't have the courage to say it.

A second guard approached and Tor smiled.

"You and the boy leaving us?" he asked.

"I'm afraid so. Take care of that wife and family of yours."

The guard nodded, and was about to speak when a voice shouted from behind. "Phoddsson! Stop yakking to that bloody orc and get back to your post! Gronk's beard! Do your job, you lazy bastard!"

His face pinked up along his cheekbones, and his gaze dropped slightly. "Yes, sir," he called back. Before stepping away he caught Tor's eye once again. "I will miss you also."

Tor smiled warmly at the man. She wanted to touch his hand to show him kindness, but knew the other guards would take it as an act of aggression. At least, the head guard would. Apparently fourteen years still wasn't long enough for him to drop his hatred.

"Take care of yourselves," she said to both guards. As she reached for her hood with one hand she placed the other on Parin's back, guiding him toward the gates.

"Where in Gronk's beard do you think you are taking that boy?" the guard on the platform yelled. "Stop her!"

Parin and Tor stopped when they were blocked by two other guards. Tor didn't know these men; they were extremely young, and as new guards this was obviously their first assignment.

"Sir," Eydis called, "the boy is of the age of consent. He can leave whenever, and with whomever, he likes."

Parin opened his mouth but Tor stepped close and gripped his wrist, silencing him.

"Is that true, boy?"

Tor gave Parin a gentle double-squeeze around the wrist.

"Yes, sir. I'm sixteen, and will be seventeen in a few short months."

"Seventeen is the age of consent, not sixteen," the guard shouted down.

"It's only two month's difference," Eydis said.

The guard stared down at them as the static in the air began to grow again; this time it came with a metallic taste. Both Parin and

Tor shared a sour look. He could taste it too. But, when the static reached its peak and the air pressure dropped, there was no thunder or lightning.

Everyone at the gate looked to the sky, waiting, but nothing happened.

Tor turned to Eydis. "May we go?"

Eydis brought his gaze down to meet hers. "I'm letting them pass," he said with an authority Tor had never heard from him before. The younger guards stepped aside, and Tor rushed Parin through the gates. As she passed the guard standing atop a raised platform to give him a better view, he spat at her, barely missing her foot. With a subtle twist of her wrist, a flick of her fingers, and a short incantation, the guard lost his balance and landed in a puddle. Her movement went unnoticed, as it had been concealed under her cloak.

As laughter erupted around her, Tor did little to hide her own smirk.

Parin waited until they were well out of earshot before saying anything. "How did you do that?"

"What makes you think I did anything?"

"Das'mut." His face was disapproving, but his tone was playful.

"There are many different types of magic in this world. You'll learn many of them at the monastery. Just make sure your healing studies are completed first."

Parin's smile was so wide that all his teeth showed. She loved to see his excitement; it was like seeing the five-year-old Parin again.

Abacuss would have applauded her standing up for herself, but High Cleric Whillem would scold her for her cruelty to the human.

Tor adjusted her pack and the two followed the road away from the castle. There was another road three hours away, which branched off and to the north, but they would be able to follow that road all the way to the monastery. Less than a week's trek away. She pushed out her stride to make better time, but Parin's shorter legs couldn't keep up.

He had to maintain a steady jog. After five minutes he protested to the pace, and to Tor's displeasure she slowed down. The tiny town where Tor had once healed a small boy's dislocated shoulder was only a day or so away. Even though it had been many years, she hoped they would remember her and allow them to stay at the inn.

CHAPTER FIFTEEN

T HE SKIES WERE BEGINNING TO darken but her eyes were slowly adjusting, so Tor wasn't worried about being able to see the road ahead. As they rounded the third bend Tor smiled.

She pointed ahead. "See in the distance—those dark spots?"

"Trees," Parin said, shrugging.

"No, it's a small town. Hopefully, we will be able to spend tomorrow night. We should get there by late afternoon."

A voice came up behind them. "I take it you have decided not go to the Fairy Fields." Her voice was familiar, and Tor knew who it was even before turning.

The two stopped. The fae was breathing a little heavy, but she had not broken a sweat. It was obvious she'd had to jog from the castle to catch up. She was dressed to travel, as well.

"Were you just sitting at the back gate, waiting for us to leave?" Tor asked.

"Yes."

"Yes? Then what took you so long? We've been walking for over three hours."

The fae shrugged. "Had a few issues with a guard. Took a little convincing to let me pass. They had closed the gates straight after the two of you left."

"What exactly did you do to convince them?" Parin asked before Tor could.

The fae smirked. "Let's just say that I won't be able to return to the High Kingdom for some time."

"You killed the guards? Why would you do that?" Tor was appalled; there were still a few she didn't like much...but to kill them?

"I told you, the future I have seen needs you to go to the Fairy Fields."

"So, you're going to try to convince me to go? After that? You expect me to trust you now?"

The fae put her hands on her hips. "I've never known an orc to be queasy about such things."

"I'm not a warrior. I denounced my orc heritage when I was sent to the monastery. My oath and my religion are that of healing. Killing—" She stopped when the realization of who had been at the gate hit her. Eydis, a good man, and one she had known for over a decade. He was family, just as Gran was. An anger she had not felt since she was a young girl flared up. The emotion that crossed her face was enough to cause the fae to drop her hands and step back.

"Das'mut," Parin said, putting a hand on her arm. "Remember your oath."

Tor clenched her jaw and tightened her fists. "Who did you kill?" Her voice was barely above a whisper as she moved in on the fae.

"The leader, he was the last there. The rest had been sent home once the gates were locked. The men you were speaking with are alive." She lifted her hands and widened her stance. "I promise you I did not harm your friends."

"How did you know who our friends were?" Parin asked.

The fae glanced around Tor, and a sly smile slide across her lips. "I have my way."

"You are not charming, nor do I wish for your company." Tor fought to remain in control, but what she really wanted to do was rip the fae's arms off and beat her with them. She spun and grabbed Parin by the arm. "Let's go."

Parin was up on his toes, trying to keep up. "Das'mut, you're hurting me."

Tor stopped and released him. Her face softened. "I'm sorry. My anger— I have no excuse. I'm sorry, Parin. But we must go."

Parin glanced over his shoulder at the fae, who hadn't moved, then nodded. Without turning back the two continued toward the town.

"Please, Tor, for centuries I've been without my trio and my visions of the future have always been fractured, disconnected. Even surrounding this child I've only received pieces, tiny glimpses—"

Tor stopped dead and spun around. It only took several long strides to close the gap between them. "The child? Do you mean the Shadow child?"

"Yes, you saw her with your own eyes. She is not so much Shadow anymore."

"What else do you know of the Shadow child?"

The fae stared at Tor for a long while.

"Well?" Tor grew impatient. She just wanted to pick up the tiny fae and shake the information out of her.

"The man you treated; he was given an elixir to feed her, to change her from a Shadow to something else. To change her blood magic."

Tor felt a bit vindicated; she'd known Jardeth had given her something. The look in his eyes, and how he changed the topic, had told her he knew a lot more than he wanted to say. "You said 'change her into something else'...what did you change her into?"

"She should be more human. Her blood magic weakened, hopefully taken."

Tor sighed. "The elixir you gave him may have changed her from Shadow, but her blood magic is strong. It's different than any magic I have ever felt, or tasted."

"I gave him nothing," the fae said, then narrowed her eyes at Tor. "You are sensitive to the static?"

"If you didn't give him the elixir, then who did?"

"You are an orc. Very interesting." The fae tilted her head. "Have you always been sensitive to the static?"

Tor shook her head. Was the fae avoiding her question on purpose, or was she just sidetracked? "You answer my question and I'll answer yours." Again, the fae merely stared. "Look, the sun has all but set and the village is still a day and a half away. I would like to find somewhere to set up camp and would prefer not to walk in complete darkness."

"Then we will walk and talk."

"No. Answer the question."

The fae tightened her jaw and crossed her arms across her chest. "You are irksome."

"As are you."

Parin chuckled, but when Tor shot a glare in his direction he stifled it very quickly.

"Very well. The man you healed first traveled to Theakredel with two other companions."

"Yes, I know. An elf and tree sprite."

"That's right." Her tone didn't hide her surprise. "How did you—"

"Jardeth told me. Now continue."

The Fae cleared her throat. "I told the elf to make the elixir, as he was gifted in magic. He gave it to Jardeth."

"Was gifted? Jardeth believes him to still be alive. Is that not the case?"

The fae sighed again. "That is why I am here seeking your help. I didn't fully understand why it had to be you. Not until this moment. But, for the first time in centuries, my visions were sharp, concise. I can no longer see Niviel, the elf. What I see is a veil being opened.... Well, one that is very small and narrow, and not really a veil because it has never existed before now. One that will take powerful magic to close."

"That time dilation thing you were talking about yesterday?"

"Yes."

"And it's happening now? This *rift*?"

"Rift...yes, that is a good word, because I'm not entirely certain that it is a veil. There appears to be no barrier between our two worlds."

Tor bit her lip and paced the width of the road in which they stood. The fae watched for several minutes, then said, "Now, you, answer my question. Have you always been sensitive to the static?"

Tor stopped and looked at the fae, then out to the horizon where the sun was setting. "Come on, let's walk and talk." Tor turned down the road, putting a hand on Parin's shoulder to guide him as the fae jogged to catch up. "I was quite young, before I reached the age of a warrior. I started noticing things, and I had heard of magic users. When I asked my father about it, he silenced me. Told me that magic wasn't for orc's, that it was a bad omen. The Goddesses would be displeased; it was why they took my mother."

Parin looped his arm through Tor's. She patted his hand, knowing he was giving her comfort.

The Fae shook her head. "I don't understand."

"My mother died in childbirth, delivering my youngest brother. My father said it was because she conspired with wizards to bring her children. He said he didn't believe it until the moment I told him I could feel the static. How during the birth I could feel it in the air." Tor touched her mouth where her tusks had once been. "When I lost my tusks he sent me away. Claimed it was because I brought him dishonor by losing a tusk completely, and not in battle. I was a shame on the family." Tor's jaw tightened. "He refused to send me to the orc's Goddess Temples in the north. Insisted that I didn't belong amongst warriors."

"That's when you went to the monastery?"

"Yes. That's where my father sent me. The clerics almost didn't take me, either, but Abacuss, my mentor, took one look at me and insisted I be brought in."

"He sounds like a kind man, wise. He must have sensed your abilities."

Tor looked down at the tiny woman, who was nothing like any fae she had ever encountered. The empathy in her voice, the kindness in her words...even with passing on information there was no arrogance there.

The three walked in silence for some time. The sun had set hours before, and the moon had begun to take its place. As if reading each other's minds, they stopped and looked to the sky. The moon felt foreboding, blood red and hanging low, and Tor felt as if she just reached up she could touch it. She was about to say something when the hair on the back of her neck stood on end.

The static in the air grew thick, strong, and even in the midnight sky she could see dark clouds roll in. Tor's mouth went dry. She knew what it meant; the shift in the magic, the heavy static. The fae looked up at Tor, and she could see a single tear roll down the fae's face. The child had been sacrificed, and that's when Tor felt it.

It was as if the ground gave out from under her, the buildup of static so strong she could barely breathe. Tor turned her attention to the castle and the air pressure seemed to drop. A flash of light nearly blinded her, and in the distance she could see a dust cloud speeding toward them. There was no time to move or react, and within seconds it had overtaken them, tossing them several feet in all directions. The explosion was so strong it leveled the trees that lined the road on one side.

Tor hit the ground hard, and for only an instant she could see the plume of smoke rise from the castle before she lost consciousness.

CHAPTER SIXTEEN

TOR WAS SHAKEN AWAKE BY a hand on her shoulder. She blinked up at the face in front of her. The sky behind them was dark, but it wasn't night. "Eydis?"

"Are you all right, Tor?" Eydis knelt next to her. "I've been searching for you all night, after the explosion nearly took out the entire castle. I think a lot of the guards died up there."

Tor pushed herself into a seated position, with Eydis's help. There was a slight buzzing in her ears, and Eydis's voice sounded muffled. She dabbed at her ears and felt the crusty stickiness of dried blood. She must have a punctured ear drum. Eydis stood and helped Tor to her feet. Her eyes searched the area. "Parin. Where's Parin?" Her first few steps were unsteady, and Eydis helped her out of the ditch and back into the road. "Parin," she shouted.

"I'm here," a voice called from the other side.

"Are you all right?" Tor shoved Eydis away as she staggered toward her son. He was sitting and holding his arm. A strange lump under his sleeve indicated a protruding bone. She knelt next to him, shaking out the cobwebs in her head and forcing herself to focus.

"It's broken. I think I landed on some rocks or something."

Tor nodded, and the two worked to get his coat off. When his arm was exposed she could see the bone poking through the skin. Behind them she heard Eydis gag. The two shared a smile.

"It's not nice to laugh," he said as he gagged again. "Some people"—gag—"just don't have—"gag—

"Stop looking already," Tor said with a laugh, and Eydis turned his head away.

Parin glanced about as he held his arm, waiting for Tor to get the right supplies together. "Where's that fae?" he asked.

Eydis faced them. "Fae? What fae?" He then turned on the spot, looking around.

"We were with a fae female when the explosion happened. I don't see her." Tor didn't particularly care where the fae had disappeared to. Her son was injured, and that was all that mattered at the moment. Again, Eydis gagged. "Perhaps you should see if you can find her."

"Right." Eydis stepped out into the road. "Fae!" he shouted. "Does she have a name?" he asked, without looking back. "I feel a little silly just calling her 'fae'."

Parin finished chewing the numbing root Tor had given him and nodded. The two took a deep breath, and Tor pushed the bone back into place with one hand while straightening his arm with the other. Parin's scream was agonizing, and Tor's stomach dropped. She couldn't stand the thought of him suffering.

Parin teetered and Tor steadied him. "You all right?"

His eyes widened as he took another breath. "I think so, but thought I might pass out for a minute. But I'm good."

"Fae!" They could hear Eydis shouting.

"Think she's dead?" Parin asked as Tor stitched up the open wound. "That explosion—" His eyes settled in the direction of the High Kingdom.

"Fae," Eydis called again.

Tor checked over her shoulder, in the direction Parin was looking. The sky above the castle, where the towers had once stood, was lit in hues of red from the fires that burned. Clouds of smoke billowed upward. Her heart sank again, certain that sweet girl, no matter if she was Shadow or not, was dead. What did that mean for the rest of them? She returned to her task and, when done stitching, wrapped it, then placed two solid pieces of wood on each side of his arm before wrapping it again to keep it in place.

After she put his arm in a sling, she helped him off the ground and put his coat on. She searched for Eydis, who had wandered further down the road calling for the fae. Parin and Tor climbed out from the ditch and she called out, "Fae, are you alive?"

"Yes, please stop yelling." Her tiny voice came from down the road, inside the ditch. Eydis rushed to her side to help her up. She was covered head to toe in mud and sludge. She held her head, unsteady on her feet.

Tor moved to stand in front of her. "Are your ears buzzing?"

The fae nodded as she tried to clear them by opening and closing her mouth. "Looks like the child has been sacrificed after all. I hoped that Niviel's man would have completed his task and got the child to safety."

"I was certain Enya was going to stop it as well."

Eydis stood in front of the two women. He stared at the fae, but said nothing. That was when Tor noticed his clothing; he wasn't wearing his armor, but was in thick leather attire usually used in training, and it fit him much better than the metal armor. "Eydis, you said the King's Guard was in the castle?"

"Yes."

"Then why are you here?"

Eydis looked from the fae to Tor, then to the castle. "Right after you left the captain told us to gather as many of the lower-town's people as we could find." His eyes had a haunted look, and Tor realized that all these years Eydis knew exactly why, and where, people were disappearing. "I couldn't let my Gran suffer that kind of fate. I rushed home, packed her and several of her neighbors to get them out of the city, sent them through the sewer tunnels. I was going to take them to the Misandria Region, or even Gloverree, but I hadn't yet figured out that much."

"Then what are you doing here?" Tor asked. "Why aren't you with them?"

"Gran refused to leave until I retrieved you two. In all the chaos I had forgotten to tell her that you had already left for the monastery. She was not happy you'd left without saying goodbye, but she told me to go after you. Said you shouldn't take this journey on your own. You know how Gran is."

"That I do," Tor said with a smile.

"Who's protecting your grandmother?" The fae asked. "Surely the journey to either of those cities will be difficult for the elderly."

Eydis stared at the fae, and Tor knew from the look on his face he was as confused by the fae's question as she was. Fae weren't known for empathy. He looked back to Tor. "As I was packing up Gran, my brother showed up. They had seen the guards gathering people, so they packed up their family and two of their neighbors followed. There is about fifteen of them all together.

"I hope they got a good enough distance away before that explosion happened. I don't know if Gran could survive that kind of impact."

"Don't worry, she's a lot tougher than many give her credit for." Tor stretched her neck and shoulders. They were stiff and tight; her shoulder ached and her lower back was tender. She must have hit the ground and rolled before coming to a stop, but she didn't remember much past the flash of light. Tor watched the fae before saying anything. "Well, it looks like we no longer need to go to the Fields now."

The Fae snapped her head in Tor's direction. "Why would you think that?"

"Because Pac is dead." Tor turned toward the castle, pointing. "What is there to do at the Fields?"

"I told you; there is a rift opening and I need your help."

"A rift?" Eydis asked. "What's a rift?"

Ignoring his question, Tor said, "Tell me why you need me and I will go."

"You obviously rattled your brain when you were knocked down. I've told you: my vision showed that you were there. You have to come. Please."

"Das'mut," Parin said, touching her arm. "What could be the harm? We go to the monastery, and then you go with the fae."

Tor set her jaw. "The harm is it's at least three months away, and gets dangerously close to orc lands."

"I'll come with you," Eydis said with a shrug. "I could use a little adventure in my life."

Parin laughed. "Plus Gran would kill you if you showed up alone."

Eydis nodded pointing a finger in agreement. "Yup, that too."

Tor sighed grabbed hers and Parin's packs, shouldering both the best she could. "Fine, we still have a couple days before we reach the monastery. Let's get moving."

"You will go to the fields then?" The fae's eyes lit up.

Such strange reactions from this creature. Nothing like any fae she has ever been in contact with, or read about. "Looks like." She looked at Eydis. "Eydis, this is...the fae. Fae, this is Eydis." It made for an awkward introduction when someone doesn't have a name.

The fae laughed. It was unnatural, but also somehow natural at the same time. "My name is Clairla."

"You have a name?" Tor did nothing to hide her surprise. "I thought fae didn't have names."

"We don't. At least, not when we are in a trio. But I haven't had a trio in a very long time. Many years ago, I named myself in memory of someone I once loved."

"What happened to them? Did they die?" Eydis asked.

Clairla turned and started down the road without acknowledging the question.

"Guess she doesn't want to talk about it," Eydis said to Tor. He walked past her and followed behind Clairla.

Tor joined Parin, and he took the lighter of the four bags and looped the pack over his good shoulder. "You'll have a very long journey ahead of you. Plenty of time to find out." He smiled up at her. "Then you can come back and tell me."

Tor and Parin shared a laugh as they walked behind the other two. It was about an hour before the static in the air began to build up. They stopped, and Tor and Clairla exchanged a glance before turning toward the castle. Even from their distance they could see dark clouds over the city. As the air pressure dropped, a large flash of lightning struck somewhere in the city and the static began to clear again.

"That is so weird; the strangest storm I've ever seen." Eydis knitted his eyebrows together and shrugged. "At least it's over there, and not pouring down on us."

Again Tor and Clairla exchanged a glance. It was obvious Eydis had no sensitivity to the static. He likely had no magical skills at all, learned or otherwise. Tor wasn't sure if this was a good thing or not.

They started their walk once again, Tor passing some bread between them and sharing some water. They traveled mostly in silence, and every half hour to hour the static would build once again. The further they got from the castle, the less they felt the effects, but the cracks of thunder echoed over the land.

When they reached the tiny village, Tor led them to the inn. She opened the door and ducked to enter the building. It was a quaint front room. A fire was burning in a hearth, with a couple of chairs to sink into around it, as well as a desk the innkeeper sat behind. It was the same as it had been when she was here fourteen years prior, but also different.

The man behind the counter stood when they entered. His eyes widened when he saw Tor. "Tor, I didn't expect to see you again."

Tor looked at the young man, smiling when she recognized him. "Tagger? Look how grown you are. A proper young man now."

"It's so good to see you again. Are you looking for a room?"

"Yes. Two rooms, please. Two beds each if possible."

Tagger smiled and pulled the same book as before from behind the counter. He wrote down her name and two room numbers. He slid the keys across the counter. "Would you like a hot meal? I assume, by the looks of all of you, you got caught out in whatever that was last night. The loudest noise I've ever heard. Do you know what it was?"

Clairla grabbed a key off the counter. "The High Kingdom blew itself up." Her impatience was evident as she headed for the stairs.

Tagger's mouth open and closed.

"It's true," Tor said. "Four hot meals when you're ready, please." She didn't want to explain. She was tired and had a horrible headache. When she looked at Parin he was having difficulty staying on his feet, and he was very pale. It was obvious he was not just tired, but in great pain.

Tor turned to Tagger one last time. "Thank you for your hospitality," she said, then ushered Parin and Eydis up the stairs.

CHAPTER SEVENTEEN

A FTER A WEEK'S COMBINATION OF walking and hitching rides on rickety farmer's wagons, they made it to the monastery. Although the sky was blue and the sun was out, not far on the horizon loomed dark and foreboding clouds. Tor wasn't positive, but she thought the clouds were slowly creeping outward.

They all knew they weren't natural, and that the magic used to create them hadn't fully dissipated. As if on a tight schedule the static would build, the air pressure dropping, and they would see a flash of light in the distance. The further they moved away from the High Kingdom, the less they could feel the effects.

Neither Tor nor Clairla thought it would last long with the clouds seemingly growing outward. They made their way through the town's cobblestone streets, which surrounded the monastery. Many of the people smiled and welcomed Tor back. She knew many of them through her years of living amongst them.

Thankfully, they were more accepting of her than pretty much anywhere else in the land of men. She guided the group through the side entrance, where the clerics would come and go. She asked them to wait as she sought out High Cleric Whillem. It was important she greet him first, much to her displeasure.

She knocked on the heavy wooden door of his office. There was a pause, and an unfamiliar voice called out for her to enter. Tor pushed the door open and poked her head through. "High Cleric Whillem?"

"Come in, come in. Don't hang around the doorway." His back was turned to her. He was a bulk of a man, and definitely not Whillem.

She noted he wasn't wearing his robes, and the shirt he was wearing showed his back muscles. He was well built, which was strange for a Rejuvenation cleric as most were quite slim.

Tor absently cleared her throat, but realized how rude it was and quickly spoke. "Hello, my name is Tor. I'm the cleric that has been stationed—"

The man turned and Tor swallowed. He was dark-skinned and sported a long beard and mustache. His hair was also longer, and mingled with his facial hair. She could see he still had a square jaw under all the hair, and he was one of the most handsome men she had ever seen.

Rarely did she find males of the race of men to be attractive, but there was something different about this one.

"You all right?" he asked, putting the papers he was holding on the desk. "Would you like to sit?"

"I...uh..." she cleared her throat again. "I-I'm fine, thank you."

He watched her for a moment longer before speaking. "I see you have returned to us from the High Kingdom. I was about to send a replacement for you, since you had been there for so long. I felt it was time for you to come home." He gestured to a large cushioned chair and sat in the one across from it. "But, I suppose, after fourteen years it must have become a home to you."

Tor took the seat, uncertain what to say. All words seemed to have dropped from her head.

"Not much of a talker?"

Tor swallowed. "I'm sorry. I guess your presence just took me off guard. Where's High Cleric Whillem?"

"Ah, I see he never sent you updates."

"Updates? No. I would send correspondence to Abacuss, but never heard anything back. I doubted my messages ever really got to him."

The handsome bearded man laughed. It was like a long song that rang in Tor's ear. She felt her heart beat a little harder and her face warm. She swallowed and cleared her throat again. "I don't remember you from when I was here."

"Ah, no, you wouldn't. I'm not from this monastery. I'm from the Deflection Monastery. There have been several changes made since King Thomas started gathering magical beings throughout this land. Many felt that High Cleric Whillem just wasn't up for the task of leadership at this time."

"Where is he now?"

The handsome man sighed. "He was sent to Mardrovend."

"To replace you?" Tor thought it strange; why would he be sent to the mountain people?

The Handsome Man laughed again. "Oh my, no. When Abacuss fell ill we sent Whillem to the Deflection Monastery."

Tor's brain seemed to stutter; all she heard was that Abacuss had fallen ill. Her stomach lurched and her heart began to pound.

Handsome Man leaned forward on his knees. His face became very somber and the hair on Tor's neck stood on end. "I'm truly sorry—"

"When did he die?" She didn't fight the tears that welled in her eyes.

The Handsome Man raised both his eyebrows and waved his hands. "Oh, no. No, I'm sorry. Abacuss didn't die, but he is quite ill. As the static and magic changed, his health seemed to start to fail as well. We tried everything we could think of. So, when nothing worked, we sent him to Ursena Lake in the hopes the people of Ursena would help him.

"At the very least, if they take him to the Deflection Monastery in Mardrovend, they can try to retrieve a sprite from Whispering Oaks."

Tor shook her head.

"What?"

"Whispering Oaks was burned to the ground several months ago. From what I heard, nothing survived."

The two were quiet for several seconds before the High Cleric spoke. "Well, then we will hope he made it to the Ursena people and they agreed to help." He came to his feet. "Now, I'm sure you're tired and hungry. You'll find your room as you left it, and you know where the dining hall is."

"Actually, I have brought my son."

"Son?"

"Yes. He wishes to learn the religion of healing and take the oath. He will be seventeen in a few months."

High Cleric smiled wide. "That would be wonderful, but perhaps he would prefer a more subtle religion of magic instead."

Tor laughed. "Are you saying the Deflection Monastery is having a difficult time finding recruits?"

He laughed a full belly laugh again. "Gronk's beard, no."

Tor was taken back by the term. It was considered derogatory and strange that a cleric would use it. But he was a mountain man, and they were a different sort of people.

"Come, introduce me to this son of yours."

Tor led him back to where she'd left the others. They were sitting on a stone bench that lined the wall, and stood when they saw Tor and the High Cleric coming.

Tor reached for Parin first. "Parin, this is High Cleric— It occurs to me that I never asked your name. I apologize."

He smiled and Tor felt butterflies in her stomach. *Pull yourself together, orc,* she scolded herself.

"Brimmere Stone," he said, holding out a hand to Parin. "It is good to meet you."

Parin smiled.

"This is Clairla, and my dear friend Eydis." Tor finished the introductions.

Brimmere held Eydis's hand. "If I'm not mistaken, you are of the mountain people, correct?"

Eydis stood a little taller. "Born but not raised, yes."

"I knew I could see a fellow countryman. I was certain you weren't raised there, though, as you would have learned to grow a better beard!" He let out a bark of a laugh and slapped Eydis on the shoulder. Eydis laughed as well, but not as hard. "Come, follow me. I'll get you a hot meal and a place to rest your heads." He turned and they all trailed behind.

"I didn't know you were from the mountains," Tor said as Brimmere led them away.

Eydis rubbed his shoulder. "There is a bit of a stigma that comes with being a mountain person. Much like there is in being an orc."

"What kind of stigma?" Parin asked from behind.

Clairla answered for them. "They are known to be a bit on the low end of the intelligence scale. A bit dim-witted."

"Well, I think I've proven that's not true," Eydis said over his shoulder.

"That remains to be seen."

Eydis opened his mouth to respond when Brimmere interrupted. "Here you are. Have something to eat. I'm sure Tor remembers where the guest quarters are."

"I do."

"How long will you be staying with us?"

Tor sighed. "I wanted to speak with Abacuss, but with him not here—"

"We'll be leaving in the morning." Clairla's tone was matter-of-fact.

Brimmere studied her for a moment. "Bossy little fae, isn't she?"

Parin and Eydis spoke at once. "How did you know?"

Brimmere laughed again. "Ah, the gifts of a well-trained Deflection Cleric. You and I, Parin, will have a few discussions on which religion suits you best."

"Yes, healing," Tor said.

Brimmere laughed again and nudged Tor. "Spoken like a true momma. Wants her baby to follow in her footsteps."

Tor couldn't help the smile that crept onto her lips and she laughed, feeling her face heat up again.

They bid their goodbyes to the High Cleric, had a hot meal, and Tor showed them to their rooms.

The next morning, Tor held Parin tight in her arms. "Das'mut, I can't breathe."

She sniffed and pulled him away. "Now, you be on your best behavior, and remember my lessons. And if High Cleric Brimmere"—she nodded to him over Parin's shoulder—"tries to lead you astray, just remember that you can study both but healing comes first." She hugged him again, kissed his forehead, and he stepped back.

"It's a shame you must leave so soon," Brimmere said as he walked Tor to the door, where Eydis and Clairla were waiting. "But it is obvious your fae has important business to attend." He reached into his robe and pulled out a journal. "Cleric Abacuss left this for you. He was certain, six months ago, you would return. He had hoped his health would keep long enough to give this to you himself, but—"

Tor took the offering. It was leather bound, had strange letters and markings on the outside, and a leather strap keeping it closed. She shoved the notebook into an inside pocket of her jacket. Thanking the High Cleric, she hugged Parin one last time before the three of them left.

CHAPTER EIGHTEEN

I T HAD BEEN FIVE DAYS since Tor had left Parin behind at the monastery. The only comfort she had for leaving him behind was that Whillem was no longer there. Brimmere seemed like a fair and open-minded man, and would teach Parin much. Just as long as he doesn't convince her son to change religions.

While they were traveling, Clairla had a vision of a small rift opening on the other side of Veil River. There was only one other place to cross, which was by the Fairy Fields. Several kilometers from the Ruins Labyrinth was a bridge, and that was to be their destination.

"But I thought you had friends you wanted to help in the village of the Ruins?" Eydis asked as they approached the swamp lands separating orc lands from the land of men.

Clairla shifted her pack. "I do, but this rift is more important. We must—" She stopped talking so quickly Tor spun around, looking for the threat.

They were traveling dangerously close to the border between lands, and the orcs would have sentries posted. They also wouldn't hesitate to kill them the instant they were spotted.

"What's wrong?" Tor asked. "Why did you stop talking? Did you see something?"

Clairla stopped and faced the other two. "I haven't been completely honest with you."

Tor clenched her jaw. She knew she couldn't trust the fae. No matter how different Clairla appeared to be, she was still a trickster.

Eydis's tone was as angry as Tor felt. "What do you mean, you haven't been honest with us?"

"Okay," Clairla said, putting her hands up. "It's not as bad as you may think."

Tor narrowed her eyes. "Then how bad is it?"

"Yes, I have friends in the Ruins Labyrinth. Or, rather, I did. They should have gone by now. Maybe. If they made it."

Tor shook her head and Eydis rested his hand on the hilt of his sword. "What do you mean, if they made it?"

Clairla paced back and forth. "My friends left Theakredel at the same time as Jardeth and his group. Only Niviel and Zaden headed for the ruins."

Tor waved her hand to usher her along. "Yes, we know this."

"We do?" Eydis said.

"Well, I did."

Clairla pointed at Tor. "Right, but by that point many Shadow soldiers had been reported in the area. The route the two of them would have took would have put them in the thick of the sightings."

Eydis let out a nervous laugh. "Shadow soldiers?"

Ignoring his question, Tor said, "So, what are we going toward?"

"I didn't lie about the rift, but I did deceive you about what we need to do."

"And that would be?"

"I saw something come from the rift. Something dangerous."

"What is this something?"

"My vision is very fractured with that. All I know is that we have to stop what is coming out of that rift. It will destroy us all." She turned her head away and whispered, "I think."

Tor's eyes widened and she grabbed Clairla's arm to turn her back to face them. "You think?" Her voice echoed through the fields and across the swampland.

"Like I said, it's fractured—"

"And this time dilation? Is that fractured too, or was it just malarkey?"

Eydis scratched his head. "Malarkey?"

Ignoring him, Clairla said, "No, I did see a time dilation."

"Where? In the Ruins?"

Clairla put a finger up and furrowed her brow. "Now, that was a little fractured."

Tor gripped her arm tighter and let out a frustrated grunt that bordered on a growl.

Eydis tapped Tor's arm. "Uh, guys. I think we may have company."

Tor glanced at Eydis, then turned her attention to where he was looking. In the distance were hills, and over the hills was where the orc lands started. Even though they were still on the other side of the swampland the hills were in clear view.

Lining the top were ten figures. The orc sentries.

"Well, that's not good." Tor sighed. Even though she wasn't a warrior, she still carried a bow and quiver of arrows. They were mostly for hunting but, if needed, for fighting.

"But we aren't even in their lands," Clairla said.

Tor pursed her lips. "Doesn't matter. They know we intend to cross the swamps."

"Do we really need to?"

"It will be faster to get to the bridge that way."

"You're with us," Eydis said. "Why would it be an issue?"

Tor quirked a brow at him, realizing they wouldn't know her standing amongst the orcs since she never spoke about it. "I'm no more orc to them as you are." A deep sadness filled her. She missed her people, her family. But so many years had passed now; would they even recognize her?

"Then we take the longer way around, and not cross the swamps if we don't have to," Clairla said.

"We'll have to stay as close to the swamps on this side as we can. But it's likely they will follow us to ensure we don't cross."

Clairla and Eydis nodded, and Tor led them along a path. It was well-worn, and in some places dipped into the swamp—likely from earth corrosion. They moved in silence, and Tor ran through the conversation in her head. She didn't fully understand why she was even still going after being deceived. If what was coming out of the rift was their world's downfall, how could she not go?

She pulled the journal from her inside pocket and ran her fingers across the lettering. Tor was surefooted even on her worst days, so she wasn't concerned about taking a wrong step while she inspected the book. The letters looked so familiar, as if she had seen them before. She was about to open the journal when the hair on her arms stood on end and a metallic taste grew in her mouth.

The static coming from the High Kingdom built up and discharged bolts of lightning, but the effects were still minimal. She shoved the journal back into her pocket and noted the static was getting stronger. She swore the dark clouds were spreading out past the High Kingdom walls at a much greater speed, and wondered how long it would take for crops to start dying without direct sunlight. With the clouds growing outward, Tor believed they would be feeling the effects a lot more and very soon.

Tor's pace was slow, and her steps deliberate. She could hear Eydis panting and swearing behind her. "If you would just stay on the path instead of stepping into the swamp every other step, you wouldn't need to stop to pull your boots free."

"It's because he's not paying attention," Clairla said from behind.

"Well, I don't want to get caught off guard by those guys"— he pointed to the orcs following them on the other side—"so I'm keeping an eye on them."

Tor glanced over her shoulder. "Stop pointing at them, Eydis. They may take it as a challenge and you'll end up with an arrow through the eye. Those ten orcs are the only ones you can see. I promise you there are more that you don't."

Eydis dropped his hand immediately and watched the ground in front of him.

Tor thought about the reason for the swampland: the orc invasion about eight hundred years ago. They'd invaded the lands and the villages of men, burning down homes and killing any living being they came across. It had started the centuries-old hatred between orcs and nearly every other race.

Tor and Clairla knew they needed to tread lightly around the humans, and Eydis was only vaguely aware of the disdain from the other groups. Tor put it to the fact that he had never actually traveled outside of the High Kingdom. Up until a few weeks before she thought he'd been born and raised behind those stone walls. So he understands, to a small degree, what it's like to be discriminated against by being a mountain man.

Once clear of the swamps and border of the orc lands, they made their way west on a road that ran horizontal to the marsh. For the orcs, it was a common trade route to the Fairy Fields and beyond. The only beings the orcs were willing to trade with were the fairies, but the land between the two areas was mostly barren. The fairies were just as fond of the orcs as they were with man, and this made trading challenging for them as well.

Tor remembered when she had to travel to the Fairy Fields for supplies as part of her training. The fairies weren't kind to her, but they were worse to the humans she'd been with.

When Tor could no longer hear the constant dragging of lazy feet behind her, she stopped and turned. Clairla did the same. Eydis was staring up at the hills and toward the north. Tor stepped toward him and looked. But she really didn't need to, as she knew what he saw.

"Come on, Eydis, we aren't going that way."

"What is that?" He nodded, knowing the orcs were still close enough to shoot him. "Why would they do that?"

"It's a warning. No man shall pass." Tor put a hand on his shoulder. "We are in dangerous land, my friend. It's best you stay close."

"But the war was so long ago." His voice trembled and he wasn't able to take his eyes from the large wooden X's that stood on both sides of the road at the top of the hill. "Do they hunt people down to put them on those things?"

Tor sighed. She didn't like it either, but it wasn't long ago her own village had been burned to the ground by an unknown race. This practice had been used long before those attacks, as the hatred of man ran deep.

"It's likely those men crossed into orc lands." She couldn't say anything else but that. There was nothing more to be said that could make any of this right.

"Come on," Clairla said. "Let's keep moving. Once we are close to the Veil River, the orcs won't be much of a concern. The fairies don't like humans either, but they won't tolerate violence so close to their borders."

"I thought they were pacifists?" Eydis said.

Clairla said, "They were, until the orcs invaded. The fairies refused to join the people of the village and fight. A clan of elves, and the humans of the village, fought back against the orcs for months. When the battle was over, the humans turned against the fairies. It really was just a huge blood bath. Orcs were killing humans, humans and elves were killing orcs then, finally, humans were killing fairies."

"That's when the fairies built the labyrinth; to block the only safe way across the river to their veil," Tor added.

The scouts followed until Tor and her group reached the crossroads that lead to the only bridge to cross the Veil River.

"Why are we going this way?" Eydis asked. "Isn't this rift in the Fairy Fields?"

Clairla shoved her hands into the high pockets of her leather jacket. "One, the fairies really don't like humans. They would sooner crush you with the large stones in the labyrinth than to let you cross. Two, the rift isn't in the Fairy Realm."

"We need to travel to the other side of the river." Tor pointed to the northeast. "We'll make camp once we cross the bridge, and are away from the orc borders. There may be five kilometers between us in this spot, but it's still a little too close for my liking." Tor made to grab for her bow, then stopped. She only wanted to hunt for dinner, but orcs could see a good distance and they might think she was prepping to attack. "When we cross the river, I'll hunt for some dinner while you set up a camp."

There was a collective agreement. When they reached the bridge they all stopped. It looked ages old and unmaintained. In many places the wood was rotting, and Tor worried she may be too heavy for it. Eydis must have been thinking the same thing because his face had lost all color.

Clairla didn't hesitate. She was the lightest amongst them, so it would hold up under her weight. She stopped and turned when she reached the midpoint.

"Aren't you coming? What's the holdup?"

Tor nodded to Eydis. "You first."

"Me? No, ladies first, I insist." He smiled and held his hand out.

"It's best I go last." She looked toward the swamps. "You know, just in case." She knew the orcs were no longer a problem at this point. They had started to pull back one by one.

"I can't swim," Eydis whispered.

Tor leaned in and whispered back. "Then don't fall in."

He straightened. "That's not funny."

"Come on," Clairla shouted. "What's the holdup?"

"Eydis, just go."

He looked down to the water. "That's moving awful quick, and this bridge—"

Setting her shoulders, she grabbed Eydis by the strap of his pack and pulled him onto the bridge. Once they stepped on, Clairla traveled the rest of the way and waited on the other side. The old, rickety bridge moaned and creaked under their feet. Tor released Eydis so she could use both hands on the railings.

It was narrow, only big enough for one person. She did her best to keep calm; she could swim, but not well. The depth of the river was unknown, and the speed would surely sweep them away. She practically jumped the last couple feet off the bridge, then spun to watch Eydis.

He was taking small, short steps, and was barely at the crest of the bridge when Tor turned.

"This is going to take forever," Clairla said. "Come on, let's go. I'm starving. The quicker you get over here, the quicker we can eat."

"Don't rush me!" This only made him move slower.

Tor sighed. "Eydis," she called.

"Stop talking to me. You're making me nervous."

Clairla cleared her throat and said, "Okay, but maybe think about this. The longer you're on that rickety old bridge, the more likely it will break and you'll fall into the river."

"Clairla, that is not helping."

There was a sudden clamoring, the wood creaking and moaning louder, and when Tor looked Eydis was running the rest of the way. When he reached them he bent over, his hands on his knees, panting.

Clairla smiled at Tor. "You were saying?"

Tor smirked back. "All right, all right. Let's find somewhere to make camp and I'll get dinner."

Tor left her bag and ventured into the woods. In a few short minutes she was able to catch two birds, and on her way back she spotted some wild mushrooms and carrots. She knelt to check the mushrooms, as the wrong kind could kill them. As she inspected the size and markings, a rustling came from behind. It wasn't human, or human-like. If it were the orcs, she wondered how they'd have got through the swamps and across the bridge without them seeing. Perhaps they'd already been on this side of the swamp when they arrived. Either way, if they were trying to sneak up on her, they were doing a piss-poor job of it.

Then the smell of sulfur hit her nose, and the air seemed to get heavy. The forest appeared darker, denser. Tor dropped her catch on the ground and pulled an arrow from the quiver on her back. She nocked it and steadied herself. She may be a cleric, but she was also a highly skilled hunter. Which meant she had perfect aim.

The rustling in the trees came from all sides, indicating there were several people. Tor squinted into the growing darkness, taking a deep breath and whispering an incantation to bring a small bit of light into the area, encircling her. It wasn't much, but it would allow her to at least see the silhouettes of her pursuers.

Not wanting to kill anyone, she spoke out. "I'm here peacefully. I am a healer from the Rejuvenation Monastery. I'm on a pilgrimage to the western region." They didn't need to know she wasn't. "Nothing more. If I have trespassed on your land, I beg your forgiveness." There was no response but for the rustling of the trees and the underbrush.

Tor rotated on the spot to ensure no one would come from behind and catch her off guard. That's when the Shadow caught her eye. The form stepped into her tiny circle of light and she couldn't contain the gasp that escaped her lips.

She had never seen anything like it before. She'd heard the descriptions and read the stories, but had never seen it with her own eyes. The creature who was once a man stared at her from behind milky-white eyes that had not seen clearly in many years.

The skin on its face was rotted away in places, and the armor it wore was dented and rusty, and centuries old. The shield, made of rotted wood, would be used better for a fire than for protection. The sword that hung from an arm that was more bone than muscle and skin was long and thin, coming to a sharp point.

"I mean you no harm," Tor said again. She knew it was foolish, and she didn't even know if the Shadow soldier understood her or let alone cared. She didn't want to raise her bow to the creature, but it moved closer and closer toward her.

She was about to speak again when a second stepped out on the other side. He was her height, had one broken tusk, and was missing an eye. One arm was much smaller, and a pale white color that was an obvious mismatch to the green skin of the Once-orc warrior.

It lifted its white arm, which held a battle-ax that looked much too small for a soldier his size. Tor couldn't hesitate or try to reason any further; she had to defend herself and go against her religion of healing. She made a small prayer to her Goddess Thanroota to stand next to her in battle. In a swift, smooth motion she lifted her bow, pulled back, and released the arrow, catching the Once-orc in his remaining eye. He staggered back, grabbing at it, as his companion charged forward.

One leg was slightly longer than the other, and he had an odd limp. Its mouth was wide, and a raspy sound she could only assume was a war cry came out. She quickly pulled another arrow and let it loose, with barely enough time. It was so close to her that the force of the arrow drove it straight through the back of its skull. It staggered and fell back.

Once-orc yanked at the arrow from its one eye and again started for Tor. She went to reach for another arrow when a third Shadow moved from behind the trees, then another, then a fifth. She was ill-equipped, foolish to not have at least brought a sword, although she had a decent hunting knife. Even if she was bare-handed, she was orc and they were born warriors.

Tor stepped to the side, angling herself to see the other three. They were attempting to surround her. She yanked her hunting knife free with one hand while still holding onto the bow in the other. It was a simple hunting bow, nothing more, and not one orc warriors carried, but it was sturdy all the same.

When the remaining four came toward her, Tor widened her stance and bent her knees. She howled a war cry she had not heard in years, surprising herself that she remembered it. "I am the sword of Thanroota!" she shouted. "You will die at my feet!"

They charged her all at once and Tor spun to the right, using her bow like a staff and striking Once-orc in the face. He staggered back a step as she came back around and sliced at a Once-man soldier, who sported a large gash down the center of his face. Tor's attack severed the tendon that seemed to be the only thing keeping his upper arm attached to his lower arm, and the part holding his weapon dropped to the ground.

Tor was struck with a shield on the back and was knocked off balance. She took two uneasy steps before regaining her balance and spun just in time to block a sword with her bow. Once-man had picked up his sword up with another arm that was not original to him. His strike cracked her bow, but did not break it.

With gritted teeth Tor shoved him back, but another attacker, a woman, half human and half elf, slashed her arm open. Warm blood ran down her bicep and she hissed in pain. But there was no time to think about the injury as she was struck again with a shield, this time pushing her closer to the Once-orc. His sword was ready, and in the right position to impale her.

Without even a second thought, instinct kicked in and she chanted a simple shielding spell. As the static grew she did what she could to avoid the blade and sidestepped, ramming into the last of the attackers.

He was shorter, but was able to grab her around the waist. He'd once been a dwarf. The static reached its peak, but Tor swore under her breath when she realized her own spell's strength and type of magic had been altered and would become unpredictable. But it was too late, she had already cast it. With a small drop in the air pressure, the magic was released and, enhanced by the High Kingdom magic, there was a small explosion.

Instead of the shield surrounding Tor in a protective bubble, it became electrified and blew her attackers away. It was if lightning had emanated from her shield and struck the four remaining soldiers, frying them into a second death.

Tor stood in the center of the destruction, and even the trees in the small circle were charred and singed. "Huh. Not quite what I wanted it to do, but I guess that works." She put her knife back in its holder, then walked over to where the Once-orc had dropped his sword and picked it up. She couldn't see the quality in the dim light of the woods, but it was heavy. It might be a good sword to have if running into Shadow soldiers was going to be a regular occurrence.

She silently thanked her goddess for helping her in battle, gathered what was left of her catch, and headed out of the woods to where the others were camped.

The little bit she understood of the Shadow creatures was that they would not come out in the daylight. As long as there was enough light outside of the woods, they would not follow. But, once night fell and they were in complete darkness, that would be another matter. If there were more Shadows in the woods they would need to keep watch overnight.

Nearly free from the woods an arm came out from behind a tree, catching her in the chest. She was thrown back a couple feet, landing on her back. Tor coughed and wheezed for breath as the air was pushed from her lungs.

A creature stepped out from its hiding spot at the edge of the trees, only a few steps away. Her safety was within reach, yet not. The creature's arm dangled from its shoulder, and only a few rotted pieces of flesh kept it from dropping to the ground.

It must have snapped loose when it struck Tor in the chest. Tor could hear the scrambling of feet behind her, and when she looked over her shoulder the woods had once again been enveloped in unnatural darkness. The sulfur in the air grew stronger, telling her there were more than just these seven creatures.

She scrambled to her feet, took a deep breath, and barreled toward the soldier in front of her. She could only hope it didn't pull out a blade of some kind as she struck him. As she got closer, she dropped her shoulder and upper body, and struck the creature in its midsection, tossing it out into the sunlight as she broke out of the woods.

It slammed to the ground, losing its arm, and hissing and howling as it tried to make its way back to the darkness. Tor heaved in a breath as she watched over a dozen Shadow soldiers line up along the tree line, staying in darkness. Then, a second later, disappear as they moved away.

She watched until she was certain she couldn't see any more of the creatures. It was going to make for a very long night if they decided to come out of the woods.

CHAPTER NINETEEN

When Tor reached the others, they were preparing to start the fire. She told them of her encounter with the Shadows and suggested they move their camp downriver, away from the trees and closer to the Fairy Fields. A river would still divide them, but at least they wouldn't be so close to the woods if the Shadows decided to finish what they started.

"How did they even get on this side anyway?" Eydis asked. "I thought their realm was in the mountains, by Theakredel."

"They are," Clairla said, setting up the wood for the fire for a second time. "But do you think they stay there? They've been spotted everywhere. Even farmers in the Walled City said they'd seen them." Once the fire was lit, Tor put the birds on a spit and added water to a pot she'd brought from the monastery. Then she set to dress the wound on her arm.

Clairla watched Tor closely, and when Tor was done she sat back and returned the stare. "What?"

"What?"

"You've been staring at me for the last fifteen minutes."

"You said there were five?"

Tor counted in her head, scrunching her face. "Five I had a close encounter with. But substantially more when I was making my escape."

"Did you—" She stopped and shook her head.

"Did I what? Kill them? Yes, the five that I—"

"No, that's not what I was going to ask."

"Then ask," Tor said with an exaggerated sigh. She was tired but knew she wouldn't likely get any sleep that night.

Clairla stared at the fire for a long while and Tor figured she had decided not to ask her question. When she finally blurted it out it caught both Tor and Eydis so off guard they jumped and reached for their weapons. "Did you see their races?"

Tor scrutinized Clairla, thinking it a strange question. Why would she ask such a thing? Perhaps she was wondering if her own kind was amongst the scavenged. "I saw several races; an orc, a man and a woman, an elf, and a dwarf."

She nodded, and Tor was certain she saw her sigh in relief. She understood. When she saw the orc as he was, mutilated and combined with other races, it had left her with a sick, hollow feeling. She could only hope that Goddess Thanroota took his soul before the Shadow Queen took his body.

Eydis looked up from the fire. "What do you mean, other races? I thought you said they were Shadow soldiers?"

Tor and Clairla responded together. "They were."

Clairla gave a half smirk. "Eydis, do you not know what a Shadow soldier is?"

"Clairla," Tor said, hoping her tone would quiet the fae; it did not.

"You really are naive to the world, just a baby."

"Hey," Eydis shouted. "You keep your teeth together. I'm no baby!" He pointed the knife he was holding at her.

Tor was taken aback by his reaction. It was so harsh and bad-tempered. "Eydis, calm down. Put the knife down. Don't be pointing that at someone unless you intend to use it." Her comment brought the attention back onto her. It surprised her as well that she said such a thing. "I-I'm sorry. I shouldn't have said that."

Eydis lowered his blade. "Just explain what you meant about

the other races." His tone was still annoyed and she could see him pressing his lips together, trying to contain whatever else he was feeling.

Tor looked to Clairla and she just waved for Tor to continue. "Okay, well, the quickest explanation is really the easiest because the Shadows are a mysterious group."

"And?" Eydis waved his hand for her to hurry along.

Tor narrowed her eyes at his rude behavior. Very uncharacteristic. She started carving the birds as she spoke. "The Shadow Queen takes the bodies of our dead. She pulls them from battlefields, graves, anywhere she can find them really. Many times she pieces them together. The orc I saw wasn't all orc; his head and body definitely were, but one of his arms, I think, was human and the other... well, I'm not entirely certain. The elf I saw was actually half an elf, its head stitched together with half a human female head."

Eydis gagged and Tor knew it was time to stop explaining. He passed on his portion of the bird, but Tor insisted he try and eat even if he felt queasy. She couldn't get Clairla to stop giggling at his discomfort, so she volunteered Clairla to take the first watch. That quieted her down.

The next morning didn't seem to come quick enough. As Tor suspected, none of them slept well. Every snap of a twig, or rustle in the distance, had them reaching for their weapons and waiting for the Shadows. What put them really on edge was a wild beast also lurking in the dark, and every so often they would hear a distant howl. It was eerie, and definitely not a beast any of them were familiar with.

As they made their way along the river the static began to grow and intensify, causing Tor's jaw to ache and her arms to tingle. Clairla continually grabbed the back of her neck, like someone was pushing down on her, and Eydis busied himself eating a handful of sweet berries he'd found, unfazed by it all.

"That can't be the Fairy Field Veil," Tor said. "It's still some distance from the actual river. It's too strong."

Clairla held her hand out toward the river and a shimmer of light sprayed out from her fingertips. She pulled her hand away and stepped back. Sharing a shocked and confused look with Tor.

"What was that?" Tor asked. "Did you feel the static change when you touched it?"

Clairla reached her hand out again.

"Be careful," Tor said.

Eydis sauntered up, having been several paces behind the girls. "What's going on? We're not crossing here, are we?" He whined as he looked at the water. "That's way too deep to walk through, and—"

Tor lifted a hand at him, silencing his inquiries. Clairla ran her hand over the barrier, and it hummed as she did. "Do you feel that?" she asked, grabbing her neck.

"Yes," Tor said through gritted teeth. "Now, stop it."

She pulled her hand away.

Eydis shoved the rest of the berries in his mouth and wiped his purple-stained hand on his belly. "What is it? Is that what a veil looks like? I've never seen one up close before." He reached out to touch it and Tor slapped his hand down. The static, the type of magic the barrier emanated, was different, and the closer they were to it, the more painful when activated.

Clairla said, "No, it looks like the fairies put up their own extra barrier."

"Can they do that?" Eydis asked.

"That is a lot of magic," Tor said as she stepped back, watching as the shimmer Clairla had caused curved and formed a dome over the area.

"They're scared," Clairla said. "The rift must be opening and causing issues."

"Rift?" Eydis asked. "What rift?"

"Haven't you been paying attention?" Clairla asked. "We talked about this several times already."

Eydis shrugged and Tor got the impression he was just trying to get on Clairla's nerves. He knew exactly what they were talking about.

Tor continued to stare at the dome. "This time dilation you mentioned, do you think this is it? Do you think the fairies...*dome* is creating it?" Tor brought her gaze to meet Clairla's.

"I don't know what is causing it." Clairla bit her lip. "But it's possible. Maybe the time is different inside that dome."

"I'm starting to see why your trio left you behind," Eydis said.

Clairla glared at him. "What's that supposed to mean?"

"Well." A tiny smirk crossed his lips. "You don't really know much. Your visions are fractured, as you said. You didn't know about the dome, and you don't know where this dilation thingy is coming from. You're not such a great future seer." He crossed his arms, wearing a smug smile, proud of his deductions.

Tor saw Clairla clench her jaw so she decided to respond for her, hoping to defuse the situation. "Eydis, Clairla's visions are fractured because she doesn't have her trio. They didn't leave her behind because she didn't help them; they didn't leave her behind at all. It wasn't anyone's choice to be separated."

Eydis dropped his arms and his smile disappeared. "Oh."

"Let's just get moving," Tor said. "Clairla, where is this rift supposed to open?"

Clairla didn't move or speak. She stared straight ahead, but her eyes looked as though they were not focused on any one thing.

"Clairla?" Tor said, moving toward her. "Are you all right?" She touched her arm and Clairla jumped.

"I'm sorry." Clairla touched her forehead and moved away from Tor. "I was getting a vision. They can be disorientating when they come unexpectedly."

"Don't they always come unexpectedly?" Eydis asked before Tor could.

Clairla's eyebrows came together as she scrunched up her face. "No, of course not. At least, not in a trio. The trio controls when the vision comes. We call to it, ask it to show us the future. But I have found, over the many years without my trio, the visions do as they please and come and go when they want. They're fractured, backward, sometimes even old. It's very frustrating."

"You talk as though these visions are living things." Tor smiled and let out a light laugh. The notion was silly at best.

"Time is fluid, my dear orc," Clairla said. "It is a living, breathing thing; it changes and grows. But the future can be tempered, for a time. It can be told what to do, how to act."

Tor put her hand up. "Wait, are you saying you can control the future? Are you saying that Destiny Custodians can change the outcome of things whenever they damn well please?"

Clairla merely blinked back at her, and had become extremely still.

"Oh, you bloody fae. Gronk's hairy balls!" Tor shouted.

Eydis's eyebrows rose and a large smile crossed his face.

"What are you smiling about?"

"I've just never heard you swear before. And using Gronk, no less." He chuckled.

Tor continued to glare at Clairla. If she and her people could have changed these events instead of playing games, then Pac would never have had to die. She wouldn't be kilometers away from home and her son, and most certainly this strange rift wouldn't be opening.

"I know what you are going to say," Clairla started.

"Really? Do you?"

"Yes, but you must understand something. Although a trio has the power to make changes to the future, they are only minor adjustments. A nudge. The effect of the adjustment depends on the size of the event." Clairla shifted on her feet. "This event, with the child, the sacrifice, the rift, well these were all too big to change. There were too many factors, and not enough trios to make any difference in the final chain of events. My own participation was incapable of making a big enough adjustment. Without my trio, time wouldn't show me the entire future. It was fractured.

"Those trios who did risk much pushed against our veil to pass the needed information in the hope of changing the future. It's possible it worked. But, as I said, time would not work with me without my trio. So I don't know if the final events are what was originally meant to be."

Tor took a huge breath. She was starting to understand a bit more but it didn't even her temper any, or her regrets for coming. At this point, there was no need to continue arguing. "Where is this rift? Is it nearby?" she asked again, wanting to get moving.

"It's not far from here. In my vision it was on the other side of the fields."

"It's probably really close to the river." Eydis shrugged. "Why else would the fairies put this barrier up, right?"

"Yeah, maybe." Tor had no idea, and she was beginning to think Clairla really had no clue either. If her vision about this rift was even right. She was going to give it one more day, then turn back. Clairla seemed nice enough, but every so often her trickster side would come out. Not to mention the fact that she was also a spy. The two combined meant that Tor and Eydis were traveling with a highly trained and natural deceiver. It was not only in Clairla's nature, but it was also her profession.

Clairla jogged to catch up with her. "Are you cross with me?"

Tor clenched her jaw.

"Tor?"

"I'd rather not speak right now if you don't mind. I have a lot to think about."

Clairla said nothing more. She dropped back several paces and walked in silence with Eydis.

CHAPTER TWENTY

Tor was exhausted, and her legs felt like lead as they moved along the riverside. The constant hum of the dome was starting to give her a headache, and the relentless static was uncomfortable. She swatted at the tiny insects that seemed to home in on her face.

She needed a distraction, something to keep her mind off her growling stomach, tired body, and the effects of the dome. She thought about the day before, and her encounter with the Shadows. It was perplexing and strange. How did the Shadow soldiers get so many out of their realm? And where were they going? The Shadow Veil was on the other side of the Fairy Realm. They had to have traveled through the mountains of Theakredel Kingdom and passed the Ruins Labyrinth, not to mention getting across the river. Had they taken a different route? Was there a different route?

As Tor's mind settled in on no exact thought, there was a deep howl that ran cold shivers down Tor's spine. "What was that?"

The three stopped and searched the area. They were at least ten kilometers from the forest where they'd encountered the Shadows the day before. Tor stepped away from the river to better listen to their surroundings. It wasn't bright out, but there was enough light that the Shadows wouldn't come out.

Clairla stepped up beside her, and a second howl echoed through the air.

There were no trees to hide behind, and the grass wasn't long enough to hide in. "Where is that coming from?" Tor asked.

Eydis joined them. "It's like it's coming from all directions."

Clairla looked around Tor and at him. "Yeah, it's called an echo."

Tor spoke before any chance of a fight could break out. "You're from this area," she said to Clairla. "What kind of animal makes that sort of noise?"

Clairla looked at her from the corner of her eye. "I'm not from around here at all. I live in the Walled City, a several weeks' walk behind us. I don't think I have ever been on this side of the Theakredel Kingdom."

"It would be helpful if we had a dwarf with us," Eydis said. When he noticed they were staring, he continued. "You know, because they would be more familiar with the wildlife in this region."

They heard another howl, but it seemed to be moving away. In the far distance Tor swore she saw a silhouette of what was howling, it was dog-like but much larger. When she tried to get a better look it was gone. "Must have been a dog of some kind." Tor did her best to sound calm and confident. "Let's keep moving."

"Yeah, it must have been." Clairla scanned the area one last time before joining the others.

"How much further do you think we need to go?" Eydis asked.

Clairla took a long drink from her canteen. "Shouldn't be that much further. If we follow this adjoining river off the Veil River, it should only be half a day's journey."

"Yes, but where about?" Eydis's voice had an impatient whine, and Tor could see it grated on Clairla.

Clairla sighed. "My vision never told me the exact location of the rift, but there were landmarks I recognized; like between the intersections where the Veil River splits off into the Sallenbrook River, but before it diverts to Thundering Rapids. It's at least a thirty or forty kilometer stretch, so not more than half a day's walk."

"I think it might be closer," Tor said.

"What makes you believe that?"

"Can't you feel the static? It's light, but it's there."

Clairla tilted her head to one side. "Are you sure that's not the hum from the barrier?"

Tor lifted her eyebrows.

"Okay, you could have just said yes."

Clairla fell in behind Tor, and Tor could hear Eydis grumbling behind them. Reaching the height of her irritation she stopped, causing Clairla to slam into her. "Enough, Eydis. You're acting like a child. Stop dragging your feet, whining that you're tired and hungry, and swinging your sword around like that." She was full-on yelling at him now. "We are all tired and hungry, and you're going to kill someone if you lose your grip while you're recklessly swinging that thing around."

Eydis clenched his jaw and curled his lip back in a snarl. "For the love of Gronk's hairy balls, who put you in charge?"

"What does it matter who's in charge?" Tor glared at him but he didn't budge. "Fine, I'm in charge then."

Clairla's brow furrowed. "Why do you get to be in charge?"

"Are you kidding me right now?" Tor pinched the bridge of her nose and closed her eyes. She took in a long, slow breath then opened them again. "The two of you can't get along long enough to decide on a meal, but you want to try and tell him what to do? But, by all means, let's put it to a vote."

Clairla put her hands on her hips, opening and closing her mouth. She tried to stare Tor down, but Tor wasn't having any of it and put her hands on her own hips and glared down at the tiny fae.

Clairla clenched her jaw then shoved her hands in her pockets. "Fine, it's not like there's much to be in charge over anyway."

Tor rolled her eyes. "Can we keep moving now?"

"You going to keep whining?" Clairla asked Eydis.

He glared at her. "I'll do my best."

Tor rolled her eyes again and continued along the river.

"You're such a child," she heard Clairla say.

"Oh, yeah, well could a child do this?"

Tor heard Clairla gasp. "You're disgusting."

"I'm not even going to turn around and see what is happening back there. So, I'm just going to tell both of you to keep your teeth together."

They walked in silence for over an hour and Tor enjoyed every second. The hum from the dome wasn't as loud now, and the pain from the different static had subsided. Now she was homing in on a different kind disturbance, one that wasn't of this world. At least not anything she had ever felt or heard of, and that made her nervous.

When Tor stopped to survey the area, Clairla moved up to stand next to her.

"Do you see something?" Eydis called from behind.

"No," Tor replied. "But I do feel it."

Clairla tilted her head again. "I still don't sense it." Tor noticed Clairla was scrutinizing her. "What?"

"It's just...I've never before heard of an orc being sensitive to the static. I don't think I've ever heard of orcs even using magic."

"They don't. We have gods and goddess's to help us. Magic is a blasphemy to orcs. It means you don't have faith in our deities." When Clairla didn't respond, Tor said, "Come on. I think we're getting close. Just over there." She pointed into the distance at a small grouping of trees in the middle of a field.

Tor had picked up her pace, high-stepping through the thigh-deep weeds, when she heard something fall behind her. When she checked to see what it was, she saw Clairla lying face down and Eydis laughing. She had tripped over a mound of dirt.

Tor rushed to her side. "Are you all right?" She brushed the grass and dirt from Clairla's front.

Clairla shooed Tor's hands away and finished the task, tugging on the bottom of her coat to even it out. "Yes. I'm fine."

"Day dreamin', were ya?" Eydis said with a playful smile and a piece of stiff weed sticking out of his mouth. "My pappy used to say, 'A wandering mind and wandering feet make terrible travel companions.'"

"Your pappy said that, did he?" Clairla said as she brushed the remainder of grass and dirt from her cloths.

"Yup. He was a bit clumsy, that one. Constantly tripping over his own feet and forgetting how he ended up in places." Eydis laughed at the memory and started walking again.

Tor smiled at Clairla and all Tor had felt about Clairla disappeared, leaving only foolishness behind. They had been traveling together for at least three months now, and she'd started to think of Clairla as a friend as she'd slowly opened up over the long nights of sitting around their camp fires. There were still many things she felt Clairla was hiding, but she was finding her company wasn't as bad as it once was.

They walked for another hour before Tor stopped and put out a hand for everyone to do the same.

"What is it? Did that creature come back?" Clairla scanned the area but it was all open field, with nowhere for anyone or anything to hide.

"Can you feel that now?" Tor asked, her hand out and palm up.

"No. It's strange, as I can normally feel the static that comes off of the veils. Why can't I feel it now?"

Tor began to walk in the direction it came. "It's not really static. It's much weaker, and more like a vibration."

"I see it," Eydis said, pointing to the center of the field.

Clairla and Tor followed his finger. "I see it too," Clairla said.

They eased ever closer to the opening, a sliver hanging four feet in the air. They could see the other side, as if looking through a window. It was not like other veils, which were murky.

They stood around the opening, contemplating it, as the edges seemed to shimmer and flicker in and out.

Tor said, "I still can't feel any static, or magic of any kind, coming from the opening. It's right and front of me, yet I still can't. It's like it's not even there. Except for that vibration." Tor walked around the rift, something that couldn't be done with a veil. When she reached the back, it was like it completely disappeared.

As she came back around she noticed Clairla looking off in the distance. Before she could ask there was a low howl, same as the night before. A cold shiver ran down her spine as the sound pulled everyone's attention from the opening.

"It's back," Eydis said.

Clairla asked, "Yes, but what is it?"

"It's not a Shadow soldier," Tor said.

Clairla pulled out her two sais from the sheaths on her hips, then took several steps toward the creature to get a better look. But before she could take a third step the creature turned and bolted in the opposite direction.

"Looks like you spooked it." Eydis sheathed his sword.

Tor put a hand above her eyes to shade the little bit of sun as she looked into the distance. "Did you at least get a good look at what it was?"

Clairla returned her weapons to their holsters. "To be honest, it looked like a dog of some sort."

"A wild dog, out here on its own, doesn't seem likely. They travel in packs from what I've read." Tor continued to look into the distance.

"Maybe that's why it's so skittish." Eydis shrugged. "It ran away this morning, too, when we got too close."

Tor dropped her hand and turned to the group. "Perhaps you're right."

"Although, it would still be nice to have a dwarf on hand to tell us what it really was," Eydis added.

"You may be right about that, too." Tor smiled and patted him on the shoulder.

Tor then turned her attention back to the rift. The other side looked like a desert, the soil brown and cracked. There were large rocks scattered about, and if she didn't know better she would swear they were spheres. She inched closer to try and get a better look, a metallic taste growing in her mouth the closer she got.

"So," Eydis said, causing Tor to jump. "How do we close it?"

Clairla had her arms crossed and was standing back about ten feet. Tor joined her. "What do your visions have to say about this? Is this the time dilation you talked about?"

"Nothing...yet. And I don't think so...maybe...I don't know."

Eydis dropped to the ground, moaning as he lifted his feet. "Oh yeah, that feels good to get off of those."

"Really?" Tor asked.

"What? I don't know how to do magic. Unless you think me hacking at it with my sword is going to help, I'm going to sit and rest."

"Well," Tor said, also crossing her arms. "The only magic I know that isn't for healing is defensive." She tilted her head back and forth, narrowing her eyes. "I suppose I could create a shield around the rift, then shrink it until it collapses."

Eydis removed his pack with a grunt. "Will that work?"

"I really don't know. What do you think, Clairla?" When she didn't respond Tor looked at her. She had the same far-off look she'd had before when getting a vision.

Tor put herself between Clairla and the rift, then bent over to look the fae in the eye. Only a minute later Clairla jumped, Tor being so close. She straightened up.

"Sorry, you went into a trance again. Learn anything new?"

Clairla sighed and had opened her mouth to speak when Eydis heaved himself off the ground faster than Tor had ever seen him move. He fumbled for his sword and pointed at the rift. Tor spun, grabbing her hunting knife as Clairla grabbed her sais.

It took a few seconds to see what Eydis had, but when they did there was no doubt it was running toward them from the other side.

The trees laugh, for time never pauses.

~From the musing of Gronk in The Chronicles of Gronk~

CHAPTER TWENTY-ONE

TOR'S HEART POUNDED, AND SHE made a silent prayer for Goddess Thanroota to join her on the battlefield. She pulled the rusted sword she'd taken from one of the Shadow soldiers from her belt, her mind racing for any incantations that may help.

Clairla was on her right and held a sais in each hand, and on her left Eydis gripped his broadsword.

They stared at the rift, the sky on the other side—wherever the place was—had grown dark. The figure ran straight toward them, but Tor couldn't see if it was human or beast.

Dark clouds began to form overhead, and the static built to a degree she had never felt before. It was both familiar and foreign at the same time. Were the magics of these two worlds mixing? What would happen when it reached its peak?

Even though Tor's heart pounded she felt calm, her mind clear. In the seconds before the air pressure dropped, Tor began to chant an incantation to shield them. With the amount of static in the area, she hoped it would enhance the power of her magic.

The figure took its final steps toward the rift and dove through. That same instant, the air pressure dropped and Tor's shield encompassed the three of them as lightning struck the rift. A loud crack echoed throughout the field, and the concussive force of the lightning strike tossed them back several feet.

Tor's head pounded, as if she'd been struck with a rock, and her shield collapsed. She and Clairla were on their feet as quickly as they'd been knocked off them, and stood in front of the new arrival. Behind them, the rift shrank until it was gone.

The newcomer wore a hood over their head, hiding their face in deep shadows. Their pale, slim yet defined arms were exposed, as the cloak they wore had no sleeves to cover them. It was long nearly touched the ground, but Tor could see they wore black pants and heavy boots underneath. They stood like a warrior, fists clenched and stance wide.

The static and the clouds had dissipated, and what little bit of sun there'd been lit the area once again. Tor steadied herself as she and Clairla nodded to each other, signaling their readiness.

Tor could hear Eydis grunting just off to her left. When she stole a glance he was lying on his back at the bottom of a small hole, his feet raised. He was trying to rock himself into a better position to get back to his feet, but the hole was too small and his belly too big.

The new arrival lifted their hands, and Tor and Clairla stood straight and alert.

"Don't move," Clairla said. "Unless you want a sharp object in your eye!"

The new arrival lifted their hands, palms up, and raised them toward their hood. They then pushed it back to reveal the face of a young woman, who couldn't be more than twenty. Her skin was pale and she had deep-set brown eyes. Her hair was braided on one side and shaved on the other, and it was a dull gray but for the streaks of red.

"I mean you no harm," she said, her voice thick and her accent strange. "There wasn't supposed to be anyone here. You took me by surprise."

"Who are you?" Clairla asked.

Tor shifted the sword in her hand, reaching for her hunting

knife. Eydis, still stuck in the hole, grunted several times with the effort to get up.

"What was that? That was no veil; where did you come from?" Clairla asked.

The young woman nodded. "It was a temporary portal. It had taken me years to get it open." She smiled, warm and inviting.

Tor studied the young woman, thinking her choice of hairstyle was strange given she wasn't from this Realm. If she'd had silver and gold rings in her braids, she would hold a dwarven military rank. It looked exactly like Enya's hairstyle.

The young woman locked eyes with Tor, and she seemed to study her as well. A look of recognition took over the young woman's face and she smiled wider. "You haven't changed at all," she said.

"I beg your pardon?" Tor said. "Do I know you?" She took a step forward.

"We only met a couple times. I was quite young, and it was nearly fifteen years ago now. Give or take a month or two."

Tor had met many children over the years, and she did help the Mothers care for the children's health. Had she been one of the young girls? How did she end up in a place with no Veil? "Are you one of the orphans from the House of Mothers' Foundlings in the High Kingdom?"

The young woman smiled but her eyebrows knitted. "No, of course not. It has been a very long time, Tor. Perhaps much has happened and your memory has slipped. But I remember you, and your kindness. You healed my dear Jardeth, and tried to warn Enya and poor Dufin."

Tor's face dropped, her mouth hanging open. She took a step back and shook her head. "How is that possible? It's only been— Pac? Is that really you?"

"Yes." She smiled so wide all her teeth showed. "It's been such a long journey to get back to this realm. So many portals to choose from, and so many destinations. Pocket Realms inside of Pocket Realms! But I finally found the right one."

"Pac, it hasn't been fifteen years for us." Tor touched the young woman's arm.

Her shoulders slumped, and the deep sigh told Tor Pac had hoped there wouldn't be such a huge difference.

"That's the time dilation," Clairla said. "It has to be. I wasn't seeing our realm, but rather wherever she came from."

"How much time has passed for you?" Pac asked.

Tor looked at Clairla, then Eydis. They all seemed to do the math in their heads. "Three, maybe four—"

"Years?" Pac interrupted. "Only three years?"

"No, Pac. Three months."

"Months!" Pac turned away from them, pacing from where the rift had been to the last spot she'd stood. She was muttering to herself. "King Thomas...how strong has he grown?"

"We haven't heard anything about the High King." Tor put the sword back in her belt and the knife in its sheath. The others followed her lead, returning their own weapons. "We left the High City before the explosion."

"Explosion?" Pac moved in close again. "Is that what it looked like to you? An explosion? Were there survivors? Jardeth? Enya?"

Tor placed a hand on the woman's shoulder. "We don't know. The night of the blood moon there was a flash of light, followed by a shock wave. Magic has been...unpredictable ever since." She dropped her hand. "We never returned to the city, but from where we were when it happened we could see that most of the castle was...gone."

"Gone?"

Eydis grunted from his hole, where he was still wedged. "Well, collapsed or destroyed." He held his hand out to Tor. "Little help?"

Tor smirked as she assisted him out. Then Clairla spoke. "Do you not remember anything from that night?"

"I was drugged, knocked out at dinner. The last thing I remember is a blinding light, someone standing over me, and loud chanting. I tried to stop what was happening, and the last thing that happened was I was thrown. When I woke up I had landed in unfamiliar woods. The air tasted different, and the grass and the trees were different colors. It was all very strange. I had large cuts on my arms, and I was bleeding. I tried to stop the bleeding with my magic, but it wouldn't work. I was certain the king must have drained all my blood magic and I was now in the afterlife.

"I don't know how long I wandered those woods, but I was eventually found by an old man–beast creature. He took me to his dwelling and patched me up, raised me. He taught me about their realm and the others. I was happy there."

"Then why did you come back?" Eydis asked.

Pac studied him, cocking her head to one side as if to see him for the first time. "Because the Realm Eater is coming."

A tiny gasp came from Clairla.

When Tor looked, she had a hand to her mouth and, impossibly, was paler than before. "What is it?"

"It's impossible," Clairla whispered, although Tor almost didn't hear.

"Are you okay?" Eydis said, moving toward her. "Maybe you should sit down."

"Maybe we should make camp," Tor said. "Then we can finish our discussion." There was too much to discuss on the move, and the sun was already low and about to set.

They decided to stay where they were, given there was a small patch of trees to protect them from any elements...and wasn't big enough to hide any Shadows.

While they were making camp the beast that seemed to be following them howled several times. Pac seemed unfazed by its presence. She helped with gathering wood and building their shelter.

When the fire was lit, and a small meal of birds was being cooked, Tor turned to Clairla. "What do you know of this Realm Eater?"

Clairla's eyes were haunted. She stared at Tor for what felt like hours.

"Clairla," Tor said gently.

Clairla cleared her throat and turned her attention to the fire. "My trio and I had visions of a powerful being who could absorb the magic that separated the Realms. We saw him consume the Veils of this world, destroying us all."

Eydis's face contorted in confusion. "Where did you see this man?"

Clairla shook her head, and set her haunted gaze on him. "He is no longer man; he is a god, a powerful being from a world nothing like our own." She grabbed Tor's arm. "If he is coming...this is a catastrophic event."

Tor did her best to keep her voice calm. It was obvious Clairla was shaken. "When did you and your trio see this future? When did it stop being a possibility?"

Clairla's eyes now fell on Pac, who was gnawing on a tiny overcooked bird leg. "Before the Shadow Realm was sealed. Many Custodians were seeing the same fate, and it was believed the Shadow Queen was working with the Realm Eater. He promised that once he drained the magic of the Veils she could have what was left of the world. When the Veil was sealed, that future ceased to be."

"Gronk's hairy balls," Eydis whispered.

Tor and Pac sighed in unison, but Tor couldn't help the smirk that formed on her face and Pac mirrored her for a brief moment.

Pac then addressed Tor. "Your friend"—she turned to Clairla—"Clairla, is it?"

Clairla nodded.

"Is a fae, a Destiny Custodian, and a keeper of the future. My friends and I encountered a few of you on our way to the High

Kingdom, many years ago." She paused and sighed again. "Or, rather, several months for you. Where is your trio now?"

"On the other side of the Veil to my realm. When the Shadow Realm was sealed, so were many others. I was trapped on this side, alone."

"Wait," Eydis said, pinching the bridge of his nose. "If I remember my history that was, like, two thousand years ago. You're over two thousand years old?"

"It appears your memory isn't so great." Clairla half smiled. "The Shadow Realm was sealed over four thousand years ago."

Eydis's mouth open and closed in surprise and he fell silent.

"What else do you know of how the Realms and their veils work?" Pac asked. Tor sensed she already knew the information, but was testing the fae. There was a great deal of mistrust, for which she didn't blame Pac. Even though Clairla has grown on Tor, there was still a bit of trust issues.

Clairla paused and studied Pac, and the look told Tor Clairla suspected the same thing as she. "As the stories say, Totriga and the connected Realms were created millennia ago. Totriga is the grounding realm, and all our Realms connected to it after. But it wasn't always like this. The Realms were once known only as worlds because they were never connected in such ways. Worlds then collided, creating the Veils between them and the magic. A type of bubble surrounded each one individually, keeping them separate..." Clairla trailed off, staring into the fire as her eyes lost focus.

Pac took over. "It's said that the universe as we know it—"

"Universe?" Tor said. "I don't know this word."

"I'm glad you said that, because neither do I," Eydis said.

Without looking up Clairla said, "Do you really understand anything we are saying?"

"Stop. Not now," Tor said, gesturing for Pac to continue.

Pac sighed deeply, and Tor could see she was trying hard not to roll her eyes. She smiled, now seeing the small child who had to explain simple concepts to imbeciles. "A universe is what encompasses all worlds, all Realms. Even those outside of this one. Totriga and her sixteen Realms is but one amongst millions like her. Some smaller, some bigger. Some still forming."

Tor turned the second bird on the spit, waving for Pac to continue. "Okay, I got it now. We are in a huge universe."

"As I was saying, it's said that the universe was not always like this. As your Custodian has said, the world's colliding and creating the Veils was what created the magic. The Realm Eater found a way to consume the magic holding the Veils together."

Eydis put his hand up. "But wouldn't that mean there would be no more Veils?"

"That is exactly what it would mean," Clairla blurted out.

Eydis opened his mouth to retort, then caught Tor's glare and closed it.

"What happens if the Veils are consumed?" Tor asked. She was certain she already knew the answer, and as much as she didn't want it said out loud she had to know for sure.

Clairla pursed her lips. "There would be nothing preventing our worlds from crashing into the others. It would be like smashing large rocks together, only for us it would be sixteen huge rocks. Resulting in mutual destruction."

"That's what all the Destiny Custodians were trying to warn us about," Tor said, pointing at Clairla. "With all their riddles and secrets, saying don't let this or that person die. Why didn't they just damn well tell us this Realm Eater was coming?"

Clairla pressed her lips tight. "They're fae."

Pac let out a low snarl. "Now I truly understand why Jardeth never trusted the fae."

Clairla shot a look at Pac, but it was one of mutual feeling and not hatred. "I don't think this was the event they saw coming."

Tor's brow furrowed. "How do you mean?"

"Like I said, all the futures with the Realm Eater changed when the Shadow Realm was sealed."

"But you also said that *your* visions are now fragmented and missing pieces because you no longer have a trio." Tor pointed the stick she used to stoke the fire at her. "So, when this one"—she pointed at Pac—"popped out of the Shadow Realm some nine years ago, that future came back into motion."

"Actually," Pac said, pushing the stick away from her with one finger then wiping the soot on the grass. "It was when the High King did the blood ritual. Or when he tried, I should say. It was done incorrectly and, when he tried to complete it, the explosion you say happened tore open a..." Pac stopped to search for the words. "A hole in the Veil of this universe."

"You mean realm," Eydis corrected.

"No," Pac pulled her attention to sit it solely on Eydis. "I mean universe. That is how the Realm Eater was alerted to the presence of our universe. Not many are like this one. There are sixteen Realms connected to Totriga. Most have no more than five. Each of these groupings are self-contained universes." She made a circle with her hands. "They don't share the same magic between universes. Only within the realms connected to each other and there is a great deal of magic surging through this realm."

"Okay, but I'm confused," Eydis said.

Clairla snorted. "Of course you are."

"Keep your teeth together," Eydis said.

Tor put a hand on his arm. "What are you confused about?"

"You've been saying sixteen Realms, but there are only twelve races. I think you might have us confused with a different— What'd you call it, unnisverse?"

"Universe," Clairla said with a sigh. "There are twelve *known* living races. There were once sixteen, which we call the four dead races. And do I need to point out that not every different race comes from different Realms?"

Tor cleared her throat.

"What?" Clairla tossed her hands up. "I'm so tired of explaining this—"

"That's fine, but at least pass on correct information if you're going to be snarky about it."

"What?" Clairla and Eydis said in unison.

"I am right," the fae said.

Now it was Tor's turn to sigh. "You are right about the twelve living races and the four dead ones. But you are wrong about the races not all coming from different Realms. Totriga is the realm of man. Every other race came from different Realms."

Pac raised her hand. "I really don't think any of that matters; living or dead races from different Realms. The Realm Eater doesn't care, he only wants the magic that is keeping those Realms separated."

As she spoke her last word, as if on cue, the static in the air grew and the skies seemed to darken further, blocking out the stars. When the air pressure dropped there was a loud thunder clap and a flash of light in the distance.

"It's that"—she pointed to the sky—"what's attracting the Realm Eater. Totriga is drawing the magic from other universes. Those lightning strikes, the storms with no rain, are from the different kind of magic combining with the magic here." She glanced at Clairla. "Surely you can feel the difference."

Clairla slowly shook her head.

"I can," Tor said. "The static is different. It leaves a metallic taste in my mouth the closer I am to the strike." It all made sense now: why her own magic didn't quite work the same way, why it turned some incantations wrong and caused more harm or turned some stronger and healed faster. As the silence fell over the four, a question burned in Tor's mind. "How did you know to come back here?" she asked Pac.

"Because this is the source of the tobloha. The Realm Eater will come before the magic is destroyed."

"Okay, I'm lost again. What is a toehaha?" Eydis scratched his head.

Pac sighed, but this time she rolled her eyes. "A tobloha is a phenomenon that pulls everything into it. It will consume everything in its path, destroying this realm and everything connected to it. The only way to stop it will be to close the tear."

"So, let me get this straight," Eydis said, pointing his bird leg at Pac. "If we don't seal the tear then this Realm Eater will come and destroy our world, or this toblawha will."

"Tobloha, and yes. This universe and everything in it will be destroyed, no matter what, as long as that tear remains open."

"Where did the tobloha come from?" Tor asked.

Pac stared at her. "Totriga is the tobloha. Totriga is pulling everything toward it through the tear."

"I see." Tor and Clairla shared a worried look.

Eydis tossed the clean bone into the fire. "Okay, closing the tear will stop this tob-thingy, so does that mean it will kill the Realm Eater as well?"

"I don't know. Maybe."

"Maybe?" Tor and Clairla said together.

"I don't have all the answers." Pac pointed at Clairla. "Why not talk to your resident Custodian?"

Clairla glared back at Pac. "I don't think I like you."

"I think the feeling is mutual." Pac sneered.

"Okay." Tor pinched her nose between her fingers. Just what she needed, more squabbling. "I'm assuming this rift, and the time dilation, is what you had seen in your vision, Clairla? Or do we still need to find it?"

Clairla nodded. "I'm certain that was what I saw in my vision."

"And in your vision you said I needed to close the rift." She pointed to where it once was. "It's gone. So I can return home?"

Clairla tightened her lips until they formed a small line.

Tor dropped her face into her hands. She was already very uncertain about her role in Clairla's vision. "This isn't the rift I am supposed to close." She wasn't asking.

"I don't believe so, no."

How was she supposed to fight someone who ate worlds? Was it even possible? She closed her eyes and made a silent prayer to her goddess, asking for guidance on what to do—who to follow, how to fight. She was a cleric of the Rejuvenation Monastery, she was a healer, and to heal was her religion, her promise, her oath. Would this fight force her to become something else? Become a warrior once again?

If at any time she had ever needed divine intervention from a goddess she wasn't even supposed to worship, now would be it.

CHAPTER TWENTY-TWO

T HE NIGHT SKY WAS SPECKLED with little dots of light that disappeared then reappeared behind the dark clouds of which only their outline could be seen. Tor stared at them, thinking of her family and how they would be in the afterlife with their goddess, fighting and dancing as warriors. She almost envied them, knowing what she knew now, about this Realm Eater that was coming and the fight ahead of them.

She was a healer, wasn't she? Never before had she been so confused about where she stood in the world; not since she was a young girl being brought to the monastery. She was born a warrior, and she was a warrior when she fought the Shadow soldiers. So, what was she now? Was she again a healer? Tor sighed as she drew her gaze down to the fire, the wood snapping and crackling and sending out tiny sparks. The static in the air was light; it had released its pressure twenty minutes prior. If the pattern continued, it would be another hour before it built up once again.

Tor pulled the leather journal from her pocket and unraveled the strap. The strange letters on the cover were also inside. She had seen designs like these before, but where? The pages were thin, so she was careful when turning them. Page after page of the markings she couldn't read, but then she opened to a part where she understood the language.

Their beastly companion could be heard in the near distance, and it briefly pulled Tor's attention away from the book. She turned back and leaned closer to the fire to better see the words. It was in Abacuss's hand, and she was about to close it, believing it was his journal, when she saw her name.

My Dearest Tor,

We are all faced with decisions in our lives that force us to choose one path or another. I was once faced with such a choice many centuries ago. My own people craved and desired a thing they could not have: power. Pure, uninhibited power. I, too, believed this was what I wanted.

In this desire, my people chose to cross a Veil into a world in which we had no place. Made deals with creat—

The howl of their beast pulled Tor out of the journal entry. Its cry held a tinge of sorrow and it pulled at Tor's heart. It was as if the beast was looking for something, perhaps a mate. The wind picked up and the smoke from the fire shifted in her direction, causing her eyes to water. She waved it off using the book, and rubbed her eyes. When she opened them Pac was sitting across from her, hair blowing gently in the breeze.

Tor didn't startle easily, but Pac's sudden appearance gave her a small start. "I didn't realize you were up." She rewrapped the journal and placed it into a small weatherproof pouch, hoping it would protect it from the elements.

"I was never asleep." Pac's smile was weak, and it was apparent she felt it impolite not to smile.

"You all right?"

"It's strange."

"What is?"

"For so many years I fought to find my way back to this world, but now that I'm here..." Her voice trailed off as her eyes looked to the sky.

"You wish you were back where you came from?"

Pac nodded, locking eyes with Tor. "I had a family there, a brother and two sisters. I miss Jardeth, Enya, and even Dufin very much. But..."

Tor nodded. "You feel guilty about missing your new family." She wasn't asking; she could see it on Pac's face. In her eyes, it was the type of mourning she felt every time the beast howled. "Did they know you were leaving? Did they help you open the rift?"

Pac's shoulders lifted, then lowered. "They knew I was trying to find a way to leave. They didn't think it would work. I had to leave home a year and a half ago just to find the right place."

"I don't understand."

"The universe I was thrown into no longer had any magic. And my magic was extremely weak because of the ceremony."

"What happened to their magic?"

"The Realm Eater. Decades before I got there he came and took the magic from their Veils. There were only a few Realms connected to their anchor Realm, so when they collided the damage wasn't catastrophic. But it did kill millions and created pockets of land that could no longer sustain life. So the people of their Realms were forced to move."

"Then how did you open the rift?"

"Like I said, I had to find the right spot. Tiny bits of magic were left behind, but they were difficult to find and get to. It was in those pockets of uninhabitable land; an area where worlds had collided. The magic was all but gone, and I barely had enough to get the rift open. And then it opened in a completely different spot than I expected. There must have been more magic in that area, and

I had to run to get to it in time. I was lucky it didn't snap shut when I was halfway through."

The beast hollowed again and Eydis moaned. "Gronk's hairy balls, how is anyone supposed to get any sleep around here?" He rolled to his back, then heaved himself up with a grunt. His hair pointed in every direction, and as he dropped down next to Tor she could see his eyes were bloodshot.

His stomach rumbled and Tor smiled. "Your stomach seems as though it is in competition with our friend out there."

Eydis grunted back, his mood foul. "How do we know that *your* friend out there isn't just hunting us, waiting for the perfect time to kill us all?"

Tor let out a small laugh. "She's been following us for several days now, and I think if she was going to do us harm she already would have."

Clairla rolled over on her bedroll and sighed. "It's a Shadow beast, and she's likely looking for a mate. Or has lost her mate. Probably got trapped on the other side, and so is alone."

Tor craned her neck to look at her. "How did you come to that conclusion? A few days ago you thought she was just a dog."

She looked to Pac then Tor, and sat up. "After Pac came through the rift I got to thinking. Well, really after we found out who she was. I had encountered many Shadows during the Shadow Realm Invasion four thousand years ago. Those natural-born, mostly females, had a way of disappearing into darkness. It was almost like they became invisible."

"Those soldiers were not invisible," Tor said with a humorous laugh.

"No, but they wouldn't be would they? They aren't naturally born. The queen would make them from the dead of other races."

Eydis sighed impatiently. "Could you just get to the point?"

Clairla looked him straight in the face. "That is my point. Our friend out there seems to disappear, vanish, whenever she is in any type of shadow."

"You think she's from the Shadow Realm?" Tor asked

Clairla grabbed her blanket and wrapped it around her shoulders. "Yes, yes I do."

Eydis nodded toward Pac. "Do those things travel in packs?"

Pac glanced to Tor then back, as if looking for the answer. "How would I know?"

"You're from the Shadow Realm, aren't ya?" Eydis laughed. "If anyone would know, it would be you."

"I was born of Shadow, but I am not from Shadow." Pac's tone was schooling.

Tor poked at the fire and Eydis scratched his head. "What in Gronk's beard does that mean?"

Pac sighed. "Not that it's any of your business but, yes, my mother was a Shadow. I was born in the Shadow Realm, but sent immediately here to Totriga. I have never really been to the Shadow Realm. I spent seven years of my life in the Dwarf King's dungeons, then I was taken to the High Kingdom to be sacrificed."

"Seven?" Tor asked. "But you were about nine when we met."

Pac smiled, but cast her gaze downward. "For a short time I was raised by dwarf nannies." Her smiled dropped and her eyes hardened. "When I was able to walk I was put in the dungeon. That is where I stayed, in the cold and dark, until Dufin and the others came for me."

"I'm so sorry, Pac." Tor wanted to reach for the girl but wasn't sure if Pac wanted to be touched.

"It's no matter, the botched sacrifice allowed me to have a real family. Both here and in the other universe."

The Shadow beast again howled in the distance.

"Why does it keep doing that?" Eydis snapped.

"Well," Clairla said with an exaggerated sigh. "I guess no one gets to sleep tonight." She pulled her blanket tighter around her.

"Beast howls keeping you up too?" Eydis nudged her.

She pulled her arm away from him and a small snarl formed on her face. "No, it's all your talking that is keeping me up."

"I'm sorry," Tor said.

Clairla shook her head. "It's not of concern. Most of my dreams were unpleasant anyway." She glanced at Eydis. "To answer your question, no the Shadow beasts do not travel in packs. They only travel in pairs, and bond with their mate early in their lives. The male provides everything for the female, and she is the only one that makes any sound."

"But you'd think she would realize her mate isn't here." Eydis shook his head. "Why doesn't she just go back to the Veil and cross back over."

Pac sighed again, and Tor could see the eye-roll from across the fire.

Eydis glared at her. "You know you don't have to do that every time I say something."

Clairla answered before Pac. "Maybe if you would actually say something intelligent once in a while."

Tor cleared her throat. "Why don't you finish your thoughts."

Pac side-eyed Eydis and said, "The Veil opening into the Shadow Realm is in the Mountains of the Dwarves. She would be killed before she got anywhere near it."

"Plus," Clairla added, "the Veil opening is only temporary. The Dwarf King got it open using a magic I'm not aware of. It's likely it's sealed back up again."

"Speaking of sealing things," Tor said. "How do you intend to seal this gaping hole in our universe?"

Pac shrugged. "Magic."

"Are you that powerful? You said you came from a place where there was no magic. How do you know you will be strong enough?"

"Oh, I'm not nearly strong enough." Her tone was almost amused.

"I don't know magic." Eydis's shoulders slumped.

Clairla said, "My magic isn't very strong either."

Everyone looked at Tor, and she raised her hands in surrender. "Don't look at me. My magic is in healing."

"Then I suppose we will need to find someone who has powerful magic." Pac shrugged, like it was an easy, everyday task.

The group fell silent and Tor could feel the static build in the air. The metallic taste in her mouth made her contort her face, and Pac mirrored her. Within a few minutes the air pressure dropped, and for a brief moment it was difficult to breathe.

With a sudden flash of light that lit the area as bright as day, a thunderous bang rang through the air as lightning struck the ground near the far-off trees. As it did there was a painful howl, a cry that made Tor's stomach drop.

"Well, that does it then," Eydis said, his tone neutral. "Looks like we no longer have a Shadow beast problem."

"She was never a problem," Tor snapped, surprising herself as much as the rest of the group with her reaction. She sympathized with the beast, knew the pain of being alone. "I hope it was quick and that she didn't suffer."

"It was a powerful strike," Clairla said in a gentle tone. "I'm certain she went quickly."

Again they fell silent, and it was hours before anyone spoke again. The fire had all but died down, and the sun did a poor job lighting the sky as it rose. The dark, ugly, and unnatural clouds could now clearly be seen. Toward the High Kingdom it looked almost pitch-black. To the west was still a slight bit of blue sky, but it was being eaten up by the ever-growing clouds.

"We might as well get a move on." Clairla stood and rolled her blanket. "We can catch some fish or something as we walk—"

She was cut short by the sound of a muffled cry.

"What was that?" Eydis asked, looking around the area.

It came again, and Tor could tell it was close. When it cried for the third time, Tor knew exactly what it was and had an idea of where came from. She spun and grabbed her medical pack, then ran in the direction of the distressed creature.

"Tor," Clairla shouted after her.

"Where are you going?" Eydis called out.

"It's the Shadow beast," Pac said, and Tor could hear her bounding behind.

Tor stopped at a grouping of bushes and Pac skidded up next to her. Trying to move with extreme caution, she pushed back the branches and saw what was making all the noise. Lifting her head it looked up at her with large brown-and-silver eyes, but after a moment dropped it back down. She whimpered, her breathing shallow and rapid.

Pac moved away as Tor knelt next to the Shadow beast, her hands raised. "It's okay," she said in a tone she saved for injured children. "I won't hurt you. I am merely here to help."

The beast heaved several breaths in Tor's direction, and although it kept a watchful eye it made no further movement.

It was much smaller than Tor had pictured, and she estimated it must weigh about fifty pounds. Her coat was black with silver streaks, which made her look as though she was shimmering. Inspecting her, Tor came to her hind legs; her left leg and hip were badly burned, and the fur was either singed or completely gone. She wasn't bleeding, the lightning strike having cauterized the wound.

Tor put down her bag and opened it, contemplating what she might use. A wound was a wound, right? As she reached for a bottle, Eydis and Clairla came up behind.

"You're not seriously going to heal it, are you?" Eydis asked.

Still crouching, Tor pivoted on the balls of her feet to face him.

"What is your problem? I never thought you to be such a heartless bastard. What would Gran say?"

Her comment stunned him to silence.

"Looks like she wasn't struck directly." Clairla knelt next to Tor. "I know some healing incantations that may help with your potions."

Tor nodded, happy to have an ally.

Pac appeared on the other side of the beast. "It looks like she has been dragging herself through the woods all night." She pointed to the west, where the lightning had struck. "There is a tree split in half and a huge scorch mark on the ground some ways back. I think she was trying to get to us for help."

Tor and Clairla nodded, then quickly got to work putting together a salve while discussing which incantations they should use. All the while, Eydis had taken to standing guard several yards away, his sword out. They were several feet into the woods, and no one knew if the Shadow soldiers were still in the area. Pac then made a comment about finding lunch and disappeared.

An hour later, the beast's back quarter was covered with a healing salve and bandages. Her breathing had begun to regulate, and Tor risked petting her. When her hand touched the beast's shoulder, her head popped up and she licked her lips. Tor quickly snatched her hand back, hoping not to lose it.

The beast made a chortling sound, almost like a bark and a laugh mixed together, and laid her head back down but still kept one eye on Tor.

"You think that means I can touch her?" Tor asked Clairla.

Clairla shrugged. "It's your hand."

Tor set her shoulders and eased her hand toward the beast once again. This time she didn't move when Tor touched her shoulder and ran her hand down her side. The beast was much softer than she'd expected, and her hand seemed to disappear into the thick coat.

The beast let out another chortle that ended with a slight whimper.

"She must still be in some pain." Clairla inspected the rest of the animal. "I never thought of checking her other side. Do you think her right side is injured as well?"

Tor stopped petting the beast. The thought had never occurred to her either. She felt foolish now; as a healer she should have known to do a full inspection of the patient. "We're going to have to move her anyway, so we'll be able to check."

Clairla opened her mouth to speak, but was cut short by Eydis. "Move her? Why would you move her?"

"Well we can't leave her here, all alone and injured. There are other predators around."

"So what? Do you think you have a pet now?"

"Eydis, seriously, what is wrong with you? She was coming to us for help. She's been following us for days." Tor paused. What *was* her intention? She wanted to help the beast, but her wounds could take days to heal. Not to mention the salve would need to be changed and the wound cleaned daily. Again she looked at Clairla, hoping for some guidance.

"Looks like we got ourselves a Shadow beast," she said, smiling.

Tor nodded and reached for it, seeing Eydis open his mouth to protest further. "Go back to the camp and restart the fire. If Pac hasn't already. And maybe think about catching some fish in that river."

He shut his mouth and she could see him clench his jaw before he stormed off.

Clairla helped Tor repack her medical bag. "Is it just me, or is he getting a bit testy lately? I remember him being much kinder when we left the High Kingdom."

Tor pursed her lips. "Yes, I've noticed that too. Perhaps it's the uncertainty about his family. He told his grandmother to leave, but the woman is stubborn. She may still have been in the city when the ceremony happened. Or, perhaps, it's the fact that you keep insinuating he's stupid."

Clairla said nothing. She stood, took the medical bag, and waited for Tor to lift the beast. "I don't think he's stupid. I'm just teasing him."

"Please don't bite me," Tor then said to the beast, "I'm only trying to help." Tor locked eyes with it, and she licked her lips and chortled. Tor set her jaw, nodded, then eased her hands under the beast, just behind the shoulders and in front of the hips. She was careful not to pull off any bandages.

The beast let out a howl of pain as her wounded leg and hip came into contact with Tor's body. Tor put her back down as quickly and as gently as possible.

"I didn't see any other wounds," Clairla said.

"Well that's something, I guess."

"Maybe if you pick her up from this side, and get her on her feet. Then you can carry her with her good side against you."

Tor nodded again and came to her feet. She moved around the beast, who still kept an eye on her. "Okay," Tor said. "Let's try this again." She eased the beast onto her feet, lifting her back leg off the ground, it was obviously too painful to bear weight. Tor picked her up again, one arm behind her shoulders and the other in front of her hips.

Tor rose to her feet, Clairla following behind as they made their way back to the camp.

Tor spoke in a tone low enough that her voice wouldn't carry and only Clairla could hear. "Maybe consider teasing Eydis less." She stretched out her stride, leaving Clairla several paces behind.

When they got back to camp Pac had what looked like rabbit and fish on the fire. It smelled wonderful, and both Tor and the beast licked their lips.

CHAPTER TWENTY-THREE

TWO DAYS PASSED, AND THE Shadow beast was now on her feet. She was slow, yet still able to move about. Tor had become quite attached to the animal, and was hoping she would choose to stay with them. Eydis, however, grew fouler as the days and hours passed. It was strange. Tor had at first believed it was the uncertainty of his family's survival and Clairla's relentless teasing, but now she was sensing it may be something else.

Clairla had voiced her worry several times in private, and she had seen Pac studying him on more than one occasion.

As they sat around the fire eating their evening meal, Clairla spoke. "I've been thinking."

"That's never a good sign," Eydis mumbled, half under his breath.

Tor shot him a glare, but the other two ignored him.

Clairla said, "You said we will need strong magic to close the rift."

"That's right," Pac said with a mouth full of meat.

"Well, I know of some pretty powerful people in this area." Clairla smiled.

"If you're thinking about the fairies, you may want to think twice," Tor said. "They wouldn't help, no matter how you ask."

"They put up an entire dome around their Veil." Clairla's face contorted as she gestured toward it. "You're telling me they don't have magic strong enough to help?"

Tor sighed heavily. It was a part of her peoples' history as to why the fairies had little to do with this world. "No, I'm saying they won't help. They put that barrier up to protect themselves. They must know something is coming, or at least they are protecting themselves from these surges of magic."

Eydis grunted. "Fairies are foul little things. They drop rocks on people for the fun of it. I don't think they care if we're all killed." His lips curled into a snarl as he glared at the dome.

Clairla waved them off. "It doesn't matter anyway. I wasn't talking about the fairies. I was thinking about other natural magic users, well, two actually."

"Who?" Pac and Tor asked.

"Would a tree sprite and an elf have the magic we need?"

"Yes," Pac's face lit up and her tone held a tinge of excitement. "They are both strong natural-magic beings. Together they would be formidable."

"I thought you said they were no longer in this area? Unless you are talking about a different sprite," Tor asked. "I don't believe Knolnt Woods outside of the Great Walled City would have any sprites willing to leave their forest. We would have to travel east to the Tilinrich Mountains, about three months away from the High Kingdom. Closer than Aweens, the Elvin Realm, which is at least a year's trek from here. Longer, since we're on foot."

"For a cleric of the Rejuvenation Monastery, you certainly know a great deal of Totriga and her inhabitants." Clairla's eyebrows rose in surprise.

"It's because I'm a cleric that I know these things. I learned about not just the practices of healing of different races, but how to heal them, as well as of the plants and herbs grown in the different areas. I may never have been to these places, but I am well-informed about them."

Pac waved them both off. "We don't have the time to travel a year in one direction and several months in another. We'll need to find another way."

"If the two of you would let me finish, I would have told you that I know where we can find them both." She gave Tor a pointed look. "No, I don't know for sure if they are still there, but it's only a day to the Ruins Labyrinth. There is no harm in us at least checking." She pointed to the east, toward the Veil River and where they had crossed the week before.

"Then we leave tomorrow morning." Pac smiled and lay out on her blanket.

"It's about time." Eydis grumbled as he threw another log on the fire, more for light than warmth. "We leaving that behind?" He nodded at the Shadow beast that lay next to Tor.

Tor looked down at the beast. She'd been absentmindedly rubbing the beast's ears, who was quite beautiful and gentle. Many of the orc tribe kids had had their own pets: big, spiky, pig-like beasts used in battle. Tor had never reached the age of receiving such a companion before being sent to the monastery.

"I was hoping she would stay with us." Tor didn't bother trying to hide the disappointment in her voice. Clairla smiled, chuckling, and Tor glanced up. "What?"

"Oh, she has bonded with you and won't leave your side. You might as well name her."

"What makes you so sure?"

"Shadow beasts are not solitary animals, and they require companionship. I suspected she had been following us in the hopes of finding just that once she discovered her mate was gone. Also why she dragged herself several kilometers to get to us when she was injured."

Pac let out a small laugh that sounded more like a sigh. She turned her head to find everyone watching her. "You all believe that Shadows are evil. All they want is to destroy everything. But look"—she pointed at the beast—"It doesn't seem so evil to me. Maybe the Shadows are just misunderstood."

Eydis snorted. "Yeah, right. So let me get this straight, not only are we going to travel with this giant, dog-like animal that could likely eat us in our sleep, but now we are going to the Ruins Labyrinth where fairies drop rocks on our heads?" His voice was becoming shrill.

His attitude was worrying to Tor. It was like he was a different person, and the Eydis she'd known, the Eydis who'd left the High Kingdom with her, was kind, generous, and adventurous. No matter the danger that may be lurking, he would always be the first person to lead the charge. More for the excitement than the glory. Being a guard for the High King hadn't suited him at all. He should have been an adventurer, a traveler.

"It'll be fine." Tor tried to sooth him, but he brushed her off.

"Will it? Will it?" He leaned toward her.

Clairla now tried. "The fairies are all behind their dome. I'm certain of that. You have nothing to fear, and with them all gone the Labyrinth will be unmanned."

"Why don't you get some sleep." Tor put a hand on his shoulder. "It'll be fine. You'll see tomorrow, when we get there, that there's nothing to be afraid of."

Eydis stood and the beast lifted her head, as if on alert, her eyes darting about. Tor rubbed her ears and whispered. "Easy now Joonee, it's all right. Easy." She laid her head back down and closed her eyes.

"Joonee?" Clairla asked. "That's different."

Tor shrugged. What should she call a beast from the Shadow Realm? Shadow beast? Somehow that felt a little too on the nose. She had once heard a child call her pet Joonee, long ago in the High Kingdom. She had always liked the name.

The static began to build and the air pressure dropped much quicker than usual, the crack of thunder coming at the exact moment the lightning struck the ground. Joonee was on her feet, Tor and the rest of the group not far behind. They all rubbed their ears.

Tor heard a buzzing in her ears and she felt a little light-headed. When she checked on the others they all seemed to suffer the same problem. The thunderclap had been loud enough to pop their eardrums, but fortunately not enough to break them. Their voices seemed muffled, as were Joonee's howls; she likely suffered the same injury.

Making quick time of it, Tor checked everyone for permanent damage, indicated by blood coming from the ears, or for any popped blood vessels in their eyes—all injuries that could be obtained from concussive explosions. They may not have been physically moved, but the thunder and lightning were now practically overhead.

It was an hour before they could all hear properly again, and Tor's ears stopped buzzing so loud. The sun had set, or so they assumed since the clouds were so dark they shielded the sun.

The night was long and uneasy, and no one slept well. The static built up faster, moving closer, throughout the night, and they were all concerned about being struck. Joonee buried herself under Tor's blankets, shaking every time the air pressure began to drop. Tor didn't blame the beast; if she had been struck and injured the way Joonee had been, she would probably want to hide too.

After the tenth lightning strike they all decided to break camp and head toward the Ruins Labyrinth. There was just no point in trying to get any more sleep.

CHAPTER TWENTY-FOUR

I T TOOK THE BETTER PART of the day to get back to the bridge. The effects of the dome the Fairies had erected were felt more strongly here, and both Tor and Clairla believed it was because of the water. It was a natural element the fairies used in all their magic, and suspected it was what they were using to keep the dome up.

Veils give off their own type of static, a powerful magic that cannot be tapped into by just any as it takes great skill and strength to use. That's what made the Realm Eater all the more terrifying. Not only did he take the magic from Veils but, from what Pac and Clairla had explained, he did it on his own and without help.

It took the twelve races and the closing of seven Veils just to seal the Shadow Realm—and the Realm Eater was going to consume it all.

Tor shook the thoughts from her head. Now was not the time to dwell on such things, and she felt it best to deal with one issue at a time. Right now, it was getting across a raging river. The issue: the bridge they'd used to cross a little over a week ago was now gone. Only the singed end poles remained standing.

"Well that's just great," Eydis shouted, throwing his hands up. "That river is too deep to walk, and it's running too fast. We'll be swept away the instant we put our toes in."

"Yes, thank you for that," Pac said. Her impatience with Eydis was growing.

Tor had watched as the tension between the two had increased during the past week, and there was constant bickering between all three. It was an odd dynamic, really. Clairla would insult Eydis, who would return the favor. But, if Pac insulted Eydis, then Clairla would stand up for him.

Pac glared at him now. "Keep giving us obvious, useful information like that. I'm sure it will help."

"Why don't you keep your teeth together," he shouted back. "This is all your fault. I wouldn't be here if it wasn't for you."

Clairla put a hand up to stop Pac from retorting. "Nobody forced you to come. If I recall, you invited yourself." She turned to Pac. "And I don't see you coming up with any ideas."

Eydis's eyes narrowed, and he opened his mouth to say something but promptly shut it again. Putting his back to them he stormed toward the dome.

Tor sighed as she watched him walk away.

"We're going to have to swim it," Pac said as she stood with her hands on her hips, looking down at the raging river.

Eydis turned and stomped back. "Are you out of your mind?" His voice squeaked just a touch before he got it under control.

"How else do you propose we get across?" Pac didn't seem fazed by his outburst. "Is there another bridge to cross?"

"Yes," Clairla said. "Well, at least there used to be. I haven't been to that area for many years, but it is in the opposite direction we want to go."

"How far out of our way?" Pac asked.

"Days; it's beyond those woods." She pointed well past where they'd found Joonee. "On the other side, where the river narrows."

"Obviously, we can't do that," Pac said with a huge sigh and turning back to the river in front of them.

Tor stepped up next to her and looked down. In places, the

rocks at the bottom could be seen, but that didn't necessarily mean the water was shallow or it was even solid enough to walk on. But she was strong and had no concerns...well, few concerns.

When she turned her gaze to Clairla, the fae's shoulders dropped. "You're going to make us swim it, aren't you?"

Tor felt for the fae; she appeared to be very light and the concern she may get swept away was real. Pac seemed a bit more solid and, as for Eydis, he was a big man and likely heavy as a stone.

"I'm afraid so."

"No way," Eydis shouted. "I'm not getting in that water."

"What is your problem?" Pac shouted back. "Are you scared to get wet? Afraid you might lose that stench you've accumulated over the past week? Are you allergic?"

"Okay," Tor said, putting a hand up. Although she didn't disagree that Eydis could do with a bath, and Clairla's smirk said she also agreed. "If you can give us a good reason *and* a solution then we won't cross."

Eydis's eyes dropped to his shoes as he dug his toe into the ground. His face pinked up and he fiddled with the straps on his pack, mumbling something no one could hear.

"I'm sorry, what?" Tor asked.

He mumbled again, refusing to look up.

"Hey, we don't have all day," Pac shouted. "Speak up, for the love of all that is holy!"

Tor and Clairla turned to look at Pac. It was a strange saying, something she had never heard before. She was about to ask exactly what it meant when Eydis shouted back.

"I don't like you very much." He made eye contact with Pac, and Tor could see not just fury but absolute fear. That's when she noticed his hands were shaking and he looked as though he might be sick.

Tor took a step closer to make it harder for the others to hear.

"Are you afraid of the water? Afraid you may drown? It's nothing to be ashamed of Eydis. I'm worried, too. But we—"

"It's not that."

"Then what?"

"I can't swim," he said, voice tense. "Gronk's hairy balls! I told you this before, but if I get in there I'll drown."

Pac huffed behind Tor, who had moved closer to listen in. Tor wasn't sure if she liked this Pac very much, either. She was boarding on abrasive and arrogant, and in Tor's opinion that was not a good combination.

Tor gave Pac a sidelong stare and the girl stepped away, her hands up.

"We're wasting daylight," Clairla said. "I'm not much of a swimmer, either, and I weigh substantially less than you, Eydis. But we have—"

Eydis threw his hand up. "I know."

"Does anyone have anything to use as a tether?" Tor asked. A collective 'no' came from the group. "What about belts? No one has a belt?"

"Yeah," Eydis said. "But it's holding my pants up."

Pac opened her mouth. Tor was certain it was to make a snide remark, so she pointed her finger and said, "Keep your teeth together, Pac. Your comments and attitude are not helping." She turned back to Eydis. "Okay, let's have it." She held her hand out.

"My belt?"

"Yes, your belt. We will tether Clairla to you. You're solid enough that you can keep her from being swept away."

"What if I get swept away?" Eydis's hands grabbed at his belt, as if trying to keep it in place.

"You won't." Tor mustered the most confident tone she could. Honestly, she didn't know if any of them would make it across, and the look in Clairla's and Pac's eyes told her they thought the same. "Come on," she said wiggling her fingers. "Times wasting, and I feel the static growing. We don't want to be in the water when the lightning touches down."

"Gronk's hairy balls," Eydis shouted. "What happens if we *are* in the water when the lightning strikes?"

"We die," Pac said with a shrug.

"Pac, that is not helpful." Tor shot a glare in her direction.

"We can't really save the world if we're dead now, can we?" Eydis shot back.

"We can't do it from this side of the river, either!" Pac balled up her fists and pulled her shoulders back. She took a strange stance, one foot slightly in front of the other, like she was making herself sturdier. Pac had lifted her hands to her waist when Tor intervened again.

"Okay," Tor said, starting to feel like she was refereeing two unruly children. "Just give me the stupid belt, Eydis."

With a grumble about Gronk's balls, Eydis reluctantly removed his belt and Tor helped fasten a tether for Clairla. No one really thought it was going to hold.

They all approached the water's edge.

Clairla touched Tor's arm. "What about Joonee?"

Tor looked down at the Shadow beast, who stared back. "Hope you can swim, or is this where we part ways?"

Joonee chortled at Tor and looked at the river, moving closer.

"Okay," Tor said, placing a hand on the beast's head. "Stay upriver from me and I'll try to act as a barrier and keep you from being dragged away." *Maybe it will work,* Tor thought.

Joonee chortled again and moved to Tor's right side.

Pac was the first in, sucking in air as she hit the cold water. Tor and Joonee were next, and her reaction was the same as the cold water soaked through her clothes. She heard a slight whimper from the Shadow beast.

"Gronk's hairy balls." She heard Eydis call from behind as he and Clairla entered the river, though Clairla didn't make a sound.

The current was strong, stronger than it had looked from the water's edge. Tor fought hard to stay on her feet and keep Joonee's head above the water. She had her by the scruff, and the beast paddled her legs as hard as she could. The rocks underfoot were loose, and made getting traction difficult at best. Her teeth began to chatter as the freezing water penetrated all her layers. It felt like tiny little daggers were stabbing her, which made the whole situation that much worse.

Pac was only several paces ahead, and she too struggled to keep her feet under her. But she made no sound or indication she needed or wanted help. Nevertheless, Tor kept a close eye on her.

Once at the other side, Pac reached for the grassy edge but lost her footing. She fell into the water and disappeared. Tor's stomach dropped as she scrambled to get closer.

"Grab her," Clairla shouted from behind.

Eydis grunted, and Tor heard a splash and a gasp of air behind her. She had no time to look over her shoulder, or to think. She pushed herself forward, gripping Joonee's scruff tighter. Ignoring the ever-growing pain of the cold she leaned forward, up to her chin in the water, and waved her free hand around.

It was the longest ten seconds she had ever lived before she felt a hand grip hers. Tor yanked up and Pac's head popped to the surface, but she still had no purchase on the riverbed and was being dragged down with the current. Tor dug in her heels, but the rocks were loose where she stood and the speed of the water—and a sudden pull from Pac—yanked Tor off balance.

Her head dipped under the water, and she had no time to suck in air. She took a gulp of the water, filling her lungs. They burned from the intake, but she resisted any urge to cough. One hand on Pac and the other on Joonee, she scrambled to get her footing. The fast, cold water made it hard to think. She managed to get her face above the surface and spurt out the water before she was pulled back under.

All she wanted to do was let go of the beast and Pac. It was as if the water called for to her to give in, but she called to her Goddess Thanroota for strength and dug deep within herself, forcing her feet down. It took every bit of her strength and willpower to get it done. When her feet touched the bottom she was able to push her head above the water, hearing Pac and Joonee take a collective breath.

Tor's feet still slipped, and she lost her footing several more times before they reached the water's edge. Joonee was the first out of the water, giving Tor the ability to grab onto any long grass or roots. With a grunt she yanked at Pac, who fought and struggled to keep her own head above the water. Her free hand flailed about, looking for something to grasp.

Pac slipped and was pulled back under, taking Tor with her, but then she felt someone grab her wrist. She yanked at Pac, who finally was close enough to grab some roots, and Tor felt herself being pulled from what she thought was to be her icy death.

When she looked up to see who her savior was, she saw a soaked and shivering Eydis. He was panting hard, and had landed flat on his ass when he pulled her free of the river. Joonee was immediately on top of her, lying flat and putting her muzzle just under her chin. Tor placed a hand on the beasts head and looked over to where Pac should be, fearing for a fleeting moment she had let go of the girl and Pac was still floating down the river.

Relief washed over her when she saw Clairla and Pac in a heap. Tor dropped back to the ground just as there was a loud clap of thunder, the air pressure dropping. The lightning struck the dome, sending a cascade of odd sparks down the river.

No one needed to say anything for each to understand just how lucky they were.

CHAPTER TWENTY-FIVE

I T WAS A LONG, COLD night for everyone. The disastrous river
crossing had left everyone soaked through and exhausted. Their
bedding and change of clothes were drenched, and there was no
wood to be could found for a fire. They spent the night curled in a
huddled mass, and morning seemed to take days to come.

Even with the dark, unnatural clouds making it overcast, it was
still bright enough to make their way to the Ruins Labyrinth.

"It's at least a day's walk," Eydis said. "How did we get so far
downriver?"

Pac stepped next to him and put a hand on her chin, as if deep
in thought. "Well, if I were to guess, I would say that it was because the current was strong and fast." She dropped her hand and
looked at him pointedly. "But that's just a guess."

"Little early to be an asshole, isn't it?" Eydis sneered back.

"Little early to be a moron, isn't it?" she said.

Eydis lifted his finger and opened his mouth but Tor interrupted
his retort. "All right, that's enough. We're all tired and hungry and
still a little wet. Yes, we were pulled a lot further downriver than
we thought last night. But at least we are alive."

Without a further word Tor, Clairla, and Pac headed for the
Ruins. Joonee bounded ahead, her back leg and hip no longer an
issue. When Tor realized they were missing someone, she stopped

and looked back. Eydis was staring at the dome then looking back toward the High Kingdom.

She walked back to her friend and stood in front of him. The bags under his eyes were not just from the lack of sleep the night before. He had been growing ever more restless the closer they got to Pac's rift. Tor now suspected it wasn't the rift at all that was making him uneasy, but rather the dome the fairies had erected around their Veil opening.

"It wouldn't be safe for you to return on your own." Tor tried locking eyes with him, but he refused to look in her direction.

"It's not safe for us to go to the Ruins. Least of all for me." He swallowed hard and looked Tor in the eye. "I'll die if I go to the Ruins."

"We aren't going through the Labyrinth, Eydis. Clairla said her friends will be in the village. The fairies don't go to the village." She pointed to the dome. "And, with that, I don't even think they are in the Ruins, or in this realm for that matter."

Eydis shook his head and stared at the dome. When he brought his hand to his mouth it was shaking. Tor tried to keep her face soft, but his reaction was strange. With everything they had encountered up to this point he had never been afraid. If anything, he hadn't been afraid enough.

"Eydis, tell me what you're thinking."

"Hey," Pac shouted from ahead. "Are we going to stand here all day?"

Tor twisted toward them, waving a hand. "You go ahead, we'll catch up."

"Don't get too far behind," Clairla shouted back.

Tor nodded and turned back to Eydis. "What are you so afraid of?"

His eyes darted from the dome to Tor and back again.

"The dome won't hurt you. It—"

"I can't explain it," Eydis blurted out. "I just have this need to get away from here. As far as I can." His eyes held a horror Tor had never seen before. It was as if he was living through a nightmare no one else could see. "I have to get out of here." His voice had dropped just below a whisper.

Tor took his hands into hers. "My goddess will protect you." She knew she shouldn't speak such blasphemy, but she doubted Eydis would punish her for it. "Goddess Thanroota is a great warrior. She will fight by your side and, when you cannot, she will fight for you. Let her guide you, strengthen your resolve, and swing a mighty sword." The prayer wasn't quite the same as the warrior prayer she had learned as a girl but, given the situation, his fear of going to the village would be considered cowardice and the prayer would never be given.

Eydis stared at her, open-mouthed. "There are no gods," he whispered. "How can you say such words to me? How dare you blanket me in your blasphemy against your monastery." He yanked his hands from hers.

Tor set her jaw, and an anger grew in Tor that she had not felt in many years. "I doubted a healer's prayer would help you here. I was merely trying to help you gain courage. It is obvious you have none. Stay, go, or come; it is your choice."

It was one thing to comment there were no gods, but to act as though she'd just spat on him was more insulting. She leaned in close, and with his height he was one of few men she could look straight in the eye. "My words are only blasphemous to my great warrior, Goddess Thanroota. Invoking her to help you is a sin against my own people. You are no warrior." She turned on her heel and stretched out her pace to catch up to the others.

As she moved closer to the girls a pang of guilt ran through her. Eydis was one of her dearest friends; he'd helped her many times in the High Kingdom. Kept her secret of using magic to heal when the king had ruled all magic illegal. Kept her safe from would-be vandals and bandits out to do harm to her and Parin. He'd been a dear friend to her, a brother. So his reaction to her blessing was perplexing. This was not the first time she'd spoken of her goddess to him, but this was the first time he'd reacted in such a harsh way. It was yet another instance of Eydis not being himself.

It only took Tor a few minutes to catch up to Pac and Clairla, and the three walked in silence.

Joonee bounded about happily in front of them as they walked, the only one seeming to enjoy their time.

"It's strange," Tor said.

"What is?" Clairla asked.

"The way Joonee is acting. I've never seen a beast act in such a way."

Clairla shrugged. "She's happy."

"Happy?" Tor raised her eyebrows.

"She was on her own for a long time, I suspect. Now she's with others."

"Makes sense," Pac said with a shrug.

Tor studied Pac. "I suppose it does." There was a look in her eye that said she knew the pain of loneliness. Knowing Pac's history as a child, raised alone in a dungeon for several years, Tor knew it would give her a perspective none of them had.

Joonee ran past them, bounding behind the group. Tor glanced over her shoulder to see Eydis following. He was at least five minutes behind, and his pace indicated he wasn't trying to catch up. She was about to turn and call to him when the static in the air grew so suddenly and so unexpectedly that the drop in air pressure made her light-headed.

A streak of light flashed through the sky, and she barely had time to react to Clairla's command to get down. She dropped to the ground and glimpsed Eydis dropping on top of Joonee and pulling her in close. The lightning struck the dome, sending out a wave of power that made Tor's flesh feel like it was on fire.

Resisting the urge to scream out in pain, she heard the others.

The clap of thunder was ear-piercing and echoed over the land. When Tor rolled over onto her back her ears were ringing painfully, and every sound she made seemed hollow and muffled at the same time. It took a minute for her to get to her feet.

As she rose, she spotted a slight shimmer run over the dome as the constant humming stopped for only a second before starting back up.

"Everyone okay?" Tor asked, uncertain if she was yelling. She opened and closed her mouth, trying and pop her ears, before plugging her nose and swallowing. There was a painful pop, but everything cleared up and she could hear normally again, although with a slight, high-pitched whine still in the background.

"That happened so quickly." Clairla was wiping the dirt and grass from her coat. "It normally takes time to build up."

Joonee and Eydis ran up. "Everyone okay?"

There was a series of nods and grunts.

Pac was staring at the dome, then said, "I think it's that. It must be attracting the magic."

"Then the quicker we get into the village and find Clairla's friends the better." Eydis was the first to start walking. The other three glanced at each other briefly, then followed.

"How can it be attracting the magic?" Eydis asked after twenty minutes of silence.

Pac shrugged. "Totriga is acting as a toblaha, a type of magical black hole, so it is pulling all the powerful magic toward it. This is why other Realms outside of this universe are being pulled in. This is why the Realm Eater is coming. That dome"—she pointed without looking—"is one of the biggest pieces of magic on this world. None of the Veils to the other Realms contain that much magic. I don't know what the fairies have done to create it, but it might be a good idea to see if we can't get them to take it down."

"Take it down?" Tor and Clairla said together.

"Yes."

Tor shook her head; the dome had been erected for a reason. "Why would they take it down? They've put it up over their own Veil. They're protecting themselves. If we close the rift over the High Kingdom, then they'll take it down. Not to mention there's no way for us to get near enough to them to ask. I doubt we would be able to cross the dome's walls."

"You don't mind that they are taking care of only themselves?" Clairla glared at Tor. "It's selfish. Typical fairy behavior."

Tor felt her anger rise again. But why? This wasn't her fight, and if Clairla didn't like the fairies then why should Tor care? But, for some reason, she did. "They have every right to protect themselves!"

"From what? They never come out of their realm anyway," Clairla shouted. "They would rather kill humans than help."

"What do you care if they kill humans?" Eydis shouted. "You fae are no better. You trap us with your riddles and deceit and take pleasure in our pain. You may not throw rocks, but you certainly would do nothing to stop the fairies."

Clairla turned on him. "You don't know me. You know nothing of what I've lived through for you humans. I've given up everything for you so her people"—she jabbed a finger at Pac—"wouldn't invade and kill everything." She now spun on Pac. "How do we know you aren't bringing the Realm Eater here? It was your people who tried to help him four millennia ago. It's a little convenient, isn't it? You just popping back into this world. And you"—she spun on Tor—"it was your war-mongering ancestors who invaded this region, burning down villages, that made the humans kill the fairies for not helping in the fight. That's why they hate humans so much!"

Pac's eyebrows rose and she was about to speak when Tor cut her off. "You're the reason I'm here," Tor said, now jabbing her finger at Clairla. "You insisted that I come, and I left my son to fend for him—"

"He's not your son," Eydis shouted. "No orc can claim a human—"

Pac raised her hands. "That's enough." Her voice was nearly as loud as a thunder clap, forcing everyone into silence. "I don't know what is getting into all of you, but I think it's best you keep your teeth together from now on." She looked pointedly at Eydis. "Before you say something I'm positive you will regret."

Tor put a hand to her forehead. She was getting a headache. "You're right. I'm sorry. I don't know what has been getting into me as of late. I've just been so angry and I don't know why."

"Me too," Clairla said. "I've never felt like this before. Ever."

Eydis cleared his throat and dug a toe into the dirt. "I'm sorry, Tor." He heaved a breath and looked up. "I've been having this feeling of dread ever since we crossed the swamps and the river came into view. The longer we are out here, the worse it's getting. Now that dread is turning into a murderous anger. Except for when..." As his words trailed off he stared up at the dome.

"When the dome shimmered," Tor said. "I felt a sense of relief for a short second when the lightning struck the dome."

Clairla nodded.

"It's the dome," Pac said. "I haven't been around it as long as all of you have, so I'm not feeling the effects to the degree you are. But, listening to you, whatever magic the fairies have used it's having an ill effect on everyone around it."

"Likely from design," Tor said. "Best way to keep people away is make them want to stay away. All I want to do right now is get as far away from this thing as I can."

Eydis nodded so rapidly Tor thought his head may fly off. "That's exactly how I've been feeling." He pointed at her. "From the moment we got close to that dome, all I have wanted to do is get away from here."

"Okay." Clairla sighed impatiently. "We've established none of us like the fucking dome." Her voice began to rise, and she took another deep breath and closed her eyes. Tor half smiled, knowing Clairla was trying to regain her composure. "Let's just get to the village, find my friends, then get as far away as we possibly can from this thing." She didn't wait for anyone before heading for the village, less than a kilometer away. The small houses could be seen in the distance.

The rest followed behind without a word. Tor thought it best no one speak further, since they risked another shouting match that could possibly end in blows. As no one else spoke, she assumed they felt the same way.

CHAPTER TWENTY-SIX

THE SKY WAS SO DARK they could barely tell it was midday. The riverbank became steeper, making it impossible to cross the river safely, and the cold gray stones of the Ruins Labyrinth towered in front of them. The stone was smooth and seemed untouched by time and weather. There would be no way for anyone to climb the Ruins' outer walls.

It had been built after the orc invasion, when the humans turned on the fairies for not helping in the battle that had wiped out most of the village. As if overnight, the fairies created the Ruins Labyrinth to keep people from the safest part of Veil River; the only place shallow enough to cross into the clearing that housed the entrance into the Fairy Realm.

"What do we do now?" Eydis asked, running his hand over the cold, smooth surface of the rock.

"We follow it around to where the village is." Clairla pointed down the stretch of stone. "Can't be much more than a ten or fifteen minute walk."

"Who lives behind these walls?" Pac asked as she stepped back to see to the top.

"No one," Tor said. "It's a test the fairies built."

Tor and Clairla were the first to walk toward the village. Pac then followed, with Eydis and Joonee close behind.

"A test?" Pac called from behind.

Tor spoke over her shoulder, not wanting to slow her pace. She was starving, and hoped someone in the village was willing to sell them a warm meal. "In order to get to the Fairy Realm, you must figure out the labyrinth. If you can get through alive, the fairies will trade with you."

No further questions were asked.

As Clairla predicted, it took fifteen minutes for them to get to the village. What they found caused Tor's heart to drop and the others to gasp in horror. Tor stared, open-mouthed, at the devastation in front of them. The tiny farming village that sat against the outside back wall of the labyrinth was all but destroyed.

Some houses were burned to ash, while others had doors and windows smashed in and broken. It appeared the village had been struck several times by lightning as well. One thing was for certain: Tor knew no one was in this village. No one alive, anyway.

"We might want to get our weapons out," she found herself saying as the hair on her arms stood on end. The static was building, but there was something else that put her on edge. Something felt different just outside of the static. Unnatural. Tor eased her sword from its scabbard, then pulled a hunting knife from her belt. She was the first to ease into the village. The Shadow beast was next to her, and Joonee's hackles were up and she barred her teeth. It was a menacing look that made Tor swallow hard.

Her steps were slow and methodical, her eyes darting from one side to the next as she studied each deep shadow for any movement. The static grew and the air pressure began to drop. It was only seconds before the flash of light struck a building several houses down, and the crack of thunder was enough from them all to drop to the ground.

Tor felt her bones vibrate from the pressure. Her ears hummed and rang for a second time that day, and she began to worry that everyone would start to lose their hearing. Once everything went back to normal the static gone, as was the other unnatural power she'd felt. Tor shook her head to get the fogginess out, then checked on the others.

"Everyone okay?" she asked, checking each of them. When they all nodded, indicating their varying states of wellbeing, she turned to Clairla. "Did you sense anything other than the static?"

"I assumed it was from the dome. We've never been this close before, so I thought it was how it was reacting to the normal static."

Tor nodded. It made sense; two distinctly different magics colliding such as this must have a different feel. She sheathed both the knife and the sword.

"Should we look around?" Eydis asked, still holding his weapon. When no one responded, but merely stared at him, he continued. "There could still be some survivors."

"Don't you mean food?" Pac asked, her eyes dropping to his large belly. "You've been grumbling for some time about how hungry you are. Like none of us are."

"Yeah okay, fine. I wouldn't be upset if we found something edible."

"We'll cover more ground if we spread out," Tor suggested.

"I think we should stick together," Clairla said.

"Are you not a trained assassin?" Tor asked. "Are you scared to search on your own?"

Clairla straightened and pulled her shoulders back. "No, of course not. It's a small village, so it just doesn't seem like a necessary measure."

Tor glanced past Clairla at the others, and they too seemed indifferent. Tor shrugged. "Whatever. Let's just get this over with. I'd like to get on the road and as far from that dome as possible before the next lightning strike."

"Yeah, I think that is a really good idea," Pac said as she stood in the doorway of a nearby home. The others joined her, and immediately Eydis was running from the shelter and vomiting around the corner.

"They've been dead for a while," Clairla said, unfazed by the sight.

Tor stepped past the two women and into the home, crouching down to get a better look at the corpses. The smell didn't bother her as much as it did the rest. She was used to the smell of decaying flesh as she'd seen and dealt with numerous injuries over the years, many that had turned gangrenous.

She pulled back the cloth of a shirt of one man, finding his belly was torn open and a knife protruded from his chest. He had no weapons of his own, and it was likely the sickle was rammed into the other occupant's head. It appeared, by their position, these two men killed each other.

When Tor came to her feet the others were no longer standing at the door. She wiped her hands on her pants and stepped into the tiny street.

"Anything interesting?" Clairla asked.

"They killed each other. But I don't know why. Happened only a few days ago by the rate of the decay."

"Well, maybe there are others that will give us a better idea of what happened." Clairla headed down the street, toward what was likely the center of the village.

"I think it's obvious what caused this unrest," Tor called after her. She could see Clairla nod, but she didn't turn or speak.

The beast ran in and out of the shadows between the buildings. Tor assumed she was doing her own patrol, as her movements were not as playful as they were in the fields.

The street opened up into a large space with buildings creating a circle around a well. This was the center of town, the buildings different shops: a baker, clothing stores, delis, and the like. Stalls were tipped on their sides, some smashed but a few burned. The meat was rotten and decaying, the bread moldy and inedible.

The four stood in the square for a short time when Tor spotted another body in the window of a shop. The glass was broken and the body was draped over the window frame, a large butcher's ax sticking out of her back. On the ground in front of her was a serrated knife, used for skinning and gutting fish.

There was no one in the shop, and looked like whoever killed this woman had left without taking their weapon.

"Maybe we should split up," Clairla said as she stepped out of the cheesemonger's store. "I need to find the Travelers Lodge. I think it's back that way"—she pointed toward the towering stone walls of the labyrinth—"at the opening of the Ruins."

"To find your friends?" Pac asked.

Clairla nodded.

"I'll go with you," Tor said. "You two search this area a bit more. There still might be some food or supplies we can take with us. Check if the well water is clean enough to drink and fill our canteens." Tor removed her canteen, and Clairla did the same.

"How would we know if it's good to drink?" Eydis said, leaning over the stone wall of the well.

Tor dug in her medical satchel and pulled out a tiny vial. "Three drops of this should do. If the water turns a murky green, it's contaminated." She handed it to Pac, who was standing closest to her. "Okay, Clairla, let's go."

Clairla nodded and headed for a different street, as the one they'd come down didn't have the building they were looking for. As they made their way back to the stone wall, Joonee walked alongside Tor. Every so often, Tor would enter a building or a home to find it in different states of disarray. She found bodies in a fraction of the homes, and the remaining ones looked as if they'd been stripped of valuables. It was like people had left in a rush and took only what they could carry.

"The dome must have caused these people to go crazy," Clairla said. She had stopped at the end of the street, was staring. Tor was too far back to see whatever she was looking at. She picked up her pace and stopped when the scene came into view.

Bodies were piled up at the opening of the Ruins Labyrinth, men and women tangled in battle, dozens crushed by large stone slabs.

"Why would they come here? The entire village just wiped each other out." Clairla's voice was thick, and Tor spotted a single tear just before Clairla brushed it away.

"I think they came here to get to the fairies. Maybe they figured out it was the dome that was driving them mad and they wanted to put an end to it." Tor hoped this gave Clairla a little peace. "I think, though, there were people who got away. Many of the homes I checked down these streets looked like they'd packed up and left."

Clairla's shoulders rose and fell, then she pulled them back and marched toward the Travelers Lodge. The two stepped through the door and were surprised to find it completely empty. No sign of struggle, no bodies left to decay.

"If your friends stayed here they'll have signed the log book," Tor said, heading for the front desk. "It'll be easier than going from room to room. This place looks pretty big."

Clairla nodded without moving from her spot. "Many come here to trade with the fairies. Sometimes, I swear people come here just to see if they can get through the labyrinth. Like some sort of thrill-seekers."

Tor found the large book that tracked visitors and their fees. She ran her finger down the list to find names that didn't have deceased or departed written next to it—the owner obviously needed to keep track of those who didn't make it out alive. One wouldn't want to be caught cleaning out valuables.

"Striden?" She read, glancing up at Clairla who shook her head. "Kepleer?"

"No."

"Dalphine?"

"No."

Tor let out an impatient sigh. "Why don't you come over here and look. It would save us a great deal of time."

Clairla stepped up next to Tor and pulled the large tome toward her. She ran her finger down the list, stopping at one.

"Prydwen," Tor read aloud. "Says they've departed. I guess that's good your friend got out."

"She isn't the friend I'm looking for." Clairla flipped the page and continued her search, then stopped again. "There, that's them."

Tor leaned in. "Niviel and Zaden. They've departed too." Tor slapped Clairla on the shoulder, then squeezed gently. "This is good news; your friends have made it out alive. About two months ago, by the looks of it." Tor headed for the door, then she turned with a frown.

"What's wrong?" Clairla asked. "You were just trying to cheer me up, now you look like *your* friends just died."

"We came here looking for them because they would be able to help us with this Realm Eater. But who knows where they've gone."

"They'll be heading toward Grashneet City. That is, if they caught up to Prydwen. My visions showed they would."

Tor contemplated her. "Are your visions telling you they're going to Grashneet?"

Clairla shook her head. "Ever since the storms started my visions are jumbled. They make little to no sense. If I still had a trio, maybe I could make sense of them, but..."

"Then how do you know—"

"I had the vision of Prydwen months ago. Eight, to be exact. Before all of this. I'm the one who told Niviel and Zaden to come here."

Tor nodded, then gestured toward the door. "Let's get back to the others so we can get out of this village. I'm starting to feel the urge to smash things. More so than earlier. Earlier I was just angry. Now I want to hurt people."

Clairla sighed and reached for the door. "Me too."

CHAPTER TWENTY-SEVEN

T HEY LEFT THE TINY VILLAGE, armed with canteens filled with fresh water and a small variety of cheeses and dried meat. With their tempers flaring, Tor and Clairla thought it best they moved away from the village and the fairies' dome as quickly as possible. There was no argument. They jogged for more than an hour down the road leading away from the farming village.

When they started feeling less of the effects, they slowed to a walk and took the opportunity to drink and have a small bite to eat. Tor shared her rations with Joonee.

Tor looked in the direction of the towers of the High Kingdom's castle. Even though the explosion had caused them to collapse, Tor knew they wouldn't be able to see them if they hadn't. With the nearly pitch-black sky over the city and surrounding area, it seemed even farther away. Only periodic flashes of light were visible. Tor couldn't feel the static, but she could imagine how unbearable it must be to those sensitive to live so close.

"Not that I'm complaining," Eydis said.

"But you're going to anyway," Pac said.

Eydis shot her some side-eye and continued. "If we cut through Misandria Region to get to Grashneet, we are going to have some issues."

"Why's that?" Pac asked.

Tor stopped, causing everyone else to do the same. She glanced at Clairla. "He has a point. I've never been through Misandria myself, but orcs this side of the swamps are rarely welcome anywhere. You don't look human enough and Eydis, being an unclaimed man, will be considered a runaway and punished."

Clairla stared at Pac, her hands on her hips.

"What?" Pac asked.

"She can pass for human. She's a little pale—"

"But who isn't right now," Tor finished for her.

Eydis and Pac studied each other, and Pac was the first to speak. "What exactly does that mean? I can only assume it has something to do with him." She jabbed a thumb toward Eydis. "I've traveled through the region—"

"When?" Eydis cut her short.

Pac narrowed her eyes and Tor could see her jaw clench. "I was a young girl, being escorted to the High Kingdom...to be sacrificed."

Eydis's mouth formed an 'O,' and he dropped his gaze to the ground.

"So, you know how it works then?" Tor was hopeful she knew enough to get them through the region without a problem.

Pac shook her head. "I was only a child, and all I remember is Enya doing all the talking and trading. Jardeth was left to care for me."

"It's really not going to be that difficult," Clairla said. "All you have to do is say that Eydis is your husband...maybe brother would be better," she said after looking at him. "You look a little too young to be married just yet, especially to an older man."

"I'm not that old." Eydis stuck his bottom lip out slightly. The sight made Tor smile and Pac giggle, and the lack of embarrassment let Tor know Eydis was playing. She was glad and relieved to see her old friend returning to his light-hearted self.

"We look nothing alike." Pac put her hands on her hips, looking Eydis up and down.

"Doesn't matter." Clairla shook her head. "As long as you say he is your brother, they won't question you. Their only concern in the Misandria Region is whether or not a man is claimed. It can be by a relative or a spouse. Tell them he's a mutt."

"A mutt?" the others asked at once.

"Yes. You will have to be a mutt, too, but that won't change anything."

Tor and Pac's brows both furrowed, but Tor was the first to speak. "Explain what that means first. It doesn't sound like a positive situation."

Confusion crossed Clairla's face for a brief moment. "Right, sorry. Forgot I'm the only one from around here." She turned back to Pac. "In this region, a mutt means that your mother's husband could not produce children. So, she bedded another man—two different men, in your case, since you both look so different."

"Seems simple enough." Eydis shrugged.

"The question may never even come up, and if you claim he's your brother they may not even ask for any other information." Clairla readjusted her pack. "Can we get moving now? My bag is getting very uncomfortable."

Tor agreed, and turned back down the tiny road leading from the village to Misandria Region. She stopped after a couple steps. "What about us? How do we explain us?"

Clairla narrowed her eyes for a moment, then smiled. "Do you have a writing implement?" she asked Tor.

"Of course." Confused by the request, she still dug in her bag and pulled it out along with a notebook.

Clairla took the utensil but waved off the notebook. She grabbed Tor's right wrist, then shoved Tor's sleeve to her elbow. After chanting several words under her breath she began to draw on Tor's forearm. It only took a few minutes for the shape of a dagger, running through an eye and with a square at the tip, to appear.

When she was done, she handed Tor the utensil once again and smiled. The three stared at the markings.

"And what is this supposed to mean?" Tor said.

"For the next few days, because this is how long it will last, you are a member of the Walled City's chapter of assassins. You show that symbol to anyone and they won't even give you a second look."

"I'm an orc."

"You could be a frog, but with that tattoo you command a great deal of respect and power in this region. Trust me."

Tor pursed her lips, and with a slight head tilt she pulled her sleeve back down. "Okay, if you say so." They started back down the road.

Eydis sidled up next to Clairla and Tor. "So, how do you know so much about this region?"

"I live in the Great Walled City."

"Ah, okay, that makes sense then." Eydis dropped back behind them again. Joonee ran from one side of the road to the other, chasing small animals, but not seeming to have any luck catching anything.

"What's the Great Walled City?" Pac asked.

"It's a city with a wall around it." Eydis responded. Tor could almost hear the smirk in his voice.

"Thank you for that; it's very helpful." Pac's tone was not amused.

Clairla talked over her shoulder. "It's the capital to the Misandria Region. It was where the King and Queen once lived, who ruled over this land centuries ago. The Walled City is a little more forward-thinking, as with it being on the outskirts of Misandria the laws for the two areas changed. In the Walled City, men have the same rights as women."

There was silence for a few moments before Pac spoke again.

"If it's the capital, then how can it be on the outskirts of the Region?"

"The Goblin Uprising pushed the boundaries back, and they never returned when the uprising was over."

Eydis sighed. "All right, enough with the history lesson."

"Maybe some of us like history," Pac said.

"Maybe some of us don't care that some of us like history." Eydis's tone was snarky, and Tor could imagine his face scrunched and him giving a mocking head wobble when he said it.

"Maybe the fact that you can't think of anything but food is part of the problem. No room for any thoughts other than roasted chicken."

"Well, maybe the accelerated growth from where you came from didn't give your brain enough time to fully develop."

"How is my wanting to learn more the sign of an underdeveloped brain?"

Eydis stuttered, then said, "Because."

"They certainly squabble like siblings," Clairla said to Tor.

Tor laughed. "That they do."

The argument went back and forth for several more minutes before they wore each other down and stopped talking altogether. Tor welcomed the silence. It was a relief the groups' feelings of anger, and the want to be violent, had begun to pass once they left the borders of the village and moved further east away from the dome. But the looming darkness that sat in front of them now left a completely different uneasiness in Tor's gut.

This Niviel and Zaden have better be in Grashneet, Tor thought. She didn't know what was so important about these two, but if Clairla believed they would be an asset then it may be worth the detour—as Tor had no idea how they were supposed to close the rift over the High Kingdom. The battle magic she knew were mostly protection spells and some nuisance magic. She doubted giving the guards a flaky scalp would do them much good.

Her mind drifted to the journal Abacuss had left for her and the letter he had written inside. Immediately, it came to her that the book may have been damaged in the river. She reached into her jacket and pulled out the weatherproof pouch. When she opened it, much to her despair, water trickled out.

"What's that?" Clairla asked.

Tor mumbled, "Nothing, just a journal." Tears threatened as she carefully opened the pages. Many had stuck together, and some tore away in her hand, and on the pages that were dry the words were smudged. She didn't have the heart to check the back, where Abacuss's final words to her were. She shook out the pouch then placed the book back inside.

"Look on your face tells me it wasn't just a journal." Clairla's voice was soft. "Do you want to talk about it?"

"No." Tor put the pouch and the book back into her pocket, and continued down the road. She would get enough courage later to check if the letter remained intact or not.

The thick forest seemed to span for kilometers, the narrow road disappearing into them. They stopped for a quick bite of a measly meal of cheese and dried meat, then put on their heavier clothes. Traveling through the woods would be much colder as it was likely no sun would get through the canopy. None of them knew how long they would need to travel through the woods, and they all hoped the road cut all the way through.

They had moved toward the woods when the static reached its peak and the pressure dropped. They all braced themselves, waiting for the lightning to strike, and a sense of relief washed over them when it struck the fairies' dome kilometers away.

One by one, they filed into the tree line. The road narrowed slightly, but a small horse and cart could still fit through with a little room on either side. The further in they moved, the darker it became and the more the temperature dropped.

Joonee stayed close to Tor who, although she didn't have any weapons out, kept a watchful eye on her surroundings. The problem was the deep shadows and the strange designs the trees cast, making it difficult to tell if they were alone or not.

The sounds of birds, bugs, and other wildlife was faint. Every so often came the snap of a branch or the rustle of leaves in the distance, but it seemed to echo and was difficult to pinpoint from where it came.

"Think we can speed the pace up a bit?" Eydis asked from the back of the group.

"You scared?" Pac asked.

"Cold," Eydis said back. His tone showed no fear, so Tor knew he was merely cold.

Perhaps she was the only one uneasy in this situation, but there was a feeling in her stomach, a pull of sorts, that nagged at her. She could often sense different types of magic being used, as the static was always different. Some would leave an odd taste in her mouth, bitter or sour. But the woods, the looming darkness, had a feel she had never felt before.

It was a magic that was dark; not blood magic, but much more sinister. The taste in her mouth was neither bitter nor sour, but rather metallic. Like she had been sucking on a copper piece for a while. It was the same taste as when Pac had come through the rift, but the one thing that made it difficult to understand was there was no static. She didn't feel as though magic was being used, rather was just present.

Perhaps the woods themselves were the magic she sensed. There were several forests in the area that had their own magical principals, and some even had beings that lived in the forests—like sprites and nymphs.

Tor decided it was perhaps best she ask instead of assume. After all, she could just be overreacting. "Does anyone know what this forest is called?"

"Caliginous Woods," Clairla said.

"Fitting." Tor shrugged.

"A bit obvious." Pac let out a humorless laugh.

Clairla shrugged. "What can I say, Misandria Region is filled with simple farmers. Why complicate things if you don't have to."

Eydis scratched his head. "Why is it so obvious and fitting? I mean, these woods are pretty dim and misty. Why not just call it the Dim and Misty Woods." He snorted a laugh. "Why call it some strange word, like caligidiouns?" He snorted again but stopped when he noticed everyone staring at him. "What?"

"You're such an idiot," Pac said.

Tor pursed her lips, and Eydis spoke, "Maybe you're the idiot, ever think of that?"

Clairla sighed. "'Caliginous' means dim or misty; they were being obvious when they named the woods that."

Pac laughed. "I guess you're even simpler than the farmers around here."

Tor spoke to Clairla to stop the inevitable argument. "You've traveled through here often?"

Clairla sighed, indifferent. "A few times. Not many. I stayed close to home, and the woods were a little further than I liked to travel."

The conversation sank into silence again. Tor figured if the woods had an odd feel to it Clairla would have noticed, certain the fae would have said something if there was a problem. More comfortable now, Tor relaxed her readiness but ran through several magical incantations for shielding in her head.

She didn't notice that Joonee's hackles were up until Clairla grabbed her wrist. Tor looked down at the fae as several snapping twigs and the sound of feet on gravel hit her ear. Clairla released her, and Tor drew her eyes up to the road ahead.

Three hooded figures stood several feet away. Their faces were covered in shadow, from both the dim light of the forest and the hoods they wore pulled down. She contemplated them; there was something familiar with the cloaks they wore. She had seen them before, but where? Tor glanced around, but couldn't make out how many were in the woods. The deep shadows hindered her being able to see human shapes against the trees; they all cast the same dark silhouettes.

"We're just passing through," Tor said to the ones in front of her. "We don't want any trouble."

The figures didn't move or make a sound.

Maybe they don't speak Totrigian, she thought. She repeated her statement again, in another common dialect. No response. She tried a rudimentary attempt at the Dragoon language, but still nothing. Her last option was her own native tongue, orc. When none of these worked, Clairla stepped up.

She tried elvish, goblin, dwarvish, and, lastly, the ancient words of the fae. It was a language Tor had never heard spoken before, but it was quite lovely and left her feeling light and airy.

Before another word could be said, Tor heard a strangled cry. When she turned, she spotted Eydis locked in battle with a figure that must have come up from behind. Pac was fighting two others, but before Tor could move she felt a blow to the side of her head.

Her knees gave out from under her, and before she could think past the fuzziness in her brain she heard a deep, guttural growl come from her Shadow beast. Joonee lunged at the first attacker, latching onto his forearm. He cried out as he stumbled away, trying to get away from the beast.

Tor pulled her short knife from her belt in time to swing out as a second attacker came at her. They jumped back out of her reach, but it was enough for Tor to get back on her feet. She towered over the person coming at her once again.

The attacker smelled of raw meat and oil—not the pleasant essential oils she used for many of her elixirs, but rather the oil used to polish and shine weapons. The meat-and-oil smelling attacker slashed out at Tor's arm; the sharp tip of the blade caught her upper arm, cutting her sleeve and catching the skin enough for it to bleed.

To Tor, it was more of a nuisance than an injury. Meat-and-Oil had barely nicked her. Tor swung out at him, using her fist rather than the blade. In that moment she still remembered her oath: She couldn't kill this person, but she could knock them out. She bore down on the smaller attacker, pushing them back. Using an open hand, Tor slapped Meat-and-Oil. When they brought their hand up to strike her, she smacked it back down.

Tor knew if she could hit them hard enough she would knock them out. Ready to strike again, Tor felt the hair on her arms stand on end.

"Not now," she mumbled as the static in the air began to rise. Perhaps the trees would protect them. That's when she noticed the change, a metallic taste grew in her mouth; never leading up to a lightning strike had this happened before.

For her to get a taste in her mouth, someone had to be casting nearby. Which meant someone in the woods was about to use magic. The metallic taste grew stronger as she tried to figure out who was doing it. She heard a small crack and a snap behind her, and as Tor began to turn she heard Clairla scream out.

"Tor!"

A rush of air struck Tor in the midsection, tossing her several feet into the woods and off the road. The tree that stopped her snapped in two, crashing to the ground. Tor pushed herself into a seated position and shook her head.

Her vision was a little fuzzy, and her back and neck ached terribly, like something was jabbing her, and her head pounded. She spotted Clairla about ten feet to her left, lying on her stomach and unmoving. Eydis was out of sight and Pac stood in the middle of the road, facing off with at least five attackers.

Tor's heart raced; the girl would be killed for sure. She had to help, had to find a way. Pac had no magic, as her blood magic had been drained during the botched sacrifice. Tor closed her eyes and chanted one of the shielding spells in her head. But, with her mind still fuzzy, she kept leaving out words or mispronouncing them. She could barely move one of her arms, and could only use one hand for the movements required.

She could see Pac was talking, but couldn't hear anything from where she lay. Panic began to rise when the group moved toward Pac. She stood her ground, one foot planted just behind the other and a look of determination on her face. As if leaning into a wind, Pac brought her hands up to shoulder height and showed her palms to the other attackers.

Was she surrendering? They stopped and stepped back. Tor struggled to get to her feet. She couldn't let Pac die. She had to help. A sharp, blinding pain ran down her back and legs when she tried to stand, causing her to drop back.

She could feel herself losing consciousness, and glanced one last time at Pac. At that exact moment, Pac brought her hands together and the static in the air built so fast, the air pressure dropping so quickly, that Tor felt light-headed from the lack of air. The clap of thunder was so loud the concussive force pushed Tor flat on her back, knocking her out.

CHAPTER TWENTY-EIGHT

TOR WOKE TO THE CRACKLING of fire and warmth on her face. She winced as she tried to sit.

Pac put a hand on her shoulder and gently pushed her back down. "You should lie still for a bit longer. You're back isn't fully healed yet. Moving may cause further damage."

Tor moved her head to see the others sitting by the fire. Clairla was tending meat on a spit, and Eydis was cleaning his blade. He had a gash on his face and one hand was bandaged. Clairla looked unscathed by the attack until she shifted and Tor spotted the sling around her arm.

"The strangers?" Tor croaked. She felt as though she hadn't talked in days. She touched her throat to find a bandage around it.

"Your neck was cut. It was superficial, but you may have some difficulty speaking for a few days." Pac smiled.

"We were all very lucky," Clairla said, giving half an unamused smile.

Eydis pointed the blade he was cleaning at Pac. "If it wasn't for her, we would all be dead. I'm sure of it." He sheathed his knife and picked up his sword.

"How long?" Tor rasped.

Pac glanced at Clairla. "Hours. I can't tell with the canopy being so thick." Clairla looked up. "But I'd say we are well past six. It was midday when we entered the woods, and we walked about an hour or so before we met our friends. I'd say it's been at least seven to ten hours since it all started." She looked at Pac, who nodded.

"That sounds about right. You were the only one that was knocked out for more than a few minutes."

Eydis didn't look up from his task, but she could hear the thickness in his voice. "We weren't sure if you would ever wake up."

Tor gave a weak smile and laid her head back down, then jolted upright and again winced against the pain. "Joonee?"

Clairla smiled and pointed to the other side of the fire. "She's fine." With her dark, black-and-silver fur she was difficult to see in the dim light of the fire. As the light flickered she appeared, then disappeared, from view.

Tor smiled again and laid back. Relieved that everyone, including her Shadow beast, had survived the encounter. Images of the battle flashed through her mind. She was about to ask Pac about the final moments she'd witnessed when Pac appeared by her head.

"Drink this," she said, holding a cup to Tor's lips. "It will help you rest and heal. We'll talk more in the morning. For now, you must rest."

Looking into Pac's eyes, Tor was mesmerized by how the young girl seemed to have grown into a mature, well-balanced woman. She needed to learn more about where Pac had come from. But for now, her eyes were just too heavy to keep open.

Birds overhead woke Tor, and she blinked to find the woods a little brighter than the last time she was up. Whatever was in the drink Pac had given her she'd been out for the entire night. Tor shifted to get her hands into a position to push herself up. The pain was gone, but she was so stiff she groaned when she moved.

The fire was all but out, and Clairla was standing closest to her. "Good to see you're finally awake. We were starting to consider dragging you out of the woods."

"How long?" She touched her throat, her voice not yet back to normal. "Drink?" she said, trying to produce her own saliva to wet her mouth.

Eydis handed her a canteen. She noted it wasn't very heavy, so only took a small drink. "You've been out all night and most the morning now."

Clairla reached her hand out to Tor. "Think you can stand?"

Tor nodded and took the tiny fae's hand. She doubted Clairla could actually bear any of her weight to get her off the ground, but then Eydis offered his. The two heaved Tor to her feet, and Eydis helped to steady her.

Tor nodded her thanks. The forest spun slightly and she nearly toppled over.

"You hit your head pretty hard when you were tossed," Pac said as she walked up to the camp. "I think it's best we get a move on. Our new friends won't stay away for much longer."

Eydis grabbed Tor's bags and handed her medical satchel to Clairla, then shouldered her other bag. "Just until you work out some of that stiffness. We need to move quickly, so we'll lighten your load."

Tor put a hand on his shoulder and nodded. He didn't need to explain. She didn't like having someone else carry her load, but she understood. Seeing as how she had barely survived the first attack from their new friends, Tor was certain she wouldn't be of any help in a second round.

Her movements were clumsy and difficult on the uneven terrain of the forest floor, but once she was back on the gravel road it was much easier to move. As the minutes passed she stretched out her legs and back, loosening up and getting all the stiffness out of her body. It didn't take long before she was taking on the weight of her own belongings.

Tor rubbed the hair on her forearm to get it to lie down. As her hand passed over the tattoo on her arm, she sighed heavily. The idea of her being a cleric healer and an assassin held an odd appeal.

With everything that had happened over the past few months, perhaps a career change would be in order. As she understood how the assassins worked, she could choose her own contracts. She shook the strange, stray thought from her mind and pulled the sleeve of her jacket down over her arm.

The static in the air was thick, and becoming a nuisance. She waited impatiently for the lightning to strike, but it never came. That's when she noticed the static wasn't quite the same. It was lighter, and although it had the same effects as the lightning static—hair on end, a drop in air pressure—it felt more like a vibration.

The metallic taste she'd had in her mouth the previous day was almost gone. It was still at the back of her throat, but there was another taste layered over top. Tor ran her tongue over the roof of her mouth and swallowed, trying to get a better taste of it. It was sweet, like just-ripe fruit. That didn't belong in this world, either. It was not natural to their magic.

Tor glanced down at Clairla. She had tucked her jacket behind her sais, making them more accessible if necessary. There was a quite hum coming from her; an odd tune, sounding almost off-key but in a strangely pleasant way.

Clairla glanced up at Tor and wrinkled her brow. "What?"

Tor noted the humming didn't stop when she spoke. She turned to glance over her shoulder. Pac was just several paces behind her and Eydis, along with Joonee, were a few paces behind Pac. Tor looked back to Clairla.

"What?" She asked again.

Tor cleared her throat. "That humming; do you hear it?"

Clairla nodded. "It's Pac, she's been doing that for most the night. Strange, isn't it? It's almost pretty, but then she just can't get those certain notes."

"And the static?"

"What about it?"

"It's not lightning static, and it tastes and feels different." She started coughing from straining her voice and took a couple sips from her canteen.

Clairla looked over her shoulder. "I noticed that, too. I don't want to make any assumptions, but I think that's Pac as well. Those friends from yesterday certainly didn't feel like this when they started using their magic."

"Who were they?"

"You should save your voice," Pac said from behind. "I'll answer your questions when we get out of these woods."

"And when will that be?" Eydis called up. "It's dark, cold, and creepy in here."

All eyes fell on Clairla and she sighed, shrugging. "Shouldn't be much longer. But, like I said before we came in here, it's been a very long time since I've been."

Not satisfied with any of the conversation, Tor remained silent. Her throat ached and her muscles were screaming, so Tor did her best to straighten and pull her shoulders back. The movement helped to relieve some tension but made her acutely aware of the worst of her injuries.

The orc side of her took over, and she said nothing about the discomfort she was in. Instead, she concentrated on other things. She tried to remember what happened the night before, during the battle. They'd tried seven different languages on the strangers. Did they not respond because they didn't understand, or because they didn't want to?

Who were they? The coats and hoods they wore were a familiar design, and they had appeared to wear black hand coverings. Or were they tattoos? She couldn't see any of their faces as they were hidden under their hoods, and they'd used the deep shadows of the woods to hide themselves further.

Tor shifted the pack, again pulling her shoulders back and down to try and get more comfortable. But her muscles were all so sore and stiff it just seemed to make things worse. She sighed, and tried to recall anything else about the fight.

The static had been thick in the air, and the metallic taste was strong—like she had a mouth full of copper pieces. Tor furrowed her brow as she tried to recall the different types of magic used in Totriga and her Realms. She had not experienced all of them, but she had read about their effects in the Rejuvenation Monastery's library.

Knowing the different magics, and how they react, was a necessary knowledge for healing. Healing magic required a delicate balance of the different magics to work most efficiently. But not one of those she'd studied claimed the taste of metal.

Her mind drifted from the fight to the journal. Abacuss talked about his people. It was the first time she had ever heard him mention them. She needed to find out if his letter had survived. She pulled the journal from her pocket and removed it from the pouch. Taking a deep breath, she opened the book near the back, where the note should be.

She sighed inwardly when it appeared intact and readable. She skimmed over the few sentences she had read already, then continued.

> *In this desire my people chose to cross a Veil into a world in which we had no place; made deals with creatures that sought the same as us: domination.*
>
> *My dear Tor, I did things that I am not proud of. I destroyed, conquered, and ruled people that I had no place doing. I sought out redemption, and I needed to make an amends for the destruction that I caused. So I fled—*

"What are you reading?" Clairla asked.

Tor tightened her lips, but was about to speak when Eydis shouted.

"Finally!" He sped past.

Tor had been so lost in the journal she hadn't noticed the break in the trees, or the road open up into the middle of two fields. She put the journal back as a pack of houses came into view, although they were at least a couple kilometers away. The sky was dark, but not a nighttime dark, and the fields were empty except for the dying wheat stalks. The lack of sun and rain had likely been their demise.

The taste of fruit and the vibrations began to dissipate, along with the tune Pac hummed.

"We should be able to find shelter in that village." Clairla pointed, then looked from Pac to Eydis. "Remember, brother and sister. The two of you are brother and sister. Eydis, you must walk behind Pac and act as subservient to her as you can."

Eydis grumbled, dragging his feet, but returned to the back of the pack.

They fell silent once again as they walked toward the village. Just ten minutes out of the woods, the lightning static began to build. It was slow and Tor found it irritating. The air pressure dropped and they all braced for the strike. With great relief, it flashed and landed in the far distance behind them. There was no smoke, so Tor assumed it hadn't hit the forest but the ground just beyond the other side.

When they entered the village there were a few people milling about, but it looked as though they were closing up shop and retiring for the day. A few women stopped to eye Eydis. Pac put a hand on his forearm and nodded at the women. It seemed to appease them enough they didn't speak up, or perhaps they really didn't care.

Tor noted the shops through the windows, the shelves were bare, and food was scarce. She supposed the last thing on her mind would be an unclaimed man wandering about when she had no food for her family. The few people they encountered appeared tired and worn down. Starving.

Tor desperately wanted to help. She wished she could give them food, but their own supplies were all but gone. Shame ran through her, as she was breaking her vow to help others. It was her way of life; her religion was to heal and care for the less fortunate. Everyone in this village certainly fell into those categories. Then a bigger regret struck when she remembered her thoughts of joining the assassins.

Clairla must have sensed Tor's struggle as she put a hand on her forearm. "There is nothing we can do for these people. You must know that."

"There is something," Pac said.

"Really?" Tor asked.

Pac pointed toward the High Kingdom. "Seal that rift and the sun will shine again, growing their crops and healing this world."

"Oh, is that all?" Eydis said with an eye roll. "Simple as cupping Gronk's hairy balls." The three women stared at him, but he didn't seem to notice and pointed down the street. "There's an inn. Let's hope they're open." He took two steps before Pac grabbed his arm. "What?"

"You can't be wandering around on your own," she said through gritted teeth.

"Oh, right. Well, then let's go." He waved his hands at the women to usher them toward the inn.

With great relief, they found the inn was indeed open and the owner was ecstatic to see them. Likely very few people traveled through this part of the region, and even fewer since the rift had opened. She gave them two rooms; Pac and Clairla sharing as Tor and Eydis had known each other for so long they were okay with sharing a room.

It had been a long day, and Tor's body ached and her throat

was itchy and scratched. She fixed herself an elixir for her throat, as well as a sedative to help herself rest.

There was no argument from anyone about going to bed early, and Eydis was snoring even before Tor thought about climbing into her bed. Joonee took up half of it, but all Tor could do was smile. She grabbed the journal from her coat pocket and climbed in. She hoped no one would disturb her this time.

So I fled to another Realm. I found my true calling as a healer. Death and destruction was all I knew, and I'd thought it was who I was going to be. Who I was born to be. Instead it was who I had to be in order to become who I truly am.

Do you understand? You were born a warrior, but you are meant to be a healer. The time will come when you must choose. When—

Tor flipped the page and found the rest had been soaked, the words smudged and unreadable. She read over the entire letter again. What did he mean by her having to choose? Where had he come from? What people had he ruled over?

Tor closed the book and put it on the nightstand next to her. She scooted down in the bed and lay on her side, giving Joonee room at the end. Sleep didn't come quickly for her; there were too many questions.

CHAPTER TWENTY-NINE

THEIR MORNING MEAL WAS MEAGER, but it was better than having nothing. Although the innkeeper was happy to have guests again, it was apparent she didn't have much else to offer outside of a bed. They didn't stay long, as it was imperative they got to Grashneet. The more time passed the more people died from starvation, their crops unable to grow and sustain life with the permanent darkness caused by the clouds coming from the High Kingdom. This was proven by the mass graves they started to see as they moved through the region.

Tor dropped back to walk next to Pac. Her voice was still raspy, but her own elixir had helped with the healing through the night. Joonee walked a couple paces ahead, her head moving back and forth—something Tor equated to her being on patrol and watching for danger. Tor would glance at Pac every so often, taking note of the changes in her. They had been together for a several weeks now, but she had only just taken real notice since Tor had been preoccupied with healing Joonee.

Pac was a beautiful young lady, and seemed to have lived a good life in this other realm, but the time dilation must have been drastic if she could age nearly fifteen years in only five months. The static around the girl had once again changed from when she was a child. Her features had seemed to soften, and though her skin tone was still quite pale, she had some color.

"You have questions," Pac said to Tor.

"You said you didn't have any magic."

"When did I say that?"

Tor tilted her head. "The first night you were back, you said you had no magic."

A half smile formed on Pac's face. It was just short of an eye roll. "No, what I said was my blood magic was nearly completely drained, and the world I was pushed into didn't have magic, or had very little magic."

Tor scrunched up her face in confusion.

"It's difficult to understand, yes." Pac readjusted the shoulder straps of her bag. "When High King Thomas tried to invoke my magic by draining my blood, he didn't anticipate it being as powerful as it was. Nor did he anticipate my fighting back."

"You fought back?" Clairla asked from behind. "How?"

"As I felt the life drain from my body, I used my magic. I was still so very young, and didn't fully understand what I was doing. But the elixir Jardeth had fed me changed my magic, made it even more powerful."

"You knew about the elixir?" Clairla asked. "Did Jardeth tell—"

"I was a child, but I wasn't stupid." She smiled, giving a light laugh with no malice or anger behind it. "I understood he was only trying to save my life. I could feel it was changing me. But I believe there was something else nobody anticipated."

"What's that?" Tor asked.

"The sun," she said with another smile.

"I don't understand," Eydis said.

"I am originally from the Shadow Realm. I was pulled across the Veil when I was just a babe by the dwarf king's son."

Eydis's eyebrows came together. "Yes, I know you've already told us this."

Tor knew Eydis's question would be answered so she ignored it and asked, "What did the sun do to you?"

"Being in the light started to change me. I was becoming less a Shadow and more of a hybrid human." She teetered her hands back and forth. Her analogy obviously had flaws. "If I were left with just the sun, I believe my magic would have disappeared. But Jardeth's elixir bonded me to my magic in a very different way. By the time we reached the High Kingdom, my magic was more than blood magic. It was the very fiber of my being. So when the king tried to take it, I cast my own spell at the same time. I'd meant to just push him away, but I misjudged my own strength and ended up punching through the Veil of this realm and into a completely different universe."

"It saved your life," Clairla said. "And no one has seen the High King since."

"I can't speak to what's happened to the king, nor do I care. But the place I was sent to, the people who raised me, they taught me how to hone my magic."

Tor said, "So you did have magic in the other world."

"Yes, but only where the worlds had collided." Her tone was condescending.

Eydis asked, "Why only there?"

Pac threw her hands up. "Do you people not understand anything about the magic you use? Do you just toss your incantations and elixirs around like wood in a fire?"

Tor lifted an eyebrow. "That tone isn't required. If you have knowledge you think we should have—"

"If? If?" Pac gave a low growl. "In order for anything to work, in order for us to close that rift, you need to understand how your magic works."

"Then explain it," Eydis nearly shouted. "Get down off this righteous pedestal you seem to be standing on and explain it!" He balled up his fists when Tor placed a hand on his arm. His breathing steadied out again.

Pac fell silent for a moment. Tor noticed Pac's cheeks pink up and she dropped her eyes. It left her with the impression that Pac had been scolded about such things before.

"It's simple," Pac said, her tone smooth, more kind than annoyed. "All magic comes from the Veils of the Realms anchored to this world. That is why the static feels different and tastes different depending on the magic that is being used. We will have to bring all the magics together, which means we will have to pull from all the Veils."

Clairla said, "I understand."

"You do?" Eydis asked.

"Yes, we used the magic from the other Veils to seal the Shadow Realm. That is why several Realms have also been sealed shut. It was the only way to contain the seal on the Shadow Realm."

Eydis said, "But those Veils are still there. If they are sealing the Shadow Realm, then why wouldn't we be able to cross—"

"Because," Pac interrupted, bordering on being condescending again. "It takes magic from the Veil to cross a Veil. These other Realms were sealed because all their extra magic is containing the Shadow Realm."

"That must be how the Shadow soldiers are crossing over." Tor spoke mostly to herself.

"But it's sealed," Clairla said.

Pac curled her lip. "No, if you're seeing a lot of Shadow soldiers—"

Tor cut her off. "We are."

Pac continued. "The rift over the High Kingdom is drawing from the Veils. So, their seal on the Shadow Realm is weakening."

Tor sighed. "Well, that's just great."

"It may not all be bad news," Eydis said.

The women looked at him.

"Well, for Clairla anyway."

Clairla's eyes widened. "How do you figure?"

"If the Veils are weakening, you can be reunited with your trio."

Tor could see Eydis truly believed this was a good thing. Clairla's expression, on the other hand, spoke to something different. "The quicker we find Clairla's friends, the better."

The others nodded, and Pac said, "I agree. If we don't close that rift soon, we may never be able to before the Realm Eater comes."

They fell into silence for a long while, each taking turns being in the lead. They felt it best not to walk in a pack, but to spread out a bit.

It took the better part of a month for them to reach the edge of the regions borders, the city of Gloverree came into sight. From what they could tell, the sun was starting to set. Joonee stopped and lowered herself, her hackles rising and a growl growing in her chest.

Tor and the beast were in the lead and she pulled her rusty sword, hearing the others behind her pull their weapons.

"What do you see?" Clairla asked.

Tor shook her head, squinting into the dusk, but she couldn't see what Joonee could. Perhaps the beast smelled something. Joonee was three paces ahead and Tor eased herself forward. She reached the beast as two men jumped out of the weeds by the side of the road.

Joonee was on the first in an instant, and the second was no match for Tor. She stood to her full height and merely pushed out her hand, palm out, and smacked the man in the face, knocking him back onto his ass.

"Stay down," she said. "Joonee, let him go." The others appeared by her side. The two men looked as though they hadn't eaten in weeks, which they probably hadn't. Their clothes were filthy and nearly rags. "We don't have anything for you." Tor's tone was kind. "I wish we could spare something, but we barely have enough to feed ourselves. I think it obvious you are no match."

The man Tor had knocked down sneered at her, while his companion cradled his arm.

"I can mend that for you," she offered, pulling out her pendant to show who she was.

"Gronk's hair balls you will!" He spat at her feet. "I'd rather die than let an orc touch me."

"Suit yourself," Pac said and pushed by. "Let's go, we don't have time to hang around." She kicked the man Tor had knocked down as she went by. "Don't follow us, or next time we'll kill you."

"Pac." Tor didn't know why she was scolding the girl. They really didn't have time and, if these men did follow, it would likely be with a much larger group of bandits. She wondered briefly where their women were. Unclaimed men running wild were unheard of in this region.

They followed Pac and walked past the two men, who indeed decided they would not follow.

———

The next week of travel was uneventful. Many of the farmers' fields were destroyed, either by obvious lightning strikes or having died out due to the lack of rain and sun. The villages, too, were sparse, with no inns in which to stay and barely any people at all.

"They must all be moving west," Eydis said.

Sensing he was worried about his family, Tor said, "I'm sure your brother got his family and Gran to safety."

Eydis smiled. "I'm sure the clerics and Parin are fine as well."

Tor smiled back, but knew they were both having the same thought as to what a beautiful lie they told each other. She was certain no one was okay, and she just hoped they were still alive.

They stayed as much to the outskirts of Gloverree as they could, and it only took an hour to get through the city with no people, horses, carts, or anything else to hinder their progress. Tor did notice the stench, and was certain she wasn't the only one. No one wanted to say anything because it meant acknowledging it.

When they passed by a building deep in shadows, Tor stopped and pulled her weapon. The smell of sulfur filled her nose.

"I don't think it's a good idea that we stop," Clairla said. "There will be too many of them for us to fight."

"Too many of what?" Eydis asked as he pulled his own sword.

"Can't you smell it?" Clairla wrinkled her nose.

Eydis shrugged. "I just assumed it was from the mass graves we passed. The winds shifted and—"

Two Shadow soldiers stepped out from dark recesses of the building Tor was watching. They didn't look as they had been dead for too long. In fact, they looked relatively fresh. Both were human, with male heads and torsos, but one had an arm that was much too small, yet it wasn't a woman's arm. Tor's eyes widened when she realized what the queen had used to piece this soldier together.

It was a child's arm, likely from one no more than eleven or twelve. Not quite at puberty yet, for the muscles had not begun to tone. Tor gritted her teeth and gripped her sword tighter. Ignoring the Shadow on the right, she dove at the one with the child's arm on the left.

She swung at its body, but it blocked it with the shield it held. Her rusty sword clanged as it hit the shiny, new shield of the King's Guard. It had a few dents, but otherwise looked as though it hadn't seen much battle.

It swung back at her using its child arm, but it was weak from the lack of muscle. Tor reminded herself that this was no longer a child, but a monster created by another monster. As the Shadow raised its arm, Tor gripped the wrist with one hand and swung her sword with the other, slicing the arm off at the shoulder.

The Shadow barely made a sound, as if nothing had happened. It dropped its shield and reached for the now-fallen sword from its other hand. Without a second thought, hesitation, or prayer of forgiveness, Tor raised her sword again and came down on the neck of the Shadow, taking its head clean off.

It rolled to Eydis's feet, who was standing over his own dead Shadow. Neither had time to speak before Eydis shoved Tor to the side and thrust his blade through the chest of another Shadow behind her. As he yanked his sword free, he pulled up and out to slice the body in half.

They stood panting and staring at each other, then looked for the rest. Clairla and Pac had engaged in their own battles, but it looked as though Pac was untouched. Tor assumed she hadn't even pulled a weapon, but used her magic instead.

"We really need to get out of here," Clairla said.

Tor dropped her rusty sword, which was now chipped in several places, and picked up the newer one from her first Shadow. "I agree, but how do we know that Grashneet isn't going to be just as bad?"

Pac grabbed a sword and two knives from the soldiers around her. "We don't. It's likely going to be much the same as here. But, think of it this way. When we reach the High Kingdom this will seem like playtime." She walked past Tor and smiled, patting her on the shoulder.

The others followed, and Eydis said, "Is that supposed to be a pep talk? 'Cause it sounded more like a warning."

CHAPTER THIRTY

THE ROAD TO GRASHNEET WASN'T as quiet as they had hoped. If not for bandits looking for food, they were fighting off Shadow soldiers who appeared to be moving toward the High Kingdom. As the city came into view, so did the billowing smoke above some sections. The only saving grace was that it appeared the city was quiet. It was difficult to tell if, or how many, people were still residing there. Tor estimated by the city size only several thousand—if that—were left.

If the Shadows in Gloverree had been any indication of what they may be walking into, she may be overestimating.

"Where do we need to go?" Tor asked Clairla.

They were kneeling in the ditch on the main road just outside the city, doing their best to stay out of sight. It was impossible to tell what time a day it was, and if not for Tor's timepiece she wouldn't have known it was just past nine p.m.

Clairla bit her lip.

"You do know where we're going, right?" Pac asked.

Now she bit her nail. "Well, to be honest—"

Eydis's eyebrows went so high Tor thought they may fly off his head completely. "To be honest? Seriously? Are you about to tell us that you don't really know if these friends of yours are in this city?" Eydis rubbed his eyes; no one had slept in several days. "I'm about to lose my mind."

"About to?" Pac said with a smile.

Clairla dropped her hand. "I've never been to Grashneet, so I'm not entirely certain where the inn for the assassins is." She bit her lip again. "And, no, I'm not positive that Niviel will be here since Zaden isn't, technically, an assassin."

Tor grunted. "Damn fae, could you not be so...so fae all the damn time!"

Pac laughed, at what Tor assumed was Clairla's confused expression.

"I'm sorry, but it's really not my fae side that has me hiding information."

"Really. What side would that be, then?"

Clairla half shrugged. "I'm a spy. Spies by nature are a secretive—"

Tor shoved her into the mud they'd all tried to avoid—because it wasn't all mud. "Keep your teeth together."

Pac and Eydis snorted, and even Joonee chortled.

Tor stood. "I'm going to assume that, since the assassins wouldn't want to be the center of attention, their inn wouldn't be in the middle of the city. I say we try the other main entrance to the south."

Eydis stood next to her. "Makes sense; quick exit and entry if needed."

Tor looked down at Clairla, who was being helped out of the mud-and-shit puddle by Pac. "You ready?"

"I didn't deserve that, you know," Clairla said as she wiped her hands on her pants and pulled her sais.

"You didn't not deserve it, either," Tor said, pulling her sword. "Let's try and get through here with the least amount of fighting."

A collective agreement was given, and they spread out into a line as they entered the city one by one. Five minutes inside the city limits, Tor wished they had taken the long way around the outside. The more they moved along the streets, the more they became acutely aware of the lack of not just people, but Shadows as well.

Tor held her sword loose in her hand, keeping her other hand free if she needed to cast a shielding spell. When they reached the inn, the street was empty. Tor glanced back at Clairla.

"This is the place," she said.

Tor asked, "So, do we just go in?"

They were hiding behind a building, and Clairla stood at the corner with Tor. "Normally, I would say no. Those who are not as-sassins are never allowed in the inn. But—"

"This isn't a normal situation," Tor finished for her.

"Exactly."

Tor nodded, then said to the others. "Let's go."

They made their way out from the side of the building and skirted the street toward the inn stairs. The streetlights were not oil-based so they were lit; not well, as the circle of light they cast was tiny. They ran up the stairs, Clairla in the lead.

She shoved open the doors and they all filed in. The lobby was pristine, like nothing out of the ordinary was happening. At the end of the long front hall sat the concierge desk. A well-dressed, clean-shaven man stood behind it.

"May I help you?" he asked politely, though his face wrinkled in disgust. Tor half smiled, knowing it had to be the smell of shit coming off Clairla.

"Yes," Clairla said, approaching with a confidence that im-pressed Tor. She lifted her sleeve and the concierge nodded. "I'm the only member here, but I was hoping—"

"I'm sorry, ma'am, but you are aware of the inn rules. No—"

Pac cut him off. "Do you understand what is happening out there right now?" She pushed past Clairla. "We don't want to stay in your crappy inn; what we want is some information on the whereabouts of one of your assassins. Then we will be on our way to save your collective asses."

Tor put a hand on Pac's shoulder, pulling her back gently. "We really got to get a place for you to take a nap." All their nerves were on edge from the lack of sleep.

The concierge didn't seem fazed by the outburst but instead directed his attention to Clairla, the only member amongst them. "You know our policy on giving information. It is not permitted."

Clairla rested her forearms on the front desk, leaving bits of dried dirt, and other things, behind. "We just came from the Fairy Fields, through Misandria Region, Gloverree, and so many other small, little villages that have been wiped out, burned down, and or overrun by Shadow soldiers. That bizarre lightning storm, and the fact that the sun is gone, should be more important to you than up-holding our privacy policy." She leaned over the desk to get closer to his face. Tor noted she was standing on her tip toes, and did her best not to laugh at the sight. "I'm not asking for a fucking contract or a client list. I am merely asking for the whereabouts of a man that may be able to help us all out of this colossal mess!"

The concierge cleared his throat, taking half a step back, just out of reach. His eyes darted about, as if looking to see if anyone was listening.

"Gronk's mighty beard!" Eydis shouted as he stormed forward and around the front desk, grabbing the man around the neck. "Where the fuck is Nived?"

"Niviel," Clairla and Tor said together.

"Not here," said a woman's soft voice from behind. She had stepped out of what looked like a lounge area to their right. Tor sized her up; she was taller than Clairla, but had a slighter build. She was dressed all in black leather with gold buckles. "You've wasted your time coming here. Niviel is a wanted man, and he has been disbanded by the Agency. You, as a fellow assassin, knows what it means to lose a client list."

Eydis shoved the concierge so hard the man fell to the floor.

He stepped around the desk as Clairla moved in front of the group. "Yes, I know. But I was hoping—"

"Hoping?" The other woman raised an eyebrow. "That is a child's pastime, to hope. Come now, you must know better."

The two assassins stepped in close to each other, keeping an arm's length between them.

The woman tilted her head as she blatantly sized up Clairla. She had a drink in one hand, and crossed her other arm over her chest. "Why were you at the Fairy Fields?"

"Why do you care?" Clairla put her hands on her hips, and Tor was certain it was so she could grab her weapons quickly.

The woman nodded and took a sip. "Just curious, really. It's odd though."

"What is?"

"Why would you return when you could have continued west, to safety? You must have noticed the lack of people."

"We noticed, but we had to come back."

The woman lifted an eyebrow and gave a lazy shrug. "Why?"

Tor was getting tired of the back and forth. The women were testing each other out. It's what they did, and this woman must also be a spy and not an assassin. Tor cleared her throat; it was rude, but she needed them to move it along.

Clairla paused. "Who are you?" Clairla asked. "You seem familiar to me, but I don't believe—" Clairla dropped her hands. "Prydwen."

The woman never flinched at her name; she merely smiled and bowed her head, lifting her glass. "The one and only. You must be Clairla. The spy from the Walled City."

"How does she know that?" Eydis asked. "Do you all know each other?"

Clairla glared at him and Prydwen laughed lightly. "Not many fae in the Agency."

Tor stepped forward. "Okay, now that the introductions are

done, can we move this along? We're all exhausted, starved, and unfortunately have a much longer journey ahead of us."

Prydwen seemed mildly amused by Tor and she focused on Tor's neck, which made her uneasy. "A healer?" Prydwen said.

Tor touched the pendant that sat around her neck. It must have dropped out of her shirt at some point. "Yes, I'm with the Rejuvenation—"

Prydwen put her hand up. "I know the pendant and where it's from. Were you at the Fairy Fields as well?"

Tor shook her head and waggled her finger. "I'm not doing this with you. Tell us where we can find Niviel and...and—"

"Zaden," Clairla finished.

"Like I said, they aren't here."

Tor gritted her teeth. "Not in the inn, or not in the city?"

Clairla let out an exasperated breath. "Look, he's a friend of mine. Well, not quite a friend, more of an acquaintance, really, but we need their help."

Prydwen's eyebrows rose. "Really? With what?"

Pac said, "To close the rift over the High Kingdom and prevent a murderous, god-like man from coming into this world and killing us all."

"Oh, is that all?" The door to the inn closed and two men in long cloaks stood in the entrance. Both had weapons in their hands, and one stood back, holding a battle-ax.

"Niviel," Clairla said, pulling her shoulders back.

Niviel's pace stuttered for only a second. "Clairla, what are you doing here?" The two stepped closer.

Tor noticed how the man carried himself: his dark hair a bit of a mess, his pointed ears sticking through. His companion was pale-skinned, and had circular markings on the side of his face. He must have been the tree sprite; the markings were of the type of tree he once inhabited.

"Sir," the concierge said over the group. "Would you like me to take your weapons and have them cleaned?"

Clairla narrowed her eyes at Niviel. "Have you not been disbanded?"

"Is that really the question you want to ask me right now?"

The concierge cleared his throat. "Sir, the weapons?"

Niviel shook his head. "No, it's fine."

"Very good, sir."

Niviel looked at the group of exhausted travelers. "Actually, could you get some food for these folks here? We'll eat in the lounge."

"But, sir, the policy."

Niviel lifted an eyebrow and gave a slight head tilt. "Seriously?"

"Right, my apologies, sir. I will get those meals right away."

Niviel gestured for all of them to follow Prydwen back into the lounge. They dropped their bags and weapons, and slumped into the cushioned chairs sitting around a large table. Tor noticed Niviel's companion staring at Pac, which Pac also noticed.

Pac shifted in her seat to face the man. "Why are you staring at me?"

He contemplated her for a minute longer. "You are not human," he said, pointing.

"Nor are you." Pac pointed back.

"There is something odd about your magic. It is familiar, but then it's not." His face furrowed as he continued to study her.

Clairla said, "You must be Zaden. I've only ever seen you in a vision."

Zaden pulled his eyes from Pac long enough to bow his head. The group fell silent.

Niviel leaned on the table to look at Pac. "There is something oddly familiar about you."

Clairla said, "Niviel we need—"

Niviel and Zaden were on their feet, weapons in hands, so fast that no one had time to react. They pointed them at Pac. "She's one of them."

"Whoa, whoa, whoa." Tor shot out of her chair and put her hands out as she slid in front of Pac. "Let's just all calm down now. I don't know who you—"

"The hooded men; she has their magic," Zaden said.

Niviel nodded. "I sense it, too. Have you not encountered the hooded men?" he asked Clairla. "They all give off that same smell, and that same vibration-like static. It's faint, as if not really there, but it is. And the metallic taste in your mouth."

Pac's expression wasn't shocked, nor did she give any indication to deny it. Tor eased away from Pac, as did the others. This whole time Tor had just thought it was the static from the storms. She had never thought it would be coming from Pac. Had this been her plan all along? Was she really helping them, or helping to wipe them out?

Pac righted her chair and sat back down. She crossed her arms and legs, and was so calm it was eerie. She nodded at Niviel and Zaden. "Sit. You can continue to hold your weapons out if you choose, but I won't hurt you." She looked at everyone else. "Everyone sit and I will explain."

One by one, they all returned to their seats. As if nothing had happened, several servants brought in plates of food and drink, putting it on the table they all sat around. It was more food than any of them had seen in months, which made it all the more difficult to pay attention.

Eydis grabbed a plate and piled it high with food. Tor put a hand on his arm just as he was about to put a forkful in his mouth and gave the tiniest of head shakes. He looked from the food to Tor, and with a small whimper put his fork back down.

"It's not poisoned," Niviel said. "Or tainted in any way."

The group didn't move, even though they were all starving to the point their stomachs were rumbling.

Niviel leaned over and grabbed some meat off of Eydis's plate, then popped it into his mouth. He chewed it and waited. "See?" he said, showing he had swallowed the food.

Tor gave a curt nod and for only a second there was a lull before they all dove in, each piling their plates and shoveling food into their mouths. Tor put several types of meat on a plate, then placed it on the floor where Joonee was waiting patiently.

Zaden leaned forward. "You have a Shadow beast."

Tor nodded in response, since her mouth was full.

"How did that happen?" Niviel asked.

"It's a long story," Tor said around the food in her mouth.

Niviel scrutinized her and the beast for a moment before turning to Pac. "I'm more interested in your story."

After several bites, Pac started. "The hooded men are called Votarions. They are not the same race as I am, and even though our magic is similar it is not the same. The Votarions have been on your world for many years, biding time and learning your magic. Many years ago, a plan was put in place. They offered the High King, and the Dwarf King's son, great power if they were to do this one ceremony. Thomas was a greedy man, just as the prince, now King Firth was a greedy dwarf. Each man needed to complete their own tasks. Firth was to kill his father and procure a Shadow child, and Thomas was to gather worshippers and their life forces.

"The Votarions were the ones who conducted the blood ceremony. They were to open a *doorway* that would allow their god-like leader to enter this world and take its magic. This was not the first time they'd done this. Many worlds have been destroyed by the Votarions and their god-like leader. But, this time, I destroyed their plans." She pointed at Tor, who'd been about to speak. "Yes, the Realm Eater is still coming, but the rift—"

"You said it was a doorway," Niviel said.

"It was supposed to be, but what I created was a rift, a tear in Totriga's Veil, which has delayed his arrival. I am not a Votarion, I am a human"—she scrunched her face and teetered a hand back and forth—"and Shadow hybrid." Pac shoved a forkful of meat into her mouth.

Niviel looked to Zaden then to Clairla, who also had a mouthful of food. "Is she...she can't be...it's not possible."

Clairla swallowed, and chased the food down with water before speaking. "She is the girl you created the elixir for. When she cast her spell during the ceremony, she ended up on a world with a much faster time than our own."

For the next hour, the group accounted the information of what needed to be done, who the Realm Eater was, and why they had a Shadow beast.

Tor sat back in her chair and crossed her legs. "Now you explain something." She pointed at Niviel.

"Ask your question."

"Clairla and your friend Prydwen both say you were disbanded and no longer allowed in the inns. If that is the case—"

"How am I here?"

Clairla pointed at Zaden. "And him, how is he allowed in? Is he an assassin now?"

Zaden snorted as he reached for, what Tor counted, his tenth sticky bun.

"When the explosion happened"—he pointed at Pac—"your botched sacrifice, Zaden and I were halfway to the Ruins Labyrinth."

Tor cut him off. "I'm not interested in any of that. I want to know what happened here, and how you are again in good standing. I may not know much about how the Agency works but I do know once disbanded, always disbanded."

Niviel took a sip of his drink. "True. I wasn't planning on returning to Grashneet, as it would have been suicide. However, after a month in the ruins the fairies put up their shield and I knew we had to." He paused and stared at his glass. "When we returned to Grashneet the chaos was only just starting. The darkness was spreading out from the High Kingdom, and with the help of Prydwen I managed to convince the Agency to allow me to stay and help."

"Help, how?"

"I'm sure you noticed the lack of people in the city and, obviously, the abundance of food."

Tor nodded. "It hasn't escaped any of us."

"We had the farmers harvest their crops, as much as they could. We also took in as much livestock as we could. Then, in groups, we sent the townspeople west. Some on foot through the dwarf mountains of Theakredel, and some along the Knolnt River."

Pac leaned forward to pour herself some water. "Why would the people do that? Harvest crops that were obviously not ready, give up livestock, and leave their homes?"

"Because," Prydwen said. "They trust us."

Eydis snorted. "They trust a group of assassins?"

Niviel lifted an eyebrow. "Yes, we keep their streets safe and we keep them safe. Do you think a city this size would allow our chapter to stay within its borders if we didn't protect them?"

Clairla said, "It's the same in the Walled City. We protect our people and in turn they help us, care for us, and share their supplies."

Niviel continued. "It was a very short time after the town was cleared out that the hooded men, the Votarions, came through. They were upset no one was left, but we had witnessed these men taking hundreds to the High Kingdom. If this Realm Eater consumes magic, as you say, it would make sense he would want as many people he could find."

"Will you help us?" Clairla asked the three of them.

Niviel, Zaden, and Prydwen seemed to have a conversation

without speaking. Prydwen was the first to speak aloud. "I will not go. We still need people to remain here and help any who seek refuge."

Tor was surprised by the information. She had no idea the assassins would put their life on the line for others. Many could be brutal and callous. She felt a pang of shame for judging them all; it was no different than how she was always judged as an orc.

Eydis cleared his throat. "Do you know if any groups escaped the High Kingdom the night of the ceremony? If there were any survivors?"

"You had family?" Zaden asked.

"Some. I told them to leave the city. I don't know if they got out. We had to go separate ways."

Zaden leaned on the table. "Many got out of the city, and those who went to Gloverree—" Zaden sat back and dropped his chin.

"What our sensitive sprite is trying to say," Prydwen said, "is that if your family went to Gloverree, it is possible they survived. But, from what our scouts have found, many in Gloverree refused to go. When the Votarions came, they took many back to the High Kingdom. Those left would have been wiped out by the Shadow soldiers. If they came here, they would have been escorted out with the rest of our townspeople."

Tor put a hand on Eydis's arm. "Then we shall believe they are safely heading west."

It was a long night of discussion that did not end until early the next morning. Niviel arranged for them all to get cleaned up and found a place to stay in an inn down the street.

The next morning they were clean, rested, fed, and on their way to the High Kingdom.

CHAPTER THIRTY-ONE

THE GROUP KEPT OFF THE main roads, instead keeping to the uneven terrain of the unbeaten path. They hoped this would help with avoiding the Votarions, as well as any Shadow soldiers. They would need to travel for at least a month and a half to get to the High Kingdom; perhaps longer, given they weren't taking the roads. Fearful the Realm Eater may arrive before they could close the rift, they ran as much as they could. This would force them onto the roads for short durations to prevent anyone from breaking an ankle or getting any other injuries from running through unexplored areas. They reached the travelers' retreat in three weeks, which meant they were making good time.

It also meant they were exhausted, their bodies spent of all energy.

"We can't stay here for too long," Pac said. The others were sitting in a circle around the fire they'd built in the already prepared pit. "It's already been close to a year, your time, since the rift was opened. And at least another ten in my time."

"We understand, Pac," Tor said from the fire. "But if we are all too exhausted to walk, we most certainly won't last in a fight. We must rest, if only for a night."

Pac dropped down next to Eydis and he handed her a mug of warm tea. They watched Zaden, who sat away from the rest. He was polishing his ax and taking tiny bites out of his last sticky bun.

Tor stood and walked over. "Mind if I join you?"

Zaden looked up from his task with a smile. "Of course not. I enjoy the company of others."

Tor sat next to him.

"I never used to," he said. "I loved my forest and the quiet. The other creatures would mind their own. But now, the quiet can be unnerving. Lonely."

Tor smiled gently. "May I ask you something?"

"Of course." He stopped polishing his ax and placed it on the ground, giving her his full attention.

"Tree sprites are a peaceful people. You are creators of life."

"Yes."

"You have obviously had to go against your nature." She nodded toward the ax.

"Yes."

"How did you come to terms with giving up that side of yourself? How do you justify taking another's life?"

Zaden readjusted himself on the pile of hay they sat on. He crossed his hands in his lap, then looked Tor straight in the eye. "You are an orc, a great warrior race."

"Yes."

"And yet, you are no more. You have taken an oath and practice the religion of healing. You take that oath seriously?"

Tor sat a little straighter. "It is who I am now. I have not been that warrior for many decades."

Zaden's smile was faint, but when the light from the fire flickered it was gone. "But you have taken lives since you took your oath."

Tor dropped her chin.

"How do you justify those actions?"

Tor lifted her head. "I had no choice."

"But you just told me that the oath of healing is your religion, it is who you are. That you are no longer that orc warrior."

"I had no choice."

"Does this mean you are no longer a healer? Are you now, once again, a proud orc warrior?"

Tor's brow wrinkled. "I don't know."

Zaden fell silent. He dropped his attention to the ground and pulled a weed that was growing in the dirt. He held it in his hand and closed his eyes. In a short minute, the weed had turned into a beautiful yellow flower. He handed the flower to Tor, and she stared at it. She had no idea what it meant, as he hadn't given her an answer to her question.

Zaden said, "I will always be a tree sprite. It will always be who I am to create life, to maintain it. But I have learned, in a short time, that sometimes we must go against who we were born to be in order to preserve who we are."

Tor stared at the yellow flower. "I am an orc warrior; it was who I was born to be."

Zaden tilted his head. "Is it? Or were you always born to be a healer, and you must become a warrior to preserve that which you really are?" Zaden picked up his ax and went to his bedroll.

Tor returned to the fire and sat next to Niviel. "Did you get the answers you were looking for?"

Tor glanced at him. "No."

Niviel raised his eyebrows. "Really? Are you sure?"

Tor turned the flower between her fingers. "I really don't know." She stood and retired to her own bedroll. She stared at the flower, Zaden's words mingled in with Abacuss's about who she was meant to be. None of it made sense; was she a warrior or a healer?

Morning came a lot quicker than Tor liked. She stretched and yawned, taking the mug of warm tea from Clairla, who greeted her with a slight grumbling about it being morning. It was one of the best sleeps she'd had in several weeks, but the feeling was short-lived when the conversation started up about how much further they had to go.

At a walking pace it would take several days; running they could get there in two, three tops. As much as any of them wanted to agree to the plan, Pac was right about the time frame. They needed to get there sooner rather than later. Another blood moon was approaching, the one-year anniversary of Pac's original ceremony. She was certain this was when the Votarions would sacrifice many to bring their god into this world.

For the first couple hours they walked to get the stiffness out of their muscles. The walls of the High Kingdom could be seen in the distance, but nothing else. The only reason they could even see the walls was because of the constant lightning flashing across the sky. The static in the air was strong, and Tor felt like she did when they crossed the river—sharp pins and needles poking and jabbing at her.

She could see everyone else feeling the same effects, except for Eydis. In that moment Tor envied the fact that Eydis had no magic, didn't do magic, and never felt the static in the air. He was rare indeed.

"Now that we're so close to the Kingdom," Eydis said. "What's the plan here? Are we just going to run in there and tell them to stop it and close the rift? How is this going to work?"

Tor was walking just behind the rest when she noticed Pac looking at her wrists, running her thumb up and down a scar Tor had never noticed before. It ran from her wrist up the inside of her forearm. When she spoke of the hooded man and King Thomas draining her blood, it had never occurred to Tor how they would have done it.

As she watched the young girl, Tor realized what Pac needed to do; why she had been keeping track of the days and nights that passed by. With the sun completely blocked out in this region, the moon and stars suffered the same, but when Pac had mentioned the blood moon a month or so back it hadn't registered.

Tor admonished herself for not figuring it out sooner. Now they were a day, maybe two, away from the biggest fight of their lives and she was only just realizing that, once again, the poor girl needed to be sacrificed.

"Pac," Tor said, clearing her throat.

Pac dropped her arm and looked forward, seeming to neither notice nor hear.

"Pac," Tor said again, but loud enough that everyone heard.

The young girl glanced over her shoulder, and in that split second Tor knew Pac's plan and that Pac knew Tor had figured it out. "It must be done," Pac said.

Tor reached out and grabbed the girl by the shoulder, spinning her around and stopping the group. "There has to be another way. You said you needed strong magical beings to help close the rift. So why would you need to sacrifice yourself?"

"Wait, what?" Eydis said, stepping closer.

Clairla's shoulders raised and lowered. Tor pointed at her. "You knew, too! You knew that was why she was here!"

Clairla raised her hands in surrender. "Okay. Calm down, Tor."

"Calm down? Calm down?" Tor could feel the anger bubbling up inside her. "If all you needed was Pac to do this, then why did you insist I be here?"

"My vis—"

Tor jabbed a finger at her. "Don't you dare say it was because of your visions!"

Clairla clamped her mouth shut.

"Tor," Pac said. "It's okay. I've always known how the rift was going to be closed. It's the only reason I returned. But I still need all of you to be there."

Niviel tilted his head and spoke. "I've taken great care in my lifetime to not prosecute the innocent." He looked at Pac. "If you can promise me that your death is the only choice, I will continue on. But, if there is another way, if you are only sacrificing yourself because you don't know what else to do, I cannot continue. Zaden and I will return to Grashneet."

Pac threw her hands up in exasperation, then put them on her hips. "All of this"—she gestured around them and to the sky—"is my fault. If it wasn't for me, this wouldn't be happening. I could have stopped it. I could have told the king to stop it before I was drugged. But I was a foolish little girl. I need you all there so that you can perform our own ceremony. The Votarions have been gathering people so they can summon their god. But, if we do this"—she pulled a piece of paper from an inside pocket—"ritual, then the rift should close. But I have to be exactly where I was the first time." She looked around at the others. "It is the only option."

Tor took the paper, and it was obvious it hadn't completely survived their river expedition. It was wrinkled and torn in places, and the words were smudged terribly, making it difficult, but not impossible, to read. "Why didn't you just tell us this from the beginning?" Tor asked. "Why wait until now?"

Pac furrowed her brow and turned to Clairla, who wrinkled her face.

Tor let out a strangled cry of frustration. "You knew! You knew this entire time and you didn't say anything. Damn you fae and your secrets!"

Clairla stepped toward Tor. "You must believe that when I approached you a year ago I didn't know. I only had a vision that you were there when Pac came returned. Then, the night Pac came through her rift, I had another vision."

"Why didn't you say anything?" Tor was doing her best not to shout. They were still exposed and could attract unwanted attention.

"She did to me," Pac said. "She told her me her second vision was of me on the altar. I told her that I already knew."

"You could have said something at that point," Eydis said, having stayed silent the entire time.

Pac nodded. "You're right. I should have, but—"

Tor nodded at Clairla, and in a much calmer tone said, "You told her not to."

"I needed you to stay with us, Tor. You were in both my visions. I knew if we told you that we were marching Pac to her death—"

Tor put a hand up to stop Clairla from speaking. She stared at the piece of paper; the words made little sense, a riddle of sorts. Her mentor's own words about the time coming when she would have to make a choice about who she was meant to be rolled through her mind. She understood, now, her true place in this world—a warrior or a healer—standing in the middle of a dead field, storms constantly rolling overhead, and the cold, stark reality of who she really was right there shown to her on that piece of paper.

Tor tucked it into her pocket, and her and Pac locked eyes. "Let's go," Tor said, moving past everyone and running for the High Kingdom.

CHAPTER THIRTY-TWO

THEY STOPPED FOR THE NIGHT. After nearly twelve hours of mostly running they were now half a day from the High Kingdom. There was a small patch of trees that would conceal them well, as long as they didn't start a fire.

Tor stared at the piece of paper, the words burning in her mind as she absently ran her hand through Joonee's soft coat of fur. Pac sat next to her.

"Where did you get this?" Tor asked.

"The world I ended up in had what they called oracles. Much like the fae here, but not so deceitful and self-serving."

Tor snorted; there was no argument about that.

"They were much stronger before the Realm Eater came, but at times they still managed to see the future." Pac pulled at strands of dead grass. "When I came through the rift to their side, as a child, they were the ones who told my father where to find me. They helped to nurse me back to health."

"So, they raised you?"

"Oh, no. Once I was healthy and back on my feet they left. Went back to the village they lived in. It wasn't for another eight years that we saw them again. They told me of the Realm Eater and his plan for this world. I wasn't going to come back. I didn't want to." Fat tears welled in her eyes, and Tor put a hand over the girl's. Pac smiled and placed her other hand over it. "My family, my father, told me it was my duty to return. That the oracles tasked me with something of great importance, and it wasn't right that I ignore it."

"These oracles," Clairla said; the group had fallen silent and were all listening in. "Did they warn you because your world would be destroyed, too?"

Pac snorted and rolled her eyes. "No, my world was already destroyed. The Realm Eater had come decades before. And the oracles don't just step in when it suits them, or when their lives are in danger. They step in because it's the right thing to do."

Tor smirked. She couldn't see everyone's faces in the dim light, but she could see they too were amused.

"What are you saying?" Clairla asked.

"Oh, come on," Eydis said with a snort.

Niviel said, "Do you honestly believe you and your people are forthcoming with information? You hid many things from me when you demanded I make the elixir and go to the Fairy Fields. You had answers, but decided to play games instead."

Tor said, "If the Destiny Custodians were straightforward with me when I was sent to the High Kingdom, I would have worked harder at getting Pac away."

Pac said, "I believe even Dufin would have refused to take me to the High Kingdom if the fae we encountered told us the truth."

"So, this is all the fae's fault?" Clairla's voice quivered.

Tor shook her head. "No, of course not. But they certainly did a poor job at helping to prevent it."

"Well," Eydis said, shifting his seated position to one of laying down. "Since we are less than a day away, what's this big plan?"

"You're going to fall asleep," Pac said.

"No, I'm not."

"Oh, please. The instant you are in a horizontal position you start snoring."

Eydis tilted his head to look at her. "If you yammer on like you always do then, yes, I will fall asleep."

"I don't yammer. When I speak it has purpose."

"What's your purpose now? Because it just sounds like yammering to me."

Pac opened her mouth and Tor put a hand on her arm. "Tell us the plan. Eydis, sit up. She's not wrong about you falling asleep."

Eydis grunted as he sat back up and Pac began explaining the plan. "It's really very simple. The Votarions won't be willing to give up the altar, so we will need to take it by force. With the magic being so strong and unpredictable, they won't use any of theirs until they are ready to proceed with the ceremony. So their defenses will be down. Everyone will be fighting while Tor performs our ceremony."

"Why don't I do the ceremony," Eydis said. "Tor knows shield magic and is an amazing fighter."

Pac shook her head. "No, it has to be Tor."

Eydis opened his mouth and Tor said, "She's right. It has to be me."

"Why?" Clairla asked. "When I saw you, I didn't see you at the altar. So why does it have to be you? What was on that piece of paper?"

Tor handed the paper to Clairla, and she leaned toward the fire to read it better. Her brow furrowed as she looked up. "This makes no sense, it's gibberish."

"It isn't," Pac said, taking it back. "It's a healing ceremony in the Votarion's language." She handed the sheet back to Tor. "The oracles wrote it for me."

Tor stared at it a little longer. "You are certain it's a healing ceremony?"

"No."

"No?" Tor and Clairla said together.

"I'm assuming it is, because it's supposed to seal the rift and heal the land." She gave a sheepish shrug.

Tor sighed and shoved it back into her pocket. "I suppose it will have to do, then. It's all we got." She laid down on her side and put an arm around Joonee. The idea of using a spell from a different world, written by a race that she had never heard of, to stave off a god-like man from destroying her own gave her a headache.

The group fell silent, and it didn't take long for them to go to sleep. They each took turns standing watch, but it was so dark it was unlikely anyone could see the enemy coming.

An ear-popping crack of thunder woke the group the next morning. It was one of the worst sleeps Tor had yet. Perhaps it was the rock she'd been sleeping on, or the pins and needles of the constant static, but it was most likely the fact that Tor was about to kill a young girl.

They made their way toward the castle, keeping an eye on the tops of the walls—or what was left of them. Many parts had been knocked down by lightning strikes. The gates were a different matter; they were wide open and looked to be untouched. So they entered through the city's main gate. If they followed this road straight up, it would take them to the castle.

They didn't have time to skirt their way up. The last eight hours it had taken them to reach the castle walls had been difficult, having to dodge constant lightning strikes and Shadow soldiers. The good thing about dealing with the Shadow soldiers was that there weren't many of them; it looked as though the Votarions had taken care of most when they moved into the city.

Eydis leaned into Tor. "Now would be a good time to ask that goddess of yours for some divine intervention."

"My goddess doesn't intervene, she assists, and I have already done so."

As Tor passed a narrow street she felt a gust of wind strike her and she was thrown into a brick building, her weapons clanking to the cobblestone road.

Eydis, who was closest to her, spun as a hooded man stepped into the light. Eydis brought his weapon up just as the hooded man raised his arm. The two connected, and the man screamed out as Eydis's sword took off his limb.

Tor pulled the knife from her belt and flung it at the hooded man, catching him in the chest. He staggered back and reached out with his remaining hand. Tor scrambled to her feet and Eydis rammed his sword into the midsection of the hooded man, who slid down the wall and into a seated position. Unmoving.

"You all right?" Eydis asked, wiping off his sword on the man's cloak.

Tor had never been close enough to these hooded men to see their faces. She knelt beside him, pulled her knife from his chest, then shoved his hood back.

He had fat black lines on one side of his face. Her heart pounded when she recognized the tattoos, the deep ridges in his forehead.

"You look like you recognize this race, even though they aren't from here," Eydis said.

Tor cleaned her blade then stood. "I do. They're the ones who killed my family and burned my village when I was eighteen. I always wondered who they were."

"At least you have an answer now."

"That I do." She stepped over the body and back into the street. The others were already at the castle steps. "We better get a move on it."

"Would be nice if they had helped."

Tor smirked. She knew he didn't need, nor want their help. He just needed to complain. They jogged to catch up, and when they reached the stairs everyone had shed their backpacks and extra gear they wouldn't need. The front doors were enormous, and of thick, heavy wood with intricate designs carved into them.

Tor had lived in the High Kingdom for fourteen years, but had never been this close to the castle. She wanted to take in the moment, and only wished the king were alive to see her standing on his front steps. She felt a surge of excitement from her defiance. Tor stood a little taller, held her head a little higher.

Eydis patted Tor on the shoulder, smiling when she looked at him. "What?" she asked.

"I've never been in front of these doors either. Wish it were under different circumstances."

With a grunt and a creak, the others pushed the doors open. "Little help?" Clairla said.

Eydis and Tor jumped in, but it felt like something was blocking the door. When they heard dragging from the other side, they realized there were benches and chairs placed in front to prevent entry.

The gap they managed to get open was just big enough for Tor, but it took Eydis some effort to squeeze his large belly through. Joonee eased in with zero issues.

"You'd think, after so much time on the road and all that running, you would have lost some weight." Pac poked him in the belly when he'd finally got through.

He swatted at her hand, but said nothing. Tor was impressed with his restraint at not snapping back, and suspected it was because it was running through his head that Pac was going to die, so why make her time more miserable.

The halls were filled with debris, and it was clear no one had lived in the castle for some time. Large holes in the roof allowed them to see the dark skies above, and the lack of coverage made Tor feel more vulnerable to the lightning. They were directly under the storms, now. It was surprisingly quieter than she had thought it would be.

They made haphazard guesses as to where the back gardens would be, where the altar stood.

Zaden, who had been keeping mostly to Niviel, and vice versa, spoke, "There is something not right about any of this."

"I agree," Niviel said.

Pac raised her eyebrows. "Really? You two have been silent for nearly a month now, and when you finally decided to speak to us it's to say something's not right?"

"Probably not the best time to get into a fight," Tor said.

"I was merely pointing out that if the Votarions are here for the altar, like us, then where are they? We haven't seen one."

Eydis put his hand up. "That's not true, Tor and I killed one just before coming into the castle."

"Just one?" Niviel asked.

"Well, yeah."

Tor patted him on the back to encourage him.

"I would say they are all at the altar," Pac said.

Tor's eyebrows rose. "And where might that be?"

Pac put her hands on her hips. "I don't know. I was nine and unconscious at the time."

"We have tried every hallway but that one." Clairla pointed. "If that's not it, then I don't know what to do."

"We are running out of time." Pac's voice rose several octaves. "If we don't do this at the right time, it will never work."

Tor raised her hands. "Okay, everybody just take a deep breath. Let's go down that hallway and see if it leads out to the garden or not."

Niviel and Zaden took the lead, then Clairla and Pac, and finally Tor looked at Eydis. "You ready for this?"

"No, you?"

"Not even a little bit."

"Excellent, let's hurry and catch up." Eydis jogged ahead. Tor sighed as she watched her old friend. He was back to his original self, albeit an odd time to do it, but it made her happy nevertheless.

She looked down at Joonee, who hadn't left her side since they'd entered the castle. She nodded for the beast to follow.

When she caught up to the others, they were standing at a door just as grand as the front door. Tor and Eydis, being the biggest of the group, pushed; it was much lighter than the front since it was not blocked by anything.

Tor poked her head out, and an arrow missed her nose by less than an inch. She pulled back.

"What's wrong?" Clairla asked. "Is it not the garden?"

"No, it's the garden, but I also found our missing Votarions."

Several shouts in a strange tongue came from the other side of the doors, which Eydis and Tor were now holding shut.

"What's the plan?" Eydis asked through his grunts.

Zaden stepped forward. "I'll create the shield that will protect us enough for Niviel to push them back. The rest of you follow us in."

Clairla shook her head and waggled her finger. "The magic is unpredictable. You could blow us all up."

The pounding and shouting was becoming more aggressive. Tor said, "Somebody needs to do something."

"We have to risk it," Pac said. "We're dead either way."

Tor gestured for Eydis to get with everyone else, and for Pac to join her. She locked eyes with Zaden. "Ready?"

He set his shoulders and brought his hands to hip level, palms down. "Ready."

Tor pulled the door open, pushing Pac to the wall and letting the door protect them. The static was already so strong the only thing that told Tor that Zaden had cast their spell was by the sound of voices shouting in pain. She couldn't understand any of the languages used, so she knew it wasn't their group.

Pac peeked around the edge of the door, then looked back. "They're through. I think I can see the altar from here."

Tor came around the door, still holding it open. Her friends were locked in battle with the hooded men. It was dark but for the streaks of lightning in the sky and the lit torches in a half moon shape where a number of bodies lay. At the front was a raised platform.

"We have to move," Pac said, rushing out into the garden.

Tor was on her heels, but when she crossed the threshold a blade came down, grazing her arm. She staggered back, gritting her teeth and grabbing at the wound. Warm blood trickled through her fingers.

The attacker swung again, and this time Tor raised her own sword to block it. Forgetting her wound, she grabbed the hooded man with her free hand and wrapped her fingers in the rough, husk-like material of his cloak.

She tossed him at the wall, ready to run him through, when she stopped. She was a healer; she didn't need to kill this man. She slammed the hilt of her sword on the top of his head and he slumped to the ground. Her heart pounding, Tor spun and was knocked back into the wall where she'd left her first opponent.

Blood trickled down her face now, and Tor dabbed at her nose. In her surprise she had dropped her sword, so when the second man sank the tip of his sword into her shoulder she had nothing to stop it.

Blinding, white-hot pain shot through her arm and shoulder. Tor called out in rage. With one hand she grabbed the sword blade, and with the other she pulled the hunting knife from her belt.

Gritting her teeth, Tor shoved herself forward into her attacker. He pulled the sword free from both her hand and her shoulder, then drove it into her other. The force slammed her back into the wall and nearly knocked the knife from her hand.

Now standing, Tor braced herself and took a step toward her attacker again. She felt the blade slice through the skin and muscle of her right shoulder, then come out the back.

The hand she'd used to grab the sword was sliced wide, and she used it to grab the head of her attacker.

Ignoring the searing pain in her shoulder and hand she raised her other arm, ramming the knife into the attacker's eye. One half-step back, and he dropped.

She grabbed the hilt of the sword and pulled the blade from her shoulder. Her hand slipped several times, slick from the blood. When she was free of the weapon, she dropped it and retrieved her knife from the attacker's eye. Scouting the area, she could see her group working in tandem with each other.

The static was still strong in the air, and she couldn't tell if anyone was using magic—or if they all were. Blood poured and oozed out of her wounds, and she felt herself getting light-headed. Tor made a silent prayer for her Goddess Thanroota to help her with the final steps of this battle. She needed to stay alive to complete the ceremony.

"Pac," Tor shouted over the noise of battle and thunderclaps. A movement caught her eye. Pac was at the top of a rock pile on the raised platform.

She started for Pac, stepping over bodies and rubble. It was difficult to tell how old either were. The smell of death was strong, and that was before they stepped out of the castle. The Votarions had to have been sacrificing people for some time.

Two steps up the rock pile, Tor felt a sharp pain in her calf. Her balance was already poor, so when she turned to see what happened the hooded man caused her to tumble back down. A knife protruded out the back of her leg.

"You have got to be—"

The man was on her, his hands were around her throat, and his strength was surprising. Blood trickled from his forehead and onto her face, and she realized he was the one she had knocked out. Thanroota would not have approved of her choosing to let this man live, for the sake of her oath, and now he was about to kill her for her weakness.

Tor's right arm was weak—the sword must had severed some tendons—so she used her left hand. With an easy thrust up, the palm of her hand connected with his chin and knocked him back. It was enough for her to grab the blade and pull it from her calf, then ram it into his throat.

"Tor," Pac shouted. "Hurry!"

Tor rolled her eyes. "It's not like I'm playing around down here." She started her climb once again. When she got to the top, Pac helped her the final couple feet. Her head was spinning now, and she was having a hard time standing.

"We have a problem." Pac pointed at a large stone slab that was split in two.

"Is that the altar?"

"It was."

"Do we need it?"

Pac shrugged. "We have no choice; the blood moon is almost gone." She pointed to a part of the sky that seemed to be clear of all clouds. The bright red moon hung low as it began its decent for the day.

"Lie down," Tor said, indicating another stone slab nearby. Pac did as she was told, her legs dangling over the edge at the knee.

Pac handed her a copper bowl she'd pulled from the satchel, which Tor hadn't noticed until that moment. "Use this to collect my blood. When there is enough in there to drink—"

"I'm not drinking your blood!"

"You have to; you must drink my blood, then say the incantation. Do you have it?"

Tor had dropped to her knees and stared down at the copper bowl. As a warrior, it was nothing to drink the blood of your enemy. As a healer, it was blasphemous and dark magic.

"Tor."

Pac's voice barely cut through her thoughts. If her father was here now he would stand in honor of her for drinking the blood of their enemy. But Pac wasn't her enemy, she was an innocent child, and not much older than her own son, Parin.

"Tor!"

What would Abacuss say if he knew of the dark magic she was about to wield? Drinking the blood alone would have her removed from the oath and stripped of her religion. Then, the words he wrote in his journal came back: *You were born a warrior, but you are meant to be a healer. The time will come when you must choose.*

"Tor!"

The words of Zaden came back to her: *Or were you always born to be a healer and you must become a warrior to preserve that which you really are?*

From her pocket Tor pulled the paper with the incantation on it. It was torn further and now smeared with blood, the words unreadable. Tor tried to wipe it clean, but only smeared more of her own blood across the page. She didn't know what to do and time was running out.

"We have a problem," Tor said.

Pac came up on her elbows. "What?"

Tor showed her the sheet. "I can't read it. Do you remember what it said?"

"It was something about a sacrifice. One giving of their self or for their self. I don't know, Tor." She stared up at the moon, which was fading fast. "We have to do something. All I remember the oracles saying is that the rift can only be sealed with a true sacrifice."

Tor understood, finally, the words of her mentor in his final thoughts to her; the constant battle she fought within herself every day; the conversation with Zaden. She knew what needed to be done, the sacrifice to be made. Tor thought of Parin and her heart pulled. She glanced down to Eydis and Clairla, fighting side by side to keep the Votarions at bay.

Eydis was locked in a battle with a man his size; he was exhausted but won the fight. Tor didn't have time to call out to him when a second man stepped in front and swung his sword up. The last image she saw of Eydis was his belly being torn open, then Pac grabbed Tor's hand and pulled her back to the altar.

"Tor, our time is almost up," Pac said, putting a hand on her shoulder.

"Yes, it is." Tor moved Pac off the altar and took her place.

"What are you doing?"

Tor handed Pac the copper bowl and the knife, then lay down on the slab. Pac shook her head.

"I know what must be done. I know what I must do, but you need to help me."

Pac's brow came together, a look of understanding crossing her face. She placed the copper bowl under Tor's already bleeding hand.

Tor closed her eyes as the blood drained from her veins and thought of a prayer, one that she had heard as a small child, given to her by her grandmother; a fierce warrior that did not die on a battlefield, but had died protecting others.

In her native tongue, Tor recited the warrior's prayer. "Come, Thanroota, here lies a warrior worthy of your guidance. She is strong and fierce, and will bring you honor on the battlefield.

"Come, Kadianea, here lies a warrior dying for the protection of others. She is worthy of your company, to sing and dance in your hall.

"Come, Great and Mighty Goddesses, and accept a worthy soul into your ranks!"

Tor felt Pac's hand on her forehead and the two recited the prayer together.

As the final words were spoken Tor felt a pull in her belly, like a string had been attached to her stomach and someone was tugging it. Her skin tingled as the static grew around her. She had begun to recite the prayer once again when the air pressure dropped and a flash of light crossed the sky—and with a shattering boom the bolt touched down on the altar. Tor was tossed from the platform, her skin charred on her right side. She was struggling to get back to her feet and stagger back to the altar when she felt a hand on her shoulder and a blade ram into her back.

Tor glanced down in time to see the sword tip protruding out her stomach disappear, then felt a second sharp pain as the sword reappeared. Tor dropped to her knees and rolled to her back. Her killer remained standing for only a second before his head was cut from his neck.

Tor gasped for air. Her ears rang and everything was muffled. Eydis stood over her, a smile across his bloodstained face. She grew cold and her sight blurred. Her final thought was of Parin.

CHAPTER THIRTY-THREE

P AC DID HER BEST TO help with the cleanup, though her right arm was bandaged. She was still quite sore from the burns to her left shoulder and neck from the lightning strike.

She had seen the lightning form, and had done her best to move out of the way before it struck the altar. She was tossed several feet, and nearly pushed off the edge of the cliff. By the time she was back on her feet, Tor had suffered a fatal blow. Eydis took the head of the Votarion who had killed Tor before he himself succumbed to his injuries.

Zaden was insistent she be buried as a warrior and not a healer. Pac understood why; Tor's final stand was as a warrior not as a healer. It was with that act as a warrior that she fulfilled her life's work as a healer and had become who she was truly meant to be.

Clairla was the only one who had any insight as to how the orc buried their dead, instructing them on how to build a pyre. Pac recited the prayer Tor had spoken while on the altar. She had a feeling it was a burial prayer, given Tor's sacrifice. She wasn't certain of the exact words, but she did her best to recite it as they had that night. She repeated them over Tor and Eydis's burning bodies.

There were no townspeople they could find in the High Kingdom, no Shadow soldiers to deal with, and if there were any more Votarions they were nowhere in the city.

The sun had not come out completely, although the storms were slowly dissipating and the static was all but gone. They figured it wouldn't happen overnight, but they were optimistic it wouldn't be more than a few months before things again returned to normal.

Clairla and Pac watched the fires burn and Clairla said, "When do you think the Realm Eater will come?"

"What makes you think he's coming? The rift has been sealed, and your universe is hidden once again."

Clairla tilted her head. "Is it though?"

Pac smiled, but she didn't really know for certain if he could find them. The rift was like a beacon in a dark room, and now that beacon had been turned off. He may not be able to find them, but she didn't know how close he really was to entering their world either.

It's possible the rift was closed while he was passing through, which meant he was dead. But no one could know for certain. "I don't think there is anything to worry about." Pac gave a reassuring smile.

"What will you do now, Pac?" Clairla asked. "Will you return to the world where you once found a home?"

Pac stared at the pyres as Niviel added a bit more fuel to ensure they burned completely. She knew where she needed to go; it was Tor's final word, the last name she'd whispered before the final breath escaped her lips.

Parin.

But the stark, cold reality of her life now was she could never return to the world she truly did call home. It was lost to her forever. Just as she hoped this world was to the Realm Eater.

"I'll let Tor's son know that his mother fought like a true orc until the very end." Pac's eyes softened. "Then I'll travel east to the clan lands. Maybe I can find my other family there." She pulled her gaze up to Clairla. "What will you do now?"

Clairla gave a gentle smile. Her skin and hair still looked as though she'd stepped out of a bath even though she was covered in blood and dirt. "I will travel with Niviel and Zaden until we reach my home, the Walled City. I will help them rebuild. From what Niviel told me, he and Zaden will travel west to gather their own townspeople and bring them home." Clairla crossed her arms. "It's going to be a long way back to what we once were." Clairla stared at the end of Tor's pyre where Joonee sat, on guard. "What of Joonee? Tor was her family."

"If she will have me," Pac said. "I'll take her with me."

The two fell silent as they watched Zaden, who was standing at the end of Tor's pyre next to Joonee. A moment later yellow flowers bloomed around her. When he was done, he picked up his pack and Niviel did the same.

"I guess that's my hint. I wish you well, Pac."

"Good and safe travels to you, too."

The two embraced, then Clairla pulled away, grabbed her things, and ran to catch up to the others. Pac took a seat and Joonee eased her way to sit next to her. Together they watched over Tor and Eydis, until there was nothing left but ash.

Author's Note

If you're reading this, then you've made it to the end of the book. I hope it was an enjoyable journey! I would love for you to leave a review on the site you purchased the book, or drop over to Goodreads and leave a review there. Reviews are like sweet little droplets of Hershey Kisses that keeps a writer writing!

Looking for more of my books to read? Want to listen to me ramble about nothing? Looking for fun and interesting character interviews? Want to see the steps behind the making of the cover art? Want to look at my world maps? Then drop by my website at:

www.bobbischemerhornauthor.ca

And, if you would love exclusive content, early cover reveals, and hear about sales and promotions, be sure to sign up for my newsletter.

My last bit of shameless self-promotion: If you would like to see strange videos I find interesting and hilarious, or just want to keep up on my activities, you can also find me on social media at:

www.facebook.com/BobbiSchemerhornAuthor

Instagram: www.instagram.com/bobbisdragons/